RAZOR

Also by Wilke Martin

unhuman series

I – Inspector Hobbes and the Blood
II – Inspector Hobbes and the Curse
III – Inspector Hobbes and the Gold Diggers
IV – Inspector Hobbes and the Bones

A Little Book of Silly Verse

Relative Disasters

Children's books as Wilkie J. Martin

All in the Same Boat
The Lazy Rabbit

RAZOR

WILKIE MARTIN

The Witcherley Book Company
United Kingdom

British Library Cataloguing in Publication Data.
A catalogue record for this book is available from the British Library.

ISBN 9781912348466 (paperback large print)

The river raged and roared like a never-ending express train. It smelled fresh, and Raymond Holmes longed for it to wash away his guilt and end his hopeless life. Overflowing with self-loathing, he stared into the blackness beneath the bridge and sneered at his own pathetic cowardice, for although half-a-dozen double whiskies had soured his stomach and muddied his brain they had so far failed to boost his courage. Pain, however brief, had always terrified him.

Suspecting that if he didn't stop dithering soon, he might never even get close to building up the nerve again, Ray forced himself to swing up a leg and straddle the parapet of the bridge. Wobbling horribly, he muttered his final farewell to the world, closed his eyes and tried to convince his hands to release their grip. All the while, his internal critic mocked the clichéd theatricality of his performance.

He might have gone through with it had a rhythmic click, click, click not broken into his thoughts. Across the river in Bindover village, the street lights lit up the kind barmaid who'd served his drinks and smiled at him in the White Hart earlier. He presumed she was on her way home. Too embarrassed to explain himself, too afraid of the void to let go, Ray slid down, ran to the far end of the bridge and crouched in the bushes there. As she drew closer, she merged into the darkness.

Not so long ago, Ray would have dashed off an angry email to the local papers, complaining about the council's failure to maintain adequate street lighting, but that version of him had died alongside Flit. Now everything seemed pointless.

The clicking stopped, a scream was stifled. Ray heard the sounds of a struggle. Not willing to engage, he stayed put and kept quiet.

And yet he couldn't forget her kindness.

'Are you alright, miss?' he asked, standing up, peering into the darkness, aware how foolish the question sounded.

Although she didn't reply, a sharp intake of breath made him certain a man was with her.

Ray emerged from the bushes and back onto the bridge. 'What's going on?' he asked, his voice tremulous and weak.

'Go away. This is private.' The man's voice was rough, his accent local.

Ray swallowed, feeling his heart might burst from his chest, but approached until he was close enough to see what was happening. The barmaid, tiny and terrified, was struggling against a thick arm around her waist and a huge hand clamped over her mouth. The man had cropped blond hair and a prominent nose, and looked worryingly large.

Ray, though neither small nor weak, fought an impulse to walk away. 'Let her go,' he said, trying to sound tough and confident.

'This is none of your business, mate.'

'It is now.'

'Fuck off, if you know what's good for you.'

Ray drew himself up and squared his shoulders. 'Let her go. Now.'

'Get lost or you're in big trouble.'

'Why?'

'Because I'll kill you.'

'I reckon you're all piss and wind, Blondie, and I'm not going anywhere,' said Ray, wondering if his bluff would be called. 'Let her go and let's see what you're made of.'

Blondie shoved the woman to the ground. Ray, surprising himself, darted forward and attempted a wild clout.

'You asked for it,' said Blondie, blocking with

his forearm and lunging at Ray, club fists swinging.

Although Ray ducked under the first, he never even saw the follow-up punch, which exploded against the side of his head, knocking him down but not out.

'Is that the best you can do?' he said, struggling back to his feet, rubbing his jaw and spitting blood, dazed but detached from the pain and fear. After all, he had nothing to lose but his life. 'I reckon my old Gran could do better… and she's been dead for ten years.'

'Then you'll soon be joining her.' The big man swaggered forward like someone who'd done such things many times before, and had done them well.

Ray ducked and dodged, amazed himself by landing a straight jab to the nose, and avoided a swinging right and left combination before a scything kick swept his legs from under him. His head hit the road and he lay stunned, though not enough that he couldn't feel the foot stamping on his face. Even so, he knew the barmaid had got away and, despite the increasing pain, felt happier than he had in months.

Blondie, blood dribbling from his nose,

picked Ray up as if he weighed no more than a child and hurled him over the parapet.

'Thank you,' Ray murmured.

Fragments of memories, as vague and insubstantial as fading dreams, returned: a plunge into darkness, the breathtaking shock of cold water, surfacing, gasping, swirling, going under, gentle hands pulling him ashore. There'd been a sweet, flowery scent. More clear was the ambulance ride, a smell of bleach and then his arrival at Glevchester Hospital, where numerous small injuries made themselves obvious as he returned to full consciousness.

Nothing was broken they said, just minor contusions and grazes. Mild hypothermia and alcohol explained his confusion. They claimed Ray was lucky, though he did not feel it, even after drugs had dulled the pain. All that remained was disappointment. His plan had failed, though it was not unpleasant to have people caring about him, even if they were only doing their jobs and would put him from their minds as soon as the next patient required attention.

He could, however, have done without the

questioning. 'What's your name? Where do you live? How are you? How did you end up in the river? Were you in a fight?' Unwilling to admit to attempted suicide, he exaggerated his befuddlement, twisted facts and even resorted to a few downright lies, including giving a false name: John Smith. He wasn't certain they believed him. A wall clock showed two o'clock. Someone mentioned the police were on their way. Reluctant to stand up to any more interrogation, Ray looked for an opportunity to get away.

An emergency came in.

Left alone, Ray checked no one was watching and hauled his battered frame from the trolley. Despite shaky legs, he felt better than he might have done, though he was wearing only a flimsy hospital robe, useless for a great escape. He was fortunate to find his own clothes screwed up in a polythene bag beneath the trolley. Discarding the robe, he hurried to dress, shivering as the clammy cloth engulfed his warm skin, but relieved to find his wallet still in a pocket. He tiptoed away, reached the main entrance unnoticed and slipped into the cool night air, hoping a taxi would be waiting and would take him home. There wasn't one, so he hurried along empty streets until he reached the centre of town where he flagged down the first one he saw.

Had he wished for a cabby who wouldn't stop talking during the entire journey, he'd have been in luck. He hadn't, of course, so endured a tortuous and inane monologue about cats for most of the forty-minute journey to the smart Cotswold village of Willoton.

Making the directions easy, Ray asked the cabby to stop outside the gates of Willoton Hall, a once grand Victorian mansion long-since turned into luxury apartments, and paid the fare with soggy money, including a tip which he hoped was adequate, but not extravagant. Once alone, he turned and hobbled back towards Riverside Cottage, his home—if he could still call it that. The dank October air, the blustery wind and the heavy clouds suggested rain was imminent. His clothing was already damp and clinging to his body, but it was only a ten-minute walk, and walking was just about the only activity that could divert him from the shapeless half-life he'd been enduring.

He was mooching along the dark and narrow winding lane towards the cottage, when a car, driven at reckless speed, forced him against the drystone wall. For a moment he was tempted to step into its path and the only thing that held him back was unwillingness to risk injuring anyone else.

On reaching the cottage, he let himself in. The familiarity of the decorations and furnishings, nearly all Flit's handiwork, struck him hard, shocking reminders of when they'd been happy. At least that was what he'd always told himself, though recently he'd started wondering if the only reason she'd done everything around the house was because he'd never bothered. He'd tried convincing himself it really hadn't been his fault. His promotion at Burke and Coe had led to work gobbling up so much of his time that he'd been too tired to do much more than slump in front of the television and eat whatever she put in front of him whenever he returned home in the evenings. The money he earned, however, had enabled them to live in a sought after area and take expensive holidays, which Ray had considered so important at the time.

His mouth was as dry as the dust covering every surface—all they'd given him at the hospital was a lukewarm plastic cup of coffee from a machine, and the whiskies he'd knocked back earlier were splitting his head. He entered the contemporary fitted kitchen with its smart granite worktops and English oak storage cupboards, once Flit's pride and joy. Something stank in there, but he couldn't be bothered to do anything about it.

He put the kettle on. When it boiled, he made tea and sat at the kitchen table, yawning and trying to remember if he had any painkillers.

It was bright daylight when he surfaced from a recurring nightmare in which an angry face he couldn't quite identify screamed accusations and abuse. His head was thumping and his mouth felt as if someone had coated it in dry flour. He poured out some tea. It was cold and stewed, but he drank it anyway.

The pong had become unbearable. He traced it to the remains of a microwaved chicken madras that had been rotting in the bin for a week. Holding his breath, his stomach heaving, he tied up the bin liner and lugged it outside to a pile beside the back gate. Marauding wasps buzzed around his head, making him flap and curse—he hated creepy-crawlies in general and wasps in particular.

Perhaps he ought to take the stuff round to the front so it could be collected before it attracted rats. But did the bin men still come round on alternate Wednesdays? He hadn't a clue—he'd left even that small job to Flit. Whatever, it would have to wait until he felt better.

He returned to the table, sat down, squeezed out another cup of tea and dozed off again.

Ray woke with a start, feeling sick and muzzy-headed. His clothes were still moist in patches and he was shivering. The doorbell was ringing and, though he couldn't be bothered to answer, the sound of a key turning in the lock made him get to his feet and stagger into the hallway.

'Oh… Raymondo, so you are home,' said the tall, slim, black-haired man in his early thirties who'd let himself in.

Ray winced, but forced a smile at his wife's former colleague from Heartfields. 'Alex.'

'Alright if I come in?'

Ray bit back on a retort that Alex was already in, nodded and stepped aside. 'Go through to the kitchen.'

It was the tidiest room downstairs though that wasn't saying much. Alex's nose wrinkled at the lingering reminders of the great stink as he sat down on the best chair, dropping his newspaper onto the table.

'I didn't know you had a key,' said Ray, sitting opposite and, despite his best efforts, admiring the cut of Alex's suit.

'You gave it me. Don't you remember?'

'Er… yeah… I suppose I must have done.'

Alex sat back. 'How are you doing?'

'Alright… in the circumstances.'

Although Alex nodded, he looked around the kitchen, taking in the pile of dirty clothing in the corner, the unwashed dishes festering in the sink, Ray's soiled clothes and his battered face. 'Are you quite sure, Raymondo? Are you really coping? With the inquest coming up and all that?'

Ray slumped.

'And what on earth have you been doing to yourself? You look terrible. Your face…'

'I… er… fell over.'

'And your hand?'

Ray glanced at his skinned, swollen knuckles. 'It's not as bad as it looks.'

Alex scrutinised him. 'Felicity… Flit… wouldn't have wanted to see you living like this. I'm sorry to have to say it, but you need to shower. And when did you last have a haircut or shave? You must start taking care of yourself. I know it'll be difficult, but you've got to get a grip. You still have a life to lead and things will get easier, I promise. It'll just take time.'

Alex's kind words and smile breached the dam of self-control that had been holding back a reservoir of unhappiness. Ray shamed himself by crying at what he'd lost. He also felt awful that he'd once been consumed by doubts about Alex who, despite being as distraught as Ray at Flit's death, had been the only one to look out for him afterwards.

'Let it all out, mate,' said Alex, getting up and placing a hand on Ray's shoulder.

Ray did, sobbing as he hadn't been able to at the funeral, when he'd been too numb to take it all in. Alex left him alone for a few minutes until he was more himself.

'It's a damned sad business,' Alex murmured. 'A bloody horrible thing that happened... what a waste... what a mess.'

'It was all my fault,' said Ray. 'If I hadn't run, she'd still be alive.' A fresh bout of sobs choked him.

'Drink this,' said Alex, placing a mug of tea in

front of him. 'You'll feel better.'

'Not in this world.'

'Don't talk like that. It was just circumstances. I'm sure the coroner will find you weren't entirely to blame.'

Ray shook his head. Alex couldn't possibly understand just how deep his guilt was, but, having calmed down after a sip or two of tea, he thought it high time to man up. 'Sorry about that,' he said, and blew his nose—his handkerchief smelled of river. He forced a crooked smile. 'What have you been up to?'

'Not a lot,' said Alex. 'Work has been busy because… well, you know?'

'How are things at Heartfields?'

Alex scowled. 'Not great, to be honest. There appears to be some sort of black hole in the accounts. They should have promoted me instead of bringing in one of the boss's mates—I deserved it and I'd never have allowed such things to happen.'

Ray nodded, trying to show interest, though he'd heard similar moans more times than he could remember. 'Have they found anyone to replace Flit yet?'

'No one could replace her, but they have brought someone in to do her job. I'm training him and it's hard work.' Alex sighed and poured more tea. 'And what do you do with your days?'

'Not much.'

'Do you feel ready to go back to work?'

Ray shook his head. He daren't face his colleagues yet, whether they were sympathetic or judgemental.

Alex shrugged. 'So, are you still moping around the house all the time?'

'No, I've started going out for long walks.'

'I'm glad to hear it—that's got to be better. Anywhere special?'

'Nowhere in particular, just wherever my feet take me, and then I find my way back. Walking is the only thing that helps, and I only sleep when I'm physically exhausted. Sometimes I walk all night.' He didn't mention that he preferred being out in the dark or in bad weather when he was less likely to bump into someone who might know him and want to talk.

'Do you ever head over to Glevchester or anywhere near there?'

Ray shook his head. 'No... well yes. I had a visit to A&E at Glevchester hospital... after my fall.'

'So you haven't visited the White Hart recently?'

'No. Where's that?' Ray tried to appear nonchalant. He had no wish to explain why he'd been there.

'Across the river in Bindover. You must remember.'

Ray shook his head.

'That's strange. Felicity said the two of you used to go there quite often once upon a time. She said you liked to sit out with a beer and have a meal and watch the river roll by.'

Ray paused. 'Oh... yeah... now you mention it I think I do, though it seems a long while ago.'

'Right. But you haven't been back there recently?'

'Not for ages.' Ray flushed and sweated.

'Oh, well, not to worry. Have you seen today's paper?'

'I'm afraid not. I don't get one delivered and I've rather cut myself off from news. Why do you ask?'

'No reason, Raymondo. Well, I'd better be going. Finish your tea, mate. I'll find my own way out. See you soon.'

'See you,' said Ray, forcing another smile. Alex departed, leaving his paper on the table.

Ray glanced at the headline: 'Woman attacked on Bindover Bridge.' The artist's impression of the unkempt suspect did look worryingly like him.

Ray could see it all—the barmaid must have blamed him!

It was too much to cope with. Panicking, he wasted no time in reading the article. Although a sensible part of his brain suggested calling the police to explain what had really happened, he knew he'd have to reveal what he'd really been doing there. How would they react? They'd certainly want to stop him trying again. And what if they locked him up for his own protection? Worse, what if they didn't believe him?

He'd become accustomed to walking away from his troubles and flight was all he could think of. Where he'd flee to and what might happen, he'd worry about later. Assuming Alex would already have called the police, he needed to get away as fast as possible. Ray pounded upstairs, put on clean clothes and chucked a change of clothing and some other essentials into his backpack. Seeing it brought back memories of the safari with Flit in Tanzania, a happy time despite multiple attacks from biting bugs and stinging things.

Ray rubbed a tear from his cheek, slung the pack over his shoulder and ran downstairs, grabbing his trusty old parka from the hook by the front door and, for once, wishing he still had his car. His hand was already on the latch when he thought to check his wallet. It was nearly empty and, although he still had credit cards, he'd heard the police could track their use.

He felt an urge to lie low for a few days. For that he needed cash—without it he'd not get far. Stumped for a moment or two, he remembered Flit concealing some money in a tin at the back of the kitchen cupboard 'in case of emergency'. He'd scoffed at the time and now wished he hadn't. After running into the kitchen, he rummaged through the cupboard, cursing his failure to pay attention when she'd told him where she'd hidden it. A distant siren made his heart surge, but he forced himself to keep calm and methodical, checking each tin until he found the right one—deceivingly labelled as pitted black olives.

The siren sounded louder.

Time to go.

He shoved the tin into his pack and sneaked out the back door, amazed to see hints of evening already greying the daylight—he must have slept at the table for hours which explained why his belly was rumbling. The clouds looked heavy and foreboding as he reached the stone wall at the end of the garden. He climbed over and set off along the side of the little River Soren. There was no footpath and he made slow progress through briars and brambles that stabbed and slashed at exposed skin. At last, he reached a rough trail trodden out by some wild animal and although it ran perilously close to the river in places and was slick with mud that grew increasingly slippery as rain started, it allowed him to keep up a good pace as the light faded. When the bank collapsed, he went in up to his knees. He dragged himself out and squelched along the trail, muttering.

Twilight arrived and a distant peacock cried out, making him jump and bang his head on a low branch. He wished he'd thought to bring a torch, though he reflected it would have cut through the gloom like a beacon, pinpointing his position to the police—assuming they were coming for him, because although he'd now heard several sirens round the end of the lane, they no longer sounded as if they were getting any closer. A sort of hopeful paranoia battled with common sense, suggesting that if the police believed him to be the bridge attacker, they might consider him dangerous and desperate. Perhaps even now they were preparing an armed response. Though he didn't entirely believe it, he hoped so—a well-aimed bullet would be quick.

The sirens fell silent and although there was still no sign of anyone hunting for him, he remained cautious. Sometimes, he felt as if someone was following, but heard or saw no one.

After about fifteen minutes, during which he'd slipped and stumbled countless times, his path took him towards a stile by the lane where flashing blue lights cut through the gloom. Creeping towards it, he peeped over the top and saw a car had crashed—it looked like the one he'd had to dodge on his way home. It now lay on its side in a ditch, with two police cars, a fire engine and an ambulance in attendance. Since all the fuss was nothing to do with him this time, his confidence returned and he climbed over the stile and marched up the lane away from his home, hoping his wet legs, mud-caked shoes and backpack would make him appear a harmless and enthusiastic rambler. It seemed to work. At any rate, no one stopped him or appeared to notice him. He turned onto the main road and sauntered past the local boozer, the Watermill Inn, which was already lit up for the night and had several cars parked outside. The inn's food and beer had a reputation that drew connoisseurs from many miles away. Ray and Flit had once been regulars, though he couldn't remember the last time he'd paid a visit. Seeing a large, rough-looking bloke leaving with another man, he wondered if standards had slipped.

Putting such trivialities from his mind, he headed up the hill away from the village centre. When he heard a car's engine approaching from the direction of his cottage, Ray dodged into the bus shelter and peeped out. Another police car approached and stopped by the accident. An officer got out, and spoke with the other cops who pointed up the hill.

It was then a bus turned up. Ray made a quick decision and stepped aboard—it was hardly likely anyone who knew him would be on a bus.

'Where to?' asked the driver.

'Er… where are you going?'

'Glevchester Central via Sorenchester and villages on the way.'

'Great. I hoped it was because that's where I'm heading… Glevchester that is.'

'Single or return?'

'Single please.'

'That'll be six pounds and sixty pence.'

Ignoring an impulse to tap his credit card on the reader, Ray fished out the olive tin from his backpack and paid with a ten-pound note. The driver grunted, poked a few buttons, and handed him a ticket and a handful of loose change, most of it small and brown, rattled into the pan.

'Sorry for all the shrapnel, mate,' said the driver. 'That's just the way it comes out.'

Ray scooped up the coins and dropped them into his trouser pockets, feeling the weight and wondering if it might have tipped the balance when he'd been in the river.

The bus set off and, being less than half full, Ray could take his pick of seats. He chose one at the back by the window from where he could keep a wary eye out for pursuing police cars. His squelchy feet felt as if encased in ice and he was shivering despite the warmth from a heater in front. He began to relax a little. He counted the roll of money in his tin—one thousand pounds, more than enough for his present needs. The rain came down heavier, sounding like someone throwing handfuls of gravel at the windows, and a thuggish wind buffeted them.

Twenty minutes later, with no sign of police pursuit, they reached the small Cotswold market town of Sorenchester and stopped by the stately old church. A handful of passengers got off and a few new ones dripped aboard. Ray gazed out at the wet street. Perhaps he'd look for a hotel in Glevchester and stay there until he'd recovered his nerve and was again ready to look death in the face. Ray's own face reflected in the window—it really did look like the artist's impression in the paper. If he didn't wish to explain himself—and he didn't—he'd have to do something. On impulse, he leapt to his feet, swung the backpack over his shoulder, and dashed for the door, squeezing out as it began to close.

'Oi! This isn't your stop,' the bus driver yelled.

Ray mumbled some sort of apology and stumbled as he struck the pavement. He would have stretched his length in a puddle had he not cannoned into a huge bloated, ugly bloke wearing a stained vest and filthy trousers who was waiting to cross the road.

'Watch it, mate!' the ugly man growled, giving him an angry glare.

'I'm so sorry,' said Ray, afraid he was going to get punched. 'I lost my footing.'

'Well, don't do it again.' The man took a deep breath, shook his head and stalked away in the direction of Vermin Street, which was otherwise deserted beneath the glow of street lights.

Ray set off down The Shambles, its smart rows of shops all closed for the night, its pubs and restaurants shining. Huddling into his parka, he headed for the Queen's Arms, a recently tarted-up hotel in the centre of town, and took refuge inside. The scent of freshly cooked food moistened his mouth and he longed to order a meal, but the bar was busy with tourists and recently released office workers—any one of them might recognise him from the paper.

He sneaked past a tired-looking businessman checking in at reception and entered the warmth of the gents' toilets, which reeked of soap and hygiene. After checking he was alone, he propped his backpack against a wall, pulled out his washbag and rummaged in it for nail scissors, razor and shaving foam. He set to work. Within a few minutes, and after a great deal of wincing as he shaved over the bruises and grazes on his face, he achieved his end. He dried up with paper towels and checked his image in the mirror, repulsed, though satisfied, by the shaven-headed thug staring back at him. Four months' growth of hair on scalp and face littered the sink. He gathered it up, determined to leave no evidence, and flushed it down the toilet. Then he took off his shoes and socks, rinsed them, shut himself into a cubicle and changed into clean, dry trousers.

By the time he left the Queen's Arms, his confidence was high—no one would recognise him now.

Back in the street, the rain was sharp enough to sting, while the wind tested every entry point, making him glad of the sturdy zips on his parka. Even so, goose pimples prickled his skin and he decided that death by exposure would take too long and be far too unpleasant. Furthermore, he was light-headed with hunger and in need of a drink. He sheltered in a posh shoe shop's doorway and looked up and down the road, deep in thought. Twelve years earlier, before Flit, the Packhorse on Vermin Street had served food and with any luck it still did. He had fond memories of the place from the time he'd lived in a small, draughty flat above an electrical shop about two minutes' walk away. In those days he'd often appreciated the pub's warmth, its meals and its company, if not its cleanliness. He doubted any of the regulars would still be around—most of them had been pensioners or lonely young people fresh to town and starting new jobs. Besides, he'd lost a lot of weight since then and had got his wonky front teeth fixed. Also, unless the pub had changed, it had the advantages of not being brightly lit and of being a little out of the way.

He entered the Packhorse, reassured that the old place appeared not to have been decorated since his day. The carpet was still faded and threadbare, the wallpaper stained and torn, just as he remembered, only more so. A scruffy middle-aged couple reading tabloid newspapers glanced up and returned to their studies. The air stank of over-boiled cabbage, stale beer and flatulence. Ray was inclined to blame an old man crouched over a half of

Guinness for the latter until an ancient and obese Labrador waddled from a corner and greeted him with a tail wag and a malodorous fart. No one else appeared to notice, but Ray rushed to the bar to avoid the toxic fumes.

A young barman looked up from a car magazine. 'Evening, guv. What can I get you?'

'A pint of Barker's Best Bitter, please,' said Ray, pointing at the hand pump.

'Barker's is off.'

'I'll have a pint of Guinness then.'

'That's off, too. Charlie finished it.' The barman nodded towards the old man, who clutched his glass as if it might be snatched away.

'Okay,' said Ray, 'tell me what you do have.'

'Lager or bottled beers. Our next delivery is tomorrow.'

'Right...' Ray studied the list on the wall. 'I'll have a bottle of brown ale, please.'

'Barkers or Trotman's?'

'Either.'

'Right you are.' The barman squatted by the chiller cabinet. 'Sorry, guv, there's none left. I can get one from the back, but it won't have been cooled. Would that be alright?'

'Yeah... okay.'

The barman disappeared behind a greasy door, leaving Ray to contemplate the view and take in the number of empty, or near-empty, spirit and wine bottles on the shelves. The man was gone for what seemed like an age and Ray was beginning to get twitchy, fearing he'd been recognised, when a head poked around the door. 'Sorry, guv, we're right out of brown ale... and just about everything else except champagne.'

'Just give me a pint of anything you've got that tastes something like beer.'

'Right you are.' The barman poured some yellow fizz into a glass and placed it in front of Ray with the satisfied smile of a man who'd done a good job. 'Anything else?'

'Yes, I'd like something to eat please.'

'Sorry, guv. I'm afraid last food orders are at eight o'clock.'

Ray glanced at his watch. 'It's one minute to.'

'Yeah, but it'd be past eight by the time I get the order to the chef. If you'd only ordered when you came in...'

Ray struggled to keep the lid on his temper. 'Come off it. If you hadn't given me the run about, I'd have been on time, wouldn't I?'

'Yeah, I suppose, but my life wouldn't be

worth living if I started giving the chef orders after eight... I only work here you know.'

'This is ridiculous.'

'We've got peanuts or crisps, and there might be a bag of pork scratchings left—unless Charlie's had 'em.'

'Forget it.' Ray turned around and stomped towards the door, muttering.

'Oi! You haven't paid for your drink.'

Ray stalked out. The rain had almost ceased and a damp wind blew tattered clouds across the gibbous moon. Now desperate for sustenance, he set off on a quest. Although drawn to the Bear with a Sore Head, which did excellent meals, he ruled it out on the grounds that, being close to the police station, it was popular with cops who fancied a beer after work. A whiff of warm bread and oregano reached his nostrils and made up his mind.

He hurried through a passageway towards Subvert, a cafe specialising in American-style sub sandwiches. It was well-lit and surprisingly busy, but Ray was confident he was unrecognisable. After a brief contemplation of the menu on the door, he went inside and ordered a Spicy Italian.

A pretty girl in a dark blue uniform at the

counter, looked him up and down, took a deep breath and asked,

'Dooyawannitwivotpippersorcrispivejis?'

'What?' Ray recognised a question, but the speed of her words and strange accent baffled him.

'Dooyawannitwivotpippersorcrispivejis?' the girl repeated, a little louder, giving him a look suggesting she was used to dealing with dimwits.

Ray felt as baffled as the time when he and Flit had tried to order train tickets in Bangkok. 'I'm very sorry, miss, but I have absolutely no idea what you said.'

'She asked if you wanted your sandwich with hot peppers or crisp veggies,' said a scruffy little man with a hoarse voice, who'd followed him in.

'Thanks.' Ray turned to the girl. 'I'll have the hot peppers, please.'

'Dooyawannadrinkwivit?'

'Do you want a drink with it,' the little man translated.

'Thanks, but I got that. Yes please, miss, I would like one.'

'Wadayoowan?'

'Coffee, please... Big as you got... Black.'

'Yoogorrit,' said the girl.

'Well done, mate,' said the little man, winking as Ray paid.

The girl constructed Ray's sandwich with well-practised efficiency, poured coffee into a capacious paper cup, and handed him the meal. A corner table became vacant, so he took occupancy of a hard chair, stretched out his legs and ate. His sandwich was tasty though the bitter coffee was barely palatable until he'd swamped it with sugar. He followed up with a giant choc-chip cookie and another coffee.

In the warmth and with a full belly, it was not surprising he dozed off.

A hand on his shoulder woke him.

'What's the matter?' he asked the girl who was standing over him.

'We'reclosing... infifeminitz.'

'What, already?' But the other customers had gone and the staff were clearing up.

She glanced at the wall clock. 'It'snearlytenaklok.'

Ray realised how pretty she looked, with her long, dark hair tied up under a white cap, her big brown eyes and sensuously full lips against lightly tanned skin. He wondered where she came from and then hated himself for having noticed her at all. It was disloyal to Flit and it was time to go. Though he felt lethargic and heavy limbed, he got up, wishing he was home and could just crawl into bed—it held so much more appeal now he'd denied himself its comforts.

Shaking his head and suppressing yawns, he opened the door, said goodnight and stepped out, where the cold air slapped his face and brought him back to life. He walked around the town, reviewing ways to end his life and discarding them as too uncertain, too messy, or too painful. Then came a moment of inspiration—last night on the bridge he'd acted almost as if he were brave and with a little more luck he would have perished at the hands of the big blond thug. That was the answer—he would become a hero, a knight errant, helping underdogs and rescuing damsels in distress. A hero who didn't know much about fighting would probably not last long, but that was surely an advantage. Although violence wasn't his bag, he had nothing of value to lose and could persuade himself that any pain would be temporary, before death took it away forever.

Such thoughts occupied him as he wandered

around the middle of town, making several circuits, until the streets were deserted and the three-quarter moon shone bright, casting weird shadows. The church clock showed the time as nearly one o'clock and all was silent—a small, quiet Cotswold town was probably not the ideal location for a hero with a death wish.

All the coffee had worked through to his bladder and nature called. He ducked down an alley by the church which, despite an old-fashioned street light halfway along, was filled with deep shadows. He undid his flies and prepared to piss in a corner.

'No, mate, please!' said a hoarse voice.

Ray jumped back and turned around, buttoning back up, ashamed and embarrassed. 'Sorry, didn't see you.'

He hurried away into the fields at the back of the church and, feeling like a dog, used a convenient tree as a target. Relieved at last, he gazed at the lake glinting beneath the moon. The peaceful scene reminded him of his honeymoon and looking out over Horseshoe Bay in the little beach bar that had turned out to be a gourmet's delight, with affordable prices and great wine. He sighed. Happy times.

Someone cried out. It was a cry of fear.

A second cry, high-pitched as if from a terrified woman, followed. Ray could envisage what was happening—the guy he'd nearly pissed on must have been lurking in the shadows awaiting a suitable victim. His first instinct was to run away, but he didn't—this might be a perfect opportunity to test his new heroism by charging to the assistance of the damsel in distress, and damning the consequences. He tried to ignore the adage about the sort of people who rush in where angels fear to tread.

Despite his good intentions, his legs proved unwilling to comply—playing the hero would not be easy for a man accustomed to driving a coward's body. Breathing heavily, he staggered forward, coming close to collapse as he entered the alley. Adrenalin kicked in, his lurching walk turned into a jog and then a sprint. Ahead, he could hear a male voice and a strange puppy-like whimpering.

'Shut up and stop grovelling,' said the voice, deep and hard. 'Give it up. You know what we want.'

'Don't think of fighting, because you've got no

chance and we'll get it anyway,' said a second voice, smoother, more cultured, but just as menacing.

Rounding the bend into the lamp post's glow, Ray made out the silhouettes of two men bending over a small, cowering figure. His initial plan was to demand what was going on and to remonstrate with the assailants, but he had a fleeting impression of something dark brushing past at high speed, clipping his ankle and making him stumble. The damp mossy slabs were as slippery as wet eels; he skidded, lost his footing, and his momentum cannoned him into the nearest man who tumbled like a skittle and flattened his comrade. The impact stunned Ray who lay on the cold ground feeling as if he'd run headlong into the wall. He tried to prepare himself for the consequences, but the two men, both at least a decade younger than him, were down. One groaned and twitched. The other lay still.

'Cheers for that,' said a hoarse male voice, 'but although the scoundrels are valiantly vanquished for the moment, we'd better get the hell out of here.'

A hand grabbed Ray's arm, dragged him to his feet and hustled him from the alley towards the town.

It was only when they were running down Vermin Street that Ray's head cleared enough to recognise the little guy from Subvert. 'Where are we going?'

'My place, before those big bullies come after us. Now, move.' He bundled Ray along until they were approaching the junction with Mosse Lane, where after a quick glance back up the street, he pulled a large rusty key from his pocket, opened a nondescript wooden gate and pushed Ray through. They were in a small moonlit courtyard in the middle of a tiny square of old houses. The little man locked the gate behind them and swaggered to the nearest house.

'Come in,' he said, as he unlocked the front door and used a cheap cigarette lighter to light an oil lamp.

Ray followed him into a diminutive room that would have felt even more cramped had it contained anything more than a three-legged stool, a beaten-up chair with a cracked leather seat and a beanbag, all standing on a threadbare rug that might have once been red. It smelled musty and dusty with an underlying pong as if something had died there some time ago. Ray could hardly complain—his own kitchen stank as much.

'Thanks for helping out back there,' said the little man, 'though there was no need—I had the situation well in hand. I'm Kevin Crumb, by the way. Most people just call me Kev. You?'

Ray paused. Anonymity might be his best policy if Alex had given his name to the cops. Memory carried him back to his first day at senior school and Mr Marks, the English teacher, asking for his first name. 'Ray, sir,' he'd replied. 'Did you say "Razor", boy?' The class had sniggered, and the nickname had stuck until an unfortunate incident on the rugby pitch, when his repeated panic in the face of the opposition's front row had cost the match. After that his schoolmates just called him Wimpy Holmes.

'Call me…'

'Ishmael?' Kev smirked.

'What? No, it's Razor,' Ray declared, already feeling a little bolder.

'Welcome to my pad, Razor,' said Kev.

'Nice place,' Razor lied, though conceding to himself that, with any amount of effort and money, it might have the makings of a pleasant little town house.

'Sure it is,' said Kev, 'but it's better than being on the street. It's mine, you know. My uncle left it to me in his will, but I don't come here often.'

'That was good of him.'

'Yeah, I suppose it was. Take a seat. The beanbag's the most comfortable, but it's smelly—I found it in a skip. The chair's okay since I fixed it... I think.'

Razor nodded and sat on the cracked leather chair. Although it creaked, it seemed solid enough.

'Would you like a cup of tea? The milk's off.'

'Yes, please,' said Razor. 'I don't mind it black.'

Kev lit a candle and disappeared through a doorway at the back, giving Razor a chance to look around, though there was precious little to see: four walls with peeling paint, two of them with battered doors, the bits of furniture, the oil lamp, a spidery fireplace and a small pile of empty beer cans in the corner. Gradually, his heart rate returned to normal and all sorts of thoughts crossed his mind concerning Kev's motives. He settled on the hope that it was merely gratitude and smiled at Kev's confidence that he'd had the situation under control—it was not how it had appeared.

Kev came back with two mugs. He handed one

to Razor, who checked it carefully before drinking. The mug was clean, its contents pale. He took a sip—it was like drinking the ghost of tea.

'It might be a bit weak,' Kev admitted, as if reading Razor's mind. 'The bag's been used too many times. I'll pick up some new ones tomorrow.'

'It's hot and wet,' said Razor. 'It'll do me fine.'

'Thank you again for helping me.'

'My pleasure. What were you doing there?'

'Hiding. I feared those fellows were intending to give me a right good working over.'

'I got that impression,' said Razor, glancing around the room. 'Were they trying to rob you, because, and forgive me for saying it, you don't appear to have much money?'

'You mean that having nothing, nothing can I lose?'

'I suppose so. They looked well off, so why pick on you?'

'The big posh one reckoned I'd nicked his wallet.'

'Why would he think that?'

'Because I had nicked it,' said Kev, grinning as he pulled a smart blue leather wallet from his back pocket and examined it. 'Louis Vuitton—

not bad, and worth a bit on its own.' He first took out a couple of credit cards, frowned and chucked them into a small bin. Then, he removed a fistful of bank notes, counted them and shrugged. 'Only ninety-five quid. I was hoping for more. Still, it'll buy a few groceries.'

'And beer?' said Razor.

'I guess that's likely as well.'

The exchange left Razor confused. Rescuing a self-confessed thief from retribution had not been the heroic gesture he'd aimed for, but for reasons he couldn't understand, it felt right to have helped this strange little man, whatever he'd done. He sipped his pale imitation of tea. 'Do you steal many wallets?'

'Not as many as I'd like. Most guys aren't as careless as Sebastian.'

'You know him?' Stealing from a friend was really low in Razor's opinion.

'No, but I've seen him about. He was in The Barley Mow, shooting off his mouth with his pal and bullying the barmaid. When he took his jacket off, I took the opportunity to teach him a lesson. Tragically, he spotted me and gave chase. I thought I'd given them the slip until I was forced to reveal my presence to prevent an unpleasantness.'

'Sorry about that. I didn't see you in the dark.'

Kev laughed. 'Thank you for restraining yourself. Not everyone in this town would be that considerate. Alas, those guys heard me and well, you know the rest. That was some charge you made to take them both out like that.'

Razor attempted a heroic devil-may-care grin, but couldn't stop laughing at himself. 'The truth is I'm not sure what I would have done, if something hadn't made me stumble. I just skidded into them.'

'Cry havoc and let slip the feet of war. Whatever your intent, I thank you.'

Razor placed his mug on the floor and stood up. 'I'm glad I could help, but I ought to be going. Thank you for the tea.'

'Go if you wish, but you're welcome to stay the night. It'll be safer. Those guys might be looking for you now.'

'I doubt it. It all happened so fast it's unlikely they even saw me.' Razor tried to act determined though the rain spattering against the window and a howling wind sapped his resolve. He felt like sleeping for a week and longed to be safe and warm in bed with Flit. Such thoughts had become a regular torture and too often the only way he could drop off was after walking himself into a state of exhaustion. Kev's motive for taking him in were another cause for concern—did the little guy intend to rob him, could he be some kind of sexual deviant, or was there another reason?

It was time to get out and return to pounding the streets, though sleep called so strongly, Razor's dozy brain wondered if he'd already been drugged. He yawned.

Razor awoke to the mouth-watering scent of frying bacon. Foggy recollections of the screaming man nightmare dispersed, leaving him alone in an unfamiliar little room, lit by dull morning light. He was enclosed in a smelly beanbag, with a soft pillow beneath his head and a musty blanket wrapped around him. His watch showed it was approaching nine o'clock and his bladder suggested he should move pretty smartly. He struggled to his feet, relieved to see he was fully dressed and, hearing movement in the kitchen, pushed open the door.

'Good morning,' said Kev, who was standing in front of an ancient cooker, attending to a blackened frying pan. 'Sleep well?'

'Yeah, apart from a bad dream. Where's the bathroom?'

Kev pointed. 'Through there and second left. Sorry.'

Razor hurried along a grubby corridor, burst into the bathroom and understood Kev's apology—it was on the sordid end of the squalid spectrum, but he had no option. When he'd finished, he used a rock-hard sliver of grey soap to wash his hands and wiped them on his trousers, trying to ignore the foetid towel dangling from a rusty hook in the corner. A glance into the smeared and spattered mirror showed the bruises on his face had spread and were taking on sunset colours, reminding him of some abstract paintings Flit had unaccountably liked.

The bacon smell drew him back to the kitchen.

'Eggs and bacon okay for you?' asked Kev.

Razor glanced around, surprised the work surfaces were gleaming clean, despite advanced years and wear. 'That would be great.'

'Take a seat.'

Kev set down a plate of bacon and eggs. Razor sat and ate greedily, washing his breakfast down with a mug of strong tea made with fresh milk. 'That was great. Where did it come from?'

'I went shopping.'

'With money?'

'Of course.'

Razor's suspicions rose. He felt his pockets. 'Where's my wallet?'

Kev shrugged. 'How would I know?'

Although Kev's expression was innocent, Razor would be no soft touch. 'I want it back.'

'But I haven't got it.'

'Who else would have it?' Anger flared.

'Sorry, mate, but I haven't seen it. Honest,' said Kev, his face creased with worry, his pale-blue eyes bugged like a frightened rabbit's.

Razor shook his head, determined to take back what belonged to him, even though the money was of little importance. It was the principle that mattered—a thousand pounds for a night's bed-and-breakfast? Ridiculous! Fury was approaching the surface, as happened too often these days, and he felt control slipping away. He wanted to give someone else a taste of pain. Kev, not a man who looked as if he could defend himself, would be an ideal subject. Razor kicked back his chair and stood up, clenching his fists.

'What are you going to do?' said Kev, backing away and knocking the frying pan from the cooker.

It crashed to the red brick floor, shocking Razor from his furious mood. He had a thought. Unclenching his fists, he returned to the tiny living room, where his parka was hanging from a nail. His wallet was in the pocket and the rest of his money was still inside the olive tin in his backpack.

'I'm so sorry,' he said, ashamed, all anger draining away as if a plug had been pulled.

He offered Kev the tin. 'Take it,' he said. 'I'm sorry for behaving like an idiot. I should have trusted you.'

'You'd be mad to trust in the tameness of a wolf,' said Kev with a grin. 'To be honest, in other circumstances, I might have pinched it, but I won't take your money now.'

'Seriously, you can have it,' said Razor. 'I don't need it.'

'Why not?'

Razor shrugged. 'Because I'm… er… planning to go away where money won't be of any use, so you might as well take it. You look as if you could use it.'

'I can always use money, mate, but I don't

understand. Why won't you need it when you come back?'

'I won't be coming back.'

'But...' Kev began.

Razor raised his hand. 'Thank you for letting me sleep here and for breakfast, but I've got to go now.' He transferred the notes from the tin to his wallet and placed twenty pounds on the table, despite Kev's protestations. 'This is for putting me up last night. Sorry for the misunderstanding. Goodbye.'

He grabbed his parka and backpack, went out the front door and tried the gate.

It was locked.

'Let me out... please.'

'Yeah, of course.'

Kev picked up his keys and released Razor back into society. 'Take care, mate,' he said and locked the gate.

Razor wandered away, up Vermin Street and towards the centre of town, trying to work out what had happened. It was weird that it felt right to have helped Kev out, though he'd have been hard put to explain why—not that he had any intention of explaining anything to anyone ever again. He'd made his mind up to depart this life in a blaze of glory, performing some heroic deed.

A glimpse of a police uniform sent him scurrying down the nearest alley—the local cops had a troubling reputation, though he wasn't sure why. Besides, he'd suffered more than enough questioning at the hospital. He strode away, slipping into the usual comfortable rhythms created by his footsteps and the beating of his heart.

He'd once been a stickler for structure in his life, but since Flit's untimely death, almost everything had been beyond him. Helpless with grief and regret, all he'd been able to do was drag his body through one guilty day after another. This, he recognised, would be unlikely to present the right opportunities—he needed to work out how and where to put himself into harm's way, though even then he suspected intervening in a crime would more likely result in a bloody nose than death. Most hoodlums, even violent ones, tended to stop short of murder. Yet, surely, if he was in the right places at the right times, the odds for a valorous ending would improve. It might take a while, but he'd got nothing better to do and, even if he couldn't be certain of a quick death, he could still carry out gallant deeds in the meantime.

He walked on, wondering where to go.

By midday, his feet had carried him into Ride Park, a vast area of grass and woodland. It was ideal for solitary walking, thinking and, most of all, for keeping away from cops. The only time he'd seen any there had been at the Sorenchester Country Fair last summer when a team of police motorcyclists had run through a rowdy routine of formation riding and other acts of skill and daring until their bravura performance was curtailed by one of the bikes bursting into flames. The fire brigade's arrival and subsequent extinguishing of the blaze, which had spread to the dry summer grass, had proved even more exciting than the display.

A middle-aged woman in a smart tweed coat was walking a black Labrador towards him. He gave her his best reassuring smile and was surprised when she deliberately took another path—he'd forgotten his shaven head and battered face. Although he'd never before considered that he could look threatening, and the experience was disconcerting, he wondered if it might prove an advantage. Perhaps looking like a hard case would provoke violence. Or maybe he'd get to like his new image—if he survived long enough.

Twenty minutes later, he was deep in the park, beyond the point where dog walkers were permitted and way beyond the limit of asphalt paths. He squelched through puddles and mud, concentrating on staying on his feet. Following a cameo appearance, the sun retired behind dark clouds that were scudding in from the southwest, hinting at another downpour before the afternoon was old. It would, however, make little difference, unless rain kept murderous criminals indoors.

A slim, young woman in jeans and a tight pink sweater ran from the trees towards him, her face screwed up, her teeth gritted, her chest heaving.

A tall, athletic man in a black top and trousers was after her, looking determined. 'I'll get you, missie,' he grunted between gasps.

Opportunity knocked. As soon as the young woman was past, Razor raised his right leg and swung it, ramming it into the tall man's midriff. The impact spun Razor around like the ballerina on Flit's music box, he lost his balance and hit the mud hard. He sprang back up, trembling, but prepared for a fight. The man lay groaning.

Something hit Razor on the back of the head and for the first time in his life he saw stars in daylight.

'Get off him!' There was fury in the young woman's voice.

She raised a hefty stick and smacked it against Razor's forehead, leaving him stunned and bewildered.

When he looked up, she was holding a mobile phone. 'Police... I want to report an attack in Ride Park.'

Still groggy, Razor stumbled away.

Razor fled deeper into the woods until his brain had unscrambled. Zigzagging, backtracking and paddling through water, he ran until he felt safe from pursuit. He subsided to a jog and put more distance between him and the incident, just in case. Now and again he looked back over his shoulder, but he was always alone and although the rational part of his mind doubted the police would mount a search after such a minor incident, he couldn't make himself entirely sure. The whole thing baffled him. He had no doubt the man had been chasing the woman, so her reaction to Razor's courageous intervention had stunned him, almost as much as her stick.

Maybe two hours later, having long ago slowed to a normal walk, he'd changed tack so many times he'd lost his bearings. However, even though the park was extensive, he could relax, for he had nowhere to be and would end up somewhere or other, sooner or later.

It came as a complete surprise when the boggy track he'd followed took him onto the broad ride up to the town gate where a police car lurked. A police officer was talking to a man with a small dog while another officer chatted to a woman with a grizzling kid in a buggy.

Razor performed a quick about turn and casually sauntered back into the woods, his heart thumping. It seemed they were out to get him after all!

'Excuse me, sir.' A loud official voice destroyed any hope they hadn't noticed him.

He engaged headless chicken mode and fled until breathlessness forced a slowdown and gave him time to think. Now he'd got his bearings back, he remembered a splendid stone side gate that led onto Duck Mill Lane in a quiet and wealthy part of Sorenchester. Keeping alert, he adjusted his route and was relieved when the gate was open and unguarded. A quick reconnaissance of the area satisfied him that no one else was around. He sneaked through, adopted a casual saunter and turned down the path by the brook, Duck Mill's water source in its working days before the church acquired the building for an old parsons' home.

All was quiet except for rippling water, the distant murmur of traffic and a feisty wren in the branches above, but despite the apparent safety he thought it wise to change his appearance again. He considered the possibilities of a wig and stick-on beard, but the only place that sold such items around town was the party shop and he could not persuade himself that comedy hair would prove convincing. Perhaps something simpler, like a new coat and hat, would suffice.

Without further thought, except to give thanks the rain was still holding off, he removed his parka, stuffed it into a rubbish bin and headed towards town, his backpack slung over one shoulder. Euphoric at his continued freedom, he punched the air in triumph until guilt reminded him that he had no right to be happy. Even so, despite his best efforts, he felt more alive than he had in months. Cursing the adrenalin and endorphins he supposed were flooding his body with this unasked for well-being, he hurried into town, trying to regain his accustomed misery.

The Shambles, a broad avenue watched over by an imposing medieval church, was far busier than usual, with an excited crowd gathered around the Corn Hall. Curiosity persuaded Razor to linger.

A rotund, red-faced woman spoke to a lanky friend who'd just arrived. 'Hiya, Sal. You hear what happened this morning?'

Sal shook her head.

'Some lunatic attacked Danny in the park...'

'No! Is he alright?' Tears started in Sal's eyes.

'He's fine, don't worry. According to my pal who works at the hospital, he was only shaken up and winded.'

'How awful.'

'Yeah, but kudos to Helen—she beat the nutter off with a stick. The cops are hunting him now.'

'Good for her. You know I always thought he was wasted on her, but maybe...'

No one had called Razor a nutter before and he wasn't sure he liked it. He slipped away, trying to work out why the names Danny and Helen had struck a chord.

The new Camping and Outdoor shop on Vermin Street had a sale on. Razor entered, nodded at the spotty youth at the till, and browsed. After a few minutes, he settled for a dull grey coat with a waterproof shell and removable fleece lining. He took it to the till, reached for his wallet and went hot and cold at the same time—he'd left it in the pocket of his parka.

'Nice composite coat, sir. I've got one myself,' said the spotty youth, as if his endorsement carried enormous weight. 'That'll be forty pounds, please—quite a bargain.'

'The thing is,' said Razor, sure he was red-faced and about to make a fool of himself, 'I... er... I left my wallet...'

'... with me,' said Kev.

Razor stared. It was his wallet. It was in Kev's hand. 'How?' was a question that formed in his mind though his mouth could not articulate.

'Are you alright, sir?' asked the till youth.

Razor pulled himself back together. 'Fine thanks... how much was it again?'

'Forty pounds. That's a lot of coat for the price, sir.'

Razor took the wallet, extracted two twenty-pound notes, and handed them over, becoming the proud possessor of an ugly new coat.

'We'd better hurry,' said Kev, dragging him to the door. 'The meeting's in twenty minutes.'

'Right,' said Razor as Kev hustled him outside. 'Er... meeting?'

'Don't say you've forgotten,' said Kev. 'Honestly, Dave, you'd forget your own head if it wasn't screwed on.'

'Dave?' The shop door closed behind them and Razor was too baffled to object when Kev shoved him along the street. 'What the hell just happened?' he asked.

'I got you out of a jam,' said Kev with a grin that showed off his glistening white teeth, 'and the false name was a brilliant subterfuge.'

'Was it? If it was, then thanks. How come you had my wallet?'

'I took it from your parka. I've got that too if you want it.'

'I was trying to get rid of it.'

'Why?'

'I fancied a new coat.'

'Anything to do with changing your appearance after booting Danny Gilbert?'

'How do you know about that?'

'I was keeping an eye on you.'

'Why?'

'Because I'm worried. There's something about you that's not quite right. Am I wrong?'

'None of your business,' said Razor.

'If you say so.'

'I do say so. Have you been following me?'

'You might think that. I would insist that I chanced to be walking in the same direction as you.'

'And then you stole my wallet.'

'No, mate, you discarded it and I happened to find it. I have your old coat, too if you want it—I'm a snapper up of unconsidered trifles.'

'What do trifles have to do with anything?' asked Razor, his mind filling with thoughts of jelly and custard. 'I made sure no one was watching, and I certainly didn't see you.'

'You wouldn't have,' said Kev, shoving him into an alleyway. 'In here.'

'Why?' said Razor, wondering what Kev's game was.

'Cops,' said Kev. 'This way.'

They scurried down the alley which was lined with dirty brick walls and stank of damp and decay. Further along, a solid-looking wooden fence replaced the wall on one side. Kev stopped, glanced around and pressed something invisible to Razor. A panel opened.

'Get in,' he said.

'What?' asked Razor, stumbling as Kev bundled him through the gap into a garden otherwise enclosed by blind stone walls. A ramshackle shed leaned casually against the far one and in the middle stood a small tree that was dropping its last leaves into a pond watched over by a wooden table and chairs.

'If you must talk, do it quietly,' Kev murmured, closing the panel and muffling the street sounds. 'I don't think the cops recognised you, but I wouldn't swear on it and they may be close behind. You should have got yourself a hat. That bald pate of yours shines like a beacon.'

'There's a hood on this coat,' Razor whispered.

'Yes, but it's not raining—you'd just look suspicious.' Kev flapped his hands, mouthing, 'Shut up!'

Two pairs of heavy feet trudged past on the alley side.

'Are you sure it was our man?' asked a bored voice.

'Not really, Sarge, but he had a shaved head and took off fast.'

'Suspicious, but there's no sign of him here. Anyway, he'll run into the patrol on The Shambles if he keeps heading this way. I wonder what made him run—he couldn't have seen us.'

'You know, Sarge, for a moment I thought someone was with him.'

'Ah well. Let's get back to our patch. We'll pick him up sooner or later.'

'Yeah. I wonder why he did it? Kicked Danny Gilbert, I mean.'

'Probably jealousy. Danny is talented, rich, and good looking too.'

'He'd have to be to pull that Helen. What a stunner!'

As the voices faded away, Razor got it at last. He'd attacked Danny Gilbert, possibly the most gifted English footballer of his generation, who'd been raised in Sorenchester. Helen, his new wife, had become the people's darling at the last Olympic Games, returning with three gold medals. Flit had mentioned it, but Razor had been too busy to take much notice.

'So, what have you got against Danny?' asked Kev.

'Nothing. I thought he was a bad guy chasing a woman, and I lashed out.'

'You really didn't recognise him? Or her?'

'Well... no, not at the time. What I saw was a young woman who appeared to be in trouble. He could have been anybody.' Razor was suddenly aggrieved. 'Why was he chasing her? They weren't in running gear or anything. It looked sinister.'

'It's what they do, mate. She credits running away from Danny for building up her speed and stamina.'

Ashamed of his ignorance, Razor changed the subject. 'Where are we?'

'In the secret garden,' said Kev.

'Does it belong to the cake shop on the corner?'

'No, it's mine.'

'How? It's not like it's connected to your house.'

'It was a legacy from Uncle Bob.'

'Yeah,' said Razor, sceptical. 'You mentioned him earlier. So, Bob's your uncle?'

'He was, and it's not uncommon to have an Uncle Bob—all my brothers and sisters had one.'

'Yeah, I suppose they would've. But isn't it strange to have a garden without a house attached?'

'Quite strange. Uncle Bob reckoned it resulted from a medieval property dispute between an earl and a bishop.'

'But why do you get into it through the fence?'

'Another peculiar vestige of times past— there's no legal access point, so I have to sneak in. It's useful to have a secret place sometimes.'

'Weird,' said Razor, suspecting Kev of pulling his leg. 'What do we do now?'

'If I were you, I'd walk to the police station and hand myself in. I doubt they'd do more than question you, and if you stick to your story, I reckon they'd soon let you go. You might get lampooned in the press, but that's the worst that could happen since no one was really hurt and your intentions were honourable. However, I suspect that's not what you intend doing.'

Razor shook his head. 'There's more to it than today's incident and to be honest, I'd rather avoid the police. It's not that I've done anything wrong, at least not on purpose, but I really don't want to... explain some things.'

'What things?'

'I'd rather not say.'

'Fair enough,' said Kev. 'You have secrets you don't want to share and so do I. I'll not pry. What would you like to do now?'

'I'd like to get something to eat.'

'Not a bad idea, mate, but first you need something to cover that brain case of yours. Tell you what, give me some cash and I'll buy you a hat.'

'How much?'

'Depends on what you want. I can probably pick up a beanie for under a tenner, but something posher, like a trilby, will cost rather more. What size is your head? It looks a little on the large side to me.'

'I have no idea,' said Razor, trying not to take offence. 'A fleece beanie, or a woollen one, would be best. I'm not aiming for a sharp fashion look.'

'Any preference as to colour?'

'Something not too distinctive... black, grey, navy blue. You know?'

'Right you are.'

Razor handed a twenty-pound note to Kev who, after listening for a moment, opened the fence and slipped out.

Risking a soggy bottom, Razor sat on a chair, and stared at the murky waters in the pond, trying to understand how Kev had known about the incident in the park. He must have been watching, but why had Razor not seen or heard him? And where had the little guy been hiding when he'd discarded his parka? No one had been in sight, and he was certain there'd been no nooks or hidey-holes where anyone, not even someone as diminutive as Kev, could secrete themselves. And what about this secret garden? He'd never heard of such a thing, although perhaps he wouldn't have if it was secret. However, Kev puzzled him the most. What was he up to? In Razor's experience people didn't just help out strangers without expecting something in return, though perhaps the little guy was just kind or grateful. Razor remained suspicious—there was something unusual about the man.

Ten minutes later, Kev returned with a knitted black beanie and pulled it over Razor's shiny skull before he could get to his feet.

'It suits you, mate, and only cost a fiver.' Kev handed back three uncreased five-pound notes. 'Put your coat on, let me carry your backpack, and the cops'll never recognise you.'

'Right,' said Razor, doing as he was told. 'Now, let's get something to eat. Where's the best place, d'you think? Is there anywhere I could keep my hat on?'

Kev glanced at the sky. 'The rain's still holding off, so what about fish and chips? We could take them into St Stephen's Park.'

Although Razor hadn't considered that option—Flit had banished fatty foods from his diet—he started salivating and nodded.

Although Razor stared hard, he couldn't see any mechanism as Kev let them back through the fence into the twisting alley. They walked along it until they reached The Shambles, where the warm aromas of fish and chips and vinegar lured them into The Fat Friar.

'What do you fancy?' asked Kev.

'Cod and chips,' said Razor, 'and a can of lemonade.'

'Battered sausage and chips for me,' said Kev. He shuffled along with the queue until he could give their order to the skinny older woman at the counter.

The woman went to work. 'Salt and vinegar?' she asked.

'Yes, please,' said Kev, 'but only on my chips.'

'No thanks,' said Razor—salt was also on the banned list.

It didn't matter. She was already shaking the condiments everywhere.

Kev glanced at Razor and shrugged. Razor reached for his wallet, but Kev got there first. 'Sebastian's treat,' he said and paid.

A crack in the clouds allowed a sliver of sunlight through, prompting a robin to burst into song in an overhead rowan tree as Razor and Kev found a dryish bench in the park and sat to open their parcels of fish and chips. Razor, as hungry as he'd ever been, wondered if the old woman had sensed this, since his portions were more than generous. He stuffed until the sharp edge of his appetite had been dulled, and slowed down to savour the delicate flavours of the fish, soft and flaky beneath a crunchy batter, and the crisp satisfaction of chips with just enough added salt and vinegar to perk them up without being overwhelming—the woman had clearly known her business. Kev munched at his side. They appeared to be the only people in the park until a harassed young mother walked past, pushing a screaming infant in a buggy. From the corner of his eye, Razor glimpsed a succulent chip spin through the air and land on the kid's chest. Fast as a snake, a pudgy hand grabbed it and shoved it into his mouth. His mother, who hadn't noticed the incoming missile, looked utterly relieved when he shut up.

Kev stared innocently into the middle distance.

'Nice shot,' Razor murmured, producing a quick grin.

Then, other than the robin that had stopped singing and was making belligerent ticking noises, all was quiet until they'd finished eating, when two puny explosions signified the opening of lemonade cans.

'Cheers!' said Kev, rapping his can against Razor's.

'Bottoms up,' said Razor, with a happy chuckle that made him feel bad.

They drank, relaxing in the sun's autumn warmth.

'Uh-oh,' said Kev, breaking the silence. 'This looks like trouble.' He nodded towards three large men, all with shaved heads like Razor's, who were lurching in their general direction, preceded by the stink of stale booze, old sweat and cigarettes.

Razor glared at them. 'Not the trouble I had in mind, but what the heck?'

'You what?' said Kev.

'Why are you staring at us?' asked the tallest man.

'Because I despise drunken imbeciles,' said Razor, forcing a sneer, even though his insides were turning to liquid.

'What?' asked the fattest of the trio, looking puzzled.

'A drunkard is a person who is habitually drunk,' Razor explained, 'and an imbecile is an unusually stupid person.'

'Are you looking for trouble?' asked the tall one.

'It has a way of finding me.'

'My friend is only joking, of course,' said Kev. 'He doesn't mean any harm.'

'Really? Well, that's alright then,' said the fat one, smiling and turning away.

Although Razor received hard looks from the other two, they appeared to be on the verge of leaving. 'No, I meant what I said, though I don't suppose intelligent words mean anything to these boneheaded buffoons.'

Kev gasped. 'What are you trying to do, mate?'

'Just having fun,' said Razor, sprawling on the bench as if he owned both it and the park.

'At our expense,' said the man who hadn't yet spoken. 'Don't you think that's rather rude?'

'Maybe,' said Razor, 'but there's a reason for it... I don't like you... any of you, and especially not you.'

The man shrugged and glanced at his mates. 'Some people,' he said. 'Let's go.'

'Snivelling cowards.'

The men walked away.

'Well, that's not what I'd call trouble,' said Razor, relieved, if disappointed.

'Not them,' said Kev, 'Him. Hello, Liam.'

A tattooed nightmare, six-foot-six of muscle and meanness with cropped blond hair was stalking towards them, oozing menace.

'I thought it was you, you little runt,' said Liam. 'Where have you been hiding? Are you going to pay for the car and give Gary back what's his, or would you prefer a taste of hospital food?'

'A friend of yours, Kev?' asked Razor, far more scared than he had been.

'Not exactly. He's a mate of my cousin, Gary.'

'You can get lost, unless you want some as well,' said Liam, fixing an unblinking stare on Razor.

'Some what?' asked Razor, struggling to stop his voice quavering.

'Some pain.'

Razor forced a laugh. 'I doubt it from a wimp like you... maybe you could hurt an ant... if it was a tiny one.'

'Shut up, mate,' murmured Kev, who'd put the park bench between him and trouble. 'He nearly killed a guy once and got locked up. That's how he met Gary.'

'Really?' said Razor, standing up slowly. 'He looks more like a frisky little puppy than a jailbird.'

'I'll smash your brains out.' Liam bunched thick fingers into fearsome fists. 'If you've got any.'

 'I've won awards for them,' said Razor, aware Kev was no longer behind him.

 'You've got guts, mate,' said Liam with a sneer, 'and now I'm going to spread them round the park.'

Hoping to protect Kev and desperate to provoke the thug to murderous violence, Razor lunged, shoving Liam in the chest with all his might. He was astonished when the big man went over backward like a felled tree—Kev had sneaked behind on all fours in just the right place to make a human tripping hazard. Liam lay still. He didn't even twitch.

'Let's get out of here,' said Kev, rubbing his back and getting to his feet.

Grabbing the backpack, Kev hustled Razor from the park. Though nervous, Razor soon slowed them to a brisk walk so they wouldn't draw attention.

Razor's head was in a spin because although Liam was clearly a blot on the landscape, he hadn't intended to hurt him. And what if he died? Getting killed in action was one thing, becoming a killer was something entirely different.

'What the hell were you trying to do back there?' asked Kev, scattering Razor's thoughts. 'Were you trying to get yourself beaten to a pulp? If you weren't, it damn well looked like it. You got lucky with that first lot.'

Razor shrugged. 'I have my reasons. Was that guy really a friend of your cousin?'

'I'm afraid so.'

'I hope I didn't hurt him too much,' said Razor. 'He went down hard.'

'Only because I tripped him,' said Kev.

'But he hit his head—I read something in the local paper about a guy who banged his head in a fight and almost died from bleeding on the brain.'

'I wouldn't worry—Liam's skull is as thick as the earth's crust, and his brains are even thicker. He got what he deserved.'

Razor shuddered and glanced back. Part of him hoped to see Liam in pursuit.

'He'll be fine,' said Kev with a nonchalant shrug.

'Perhaps,' said Razor, unconvinced. 'What was that about a car? Did you steal it?'

'A misunderstanding,' said Kev dismissively as they walked up Moorend Road towards the centre of town.

Razor continued. 'And he reckoned you'd taken something of your cousin's. Did you steal that too?'

'He thinks so, but he thinks too little. Such men are dangerous.'

'What?'

'He thinks Gary should have received something that was bequeathed to me.'

'Why?'

Kev sighed. 'Uncle Bob adopted Gary and brought him up with all the advantages. Unfortunately when Gary reached his teens he seemed determined to prove a villain. He got arrested many times for robbery and violence, but Uncle Bob paid the fines and forgave him. However, the last straw was when Gary got caught selling drugs to school kids.'

'Was that why he went to prison?'

Kev nodded. 'For that and for attacking a shopkeeper with an axe. Much of what I inherited would have gone to him if he'd not been such a dick.'

'From what I can see, it all worked out very nicely for you, even though you're a self-confessed thief,' said Razor.

Kev shrugged. 'I'm only a thief in the eyes of the law.'

Razor laughed. 'That's preposterous!'

'I admit thieving is against the law—where laws exist, but I put it to you that while many thieves are greedy, lazy or selfish, not all are bad. I'm one of those, because I don't steal for myself.'

'Yeah, right—you're an altruist!' Razor couldn't stop chuckling at the outrageous statement.

'You might say that,' said Kev.

'What about last night? You bought food with the money you stole.'

'A worker deserves his wages, and I'd be no good to anyone if I was starving.'

'So, you're a regular Robin Hood,' said Razor, grinning.

'Maybe I am,' said Kev, his face serious.

'And the rest of last night's money will go to a

good cause, will it?' scoffed Razor.

'It already has.'

'What do you mean? Beer?'

'I gave it to someone who needed it.'

'Who?'

'Someone in need.' Kev would say no more.

Although unconvinced, Razor had no wish to antagonise the little guy. He did, however, think it high time to fulfil his destiny. 'Well, Robin Hood, thanks for lunch and for your company. I appreciate it.'

'You're welcome, mate. Do you want to come back for a cup of tea?'

'I'll pass on that. There's something I must do, so I'd better get a move on. Thanks again. See you.'

'Where are you going?'

'Somewhere I have to be.'

'Alright then, mate, have it your way. Look after yourself.'

'You too.' Razor glanced at his watch and strode away as if hurrying to an appointment.

A few moments later, the thought struck him that he really did have an appointment—with Death. Although his internal cynic sneered at such a cliché, hyperactive butterflies took wing in his guts, his stride faltered, and he wanted to curl up warm and safe at home, though it had offered little comfort since Flit's passing. For a moment he considered reverting to the original plan of throwing himself off the nearest bridge, but knew he'd never again summon up the courage. With any luck he would, however, find an obliging murderer elsewhere. Maybe in Glevchester. Looking back, it was hardly surprising he'd messed up killing himself—Flit had always regarded his rare attempts at DIY with incredulous hilarity. The memory triggered a brief smile.

The centre of town still looked full, with far more than the regular number of uniformed police officers patrolling and at least one keeping a beady eye on the bus stop. Head down, alert in case his disguise turned out less brilliant than Kev had made out, Razor mooched past the church towards Glevchester Road, trying to appear casual and innocent while he forged a cunning plan.

No one gave him a second glance as he walked away from town, first using quiet side streets and then a miry footpath by the river. When the tail ends of Sorenchester were behind him, he turned onto the main road and after ten minutes reached a bus stop. The rain returned and threatened to become a downpour. Condensation made the timetable blurry, but he deciphered enough to see that buses came by at seven minutes after the hour—the next was due in about twenty minutes. He sat on the soggy Cotswold stone wall and waited, and though his new coat kept his upper half dry, the runoff soaked through the top of his trousers. Fortunately, he didn't have to endure for too long and the bus arrived dead on time.

'A single to Glevchester, please,' he said as he stepped aboard.

'That'll be four pounds, sir.'

Razor handed over the money. 'When do we get there?'

The driver glanced at the clock. 'We make a ten-minute stop in Sorenchester and then, assuming no delays, we should reach Glevchester at sixteen nineteen.'

'Right, twenty past four.'

'Nineteen past,' said the driver, a stickler for exactitude.

Although the bus looked packed, a free seat was available next to a bulky middle-aged woman in an even bulkier puffer jacket. As he made his way towards it, the bus pulled away. The jolt threw him off balance, he lost his footing and sprawled across the woman's ample thighs. She screamed and swore.

'Sorry,' he said. 'Are you alright?'

Although unharmed, she was perfectly pissed off, which she demonstrated with an outpouring of scorn, insults and slaps. Razor struggled to escape. Still apologising, he backed away, trying to ignore the semi-suppressed sniggers and remarks from fellow travellers as he searched for another seat. He found one, near the back beside a small, slim woman, enveloped in a dark coat with the hood up. Razor assumed she was cold. He, on the other hand, could feel his cheeks burning with embarrassment, though his legs were chilled and damp.

'Is this seat free?' he asked.

Without looking up, the young woman nodded, and turned her face to the window, clearly not wishing to talk. Razor inhaled her warm flowery scent as he sat down. The bulky woman turned and stared, but he avoided eye contact.

The bus carried Razor back towards town, weaving through the narrow old streets before stopping outside the church where some passengers, including the bulky woman got off. Razor feigned not to notice her final gorgon glare. He did, however, spot the police officer scrutinising the new passengers as they embarked, though paying no attention to those already aboard. Allowing himself a smug smile, Razor settled back into his seat.

The heavy clouds were already making it dark, though evening was still a couple of hours away. The bus's lights came on and he glimpsed the reflection of the woman at his side in the window. She looked young, pale and pretty, and a little sad. Razor forced himself to stop staring and pretended to doze off, though her image kept forcing itself into his mind, making it difficult to maintain his comfortable misery. The bus departed on time, its windscreen wipers beating out a monotonous rhythm that the rain did its best to drown out. It wasn't long before Razor had no need to feign sleep.

He awoke as the bus slowed. They had reached the dual carriageway to Glevchester and a long line of red brake lights snaked ahead. Soon everything came to a standstill. Five minutes later, with no sign of further progress, some passengers muttered about being late, others cursed the lousy British weather and one or two swore.

The driver looked back over his shoulder. 'Sorry about this, folks, but it's out of my hands. There's some sort of holdup.'

'Why?' asked a large and belligerent middle-aged man.

'I suspect an accident... this weather, you know?'

'Why can't the idiots bloody well learn to drive?' asked the belligerent man.

'I have no idea,' said the driver, staring ahead.

Other than streams of rainwater rushing down gutters, nothing moved. Ten minutes later, still nothing moved, and the belligerent man's complaints grew louder as his face grew redder. Then the bus edged forward, pressing close to the roadside, to allow a police car with blinding blue flashing lights to squeeze through with a fire engine and an ambulance close behind.

'Follow them,' said the belligerent man. 'There's space now, and I'll miss my connection if you don't.'

'What you are suggesting is illegal and

dangerous,' said the driver, shaking his head. 'I'd lose my job.'

'Bloody jobsworth.' The man got to his feet. 'You'd better get me to Glevchester on time, or else.'

'Why don't you sit down and be quiet?' said a skinny old man with wispy white hair, sounding exasperated. 'There's nothing anyone can do.'

The belligerent man bustled down the bus and grabbed the old chap by the lapels on his overcoat. 'Don't you go telling me what to do, mate. Not if you want to keep all your teeth.'

Razor, though still sleepy and with his prejudice against personal pain undiminished, saw an opportunity. He forced himself to stand up. 'That's enough, sir. Put him down and relax. We're all stuck here, there's nothing anyone can do, and it would be much pleasanter if everyone just kept calm and carried on.'

His speech had half the desired effect in that the belligerent man released his victim. He did not, however, calm down, but launched himself at Razor, knuckles tight and white as he swung a thudding right fist.

Razor felt no pain. At least not until he came

round. Then he felt it in his head and jaw. Tasting blood, he groaned and tried to sit.

'Stay where you are, my lovely,' said a soft female voice with a slight lilt.

A hand pressed him down. 'Alright. Where am I?'

'On the bus to Glevchester,' said the woman.

As he opened his eyes, he glimpsed a pale, pretty face and forget-me-not eyes before they retreated into her hood. The other bus passengers were staring, some concerned, others curious.

'Why am I on the bus to Glevchester?' he asked. 'I live in Willoton. My head hurts.'

'Because you are travelling there,' said the pretty woman. 'At least you will be if we ever move again. You got punched.'

Razor's discombobulated brain began to recombobulate.

'How long was I out?'

'Two days.'

'What?'

'I'm joking. It was only for a minute or two.'

'But what about the guy who hit me?'

'Don't worry, my lovely. He won't hurt you anymore.'

'Good.' Razor believed her and relaxed,

closing his eyes and lying back. Something soft was cushioning his throbbing head, a delicate flowery scent filled his nostrils and despite his temples pounding like a heavy metal drummer, he almost felt happy.

Sometime later there was a cheer. A few seconds after that, the engine rumbled back into life and they began to inch forward.

Razor, his head full of pain and with numbness down the left side of his face, recovered in slow stages. He sat up and looked around. 'Where's he gone?'

'I beg your pardon?' said the young woman.

'Where's the guy who hit me?'

'He got off.'

'In the middle of nowhere? In a storm?'

'Yes.'

'Really?'

She nodded.

'He didn't leave of his own volition,' a grinning youth across the aisle explained. 'It was an assisted departure.'

'For which we can all be grateful,' said the old man.

'He'll catch his death,' said Razor.

'Then he'll get what he deserves,' said the old man.

'Got off lightly, if you ask me,' said a woman. 'It's a good job some people are public spirited.'

'Who persuaded him to leave?' asked Razor. No one on the bus struck him as the physical type. A couple of fingers pointed at the young woman.

Despite this, Razor guessed the grinning youth had done the daring deed and was being modest, as a hero should be.

Soon, Razor felt strong enough to retake his seat. Rising to his feet, he picked a soft woollen scarf from under his head. 'Whose is this?'

'Hers,' said the grinning youth, pointing at the woman, who was still enveloped in her coat.

Razor handed the scarf back as he sat down beside her. 'Thank you, miss... and for looking after me.'

She took it with a nod and a hint of a smile.

'I like the pattern,' said Razor. 'Is it rowan berries?'

She nodded.

'It's lovely—where did you get it from?'

'A charity shop,' she said, and turned to look out the window.

Razor took the hint, hoping she hadn't thought he'd been trying to chat her up, because he hadn't been. Definitely not. However, her sympathy and soft touch had almost made him feel life could become worth living again, though such feelings came pre-loaded with guilt. Convinced he'd let Flit down again, he tried to force himself back to his usual state of misery and desolation—without much success.

The traffic ahead kept moving in a stop and start manner for a mile or more, until they reached a place of bright white and flashing blue lights. As they crept by, morbid curiosity took over and he shuddered at the results of a spectacular collision. A car was on its roof. It appeared to be the same type as the company car he'd once taken huge pride in. He had no idea what had happened to it after Flit's death and didn't care.

Once past the accident, the traffic sped up and there was a frenzy of mobile phone use as passengers updated friends and family on the delay before the bus returned to a moody silence. They were already over an hour late by the time they reached the outskirts of Glevchester, by which time rush hour was at its peak. A burst drain meant a long detour delayed them even further, though Razor, with nowhere to go and nothing to do but die, was unconcerned. The rain and increasing condensation on the windows meant he could see little other than blurry lights from vehicles and shops as the bus crawled through town.

It was gone half-past six when they pulled into the bus station, a grim grey concrete and glass construction that might have seen better days, but had probably always looked like a Soviet prison. All those aboard stood up, gathered their belongings and shuffled off, going their separate ways. Razor lost sight of the young woman which saddened him more than he could explain. He zipped up his coat and wandered away to seek his destiny on streets the rain had swept clear of all but the most determined or desperate pedestrians.

He was heading towards Glevchester's Severn Wharves, where the attack had happened all those months ago. It was the first time he'd been back and memories, feelings and images almost overwhelmed him: the cinema, the shortcut back towards the car, the knife in a gloved hand, the hooded attacker, Flit's scream, and most of all his helplessness as the lorry bore down on her. It seemed so long ago, and at the same time so recent. He wished he hadn't run. Why had he not stood his ground and fought to protect her? Though he might have been injured or killed, it would have been better than living without her and with the guilt. Yet flight had not seemed such a bad idea at the time—Flit had been a good runner, much faster and fitter than him, and they should have got away.

'Watch it, mate!'

Lost in the past, he'd walked straight into the present, in the form of a sad-faced man wearing a cheap cagoule.

'Sorry,' said Razor, 'I was miles away.'

'I wish you had been. Still, no harm done. Just take care.'

Razor carried on until he reached the Severn Wharves, a network of old canals dotted with tall buildings that had once been warehouses. When they'd become obsolete, many had fallen into dereliction. A developer had bought them up and converted them into flats, shops, restaurants and night clubs. There'd also been the cinema. Razor had no memory of what they'd seen there on that last night.

His head was still aching and his stomach was rumbling. Lunch had been many hours ago and heroics would be easier after a decent meal. He entered the first place he saw, a large chain restaurant. It was warm, bright, dry and surprisingly busy. A young waitress, after looking Razor up and down as if he might be trouble, guided him to a booth at the back and took his order.

6

The waitress was polite and efficient, but the greasy burger she delivered was dreary at best, even after Razor had plastered it with some alleged mustard, a bland, yellow gloop in a plastic bottle. He found some consolation in the mug of not-bad coffee, which the waitress refilled whenever he drained it, but after paying, he walked away with a sense of relief—he'd never have to eat there again.

While he'd been inside, the rain had diminished to an annoying drizzle and the wind to damp gusts. He started patrolling the Wharves, looking out for anyone acting suspiciously, as well as for the police—though he doubted they'd really be looking for him in Glevchester or that they'd be able to see through his new appearance and bruises. After walking for hours and coming across nothing even mildly untoward, he yawned. Perhaps it was time to cut his losses and find a hotel?

A burst of raucous shouting suggested something might be kicking off. He ran towards it, ready to leap into heroic action should an innocent member of the public need his assistance, but it was only a bunch of high-spirited lads cheering on one of their mates, who'd somehow wedged his head between the seat and the back of a bench. The unfortunate lad was roaring and cursing, his legs kicking the air, as he tried to break free while his audience laughed, made fatuous remarks and filmed the titanic struggle on their mobiles.

A posse of young women, inappropriately dressed for the outdoors, stopped and goggled.

'How did Wayne get like that?' one asked, teetering on towering heels.

'He was dropped on his head as a baby,' said one of the friends, causing further laughter.

'I mean in that position?' The woman laughed and gestured at Wayne, her expression incredulous.

'He was bragging that he could do a handstand, even when he was pissed as a fart. No one believed him, so he thought he'd show us and since he didn't want to get dirty, he had the brilliant idea of doing it on the bench. Then his hands slipped, and you can see what happened. This is so going on YouTube.'

'Yeah,' added another lad, 'you're going to be famous, mate!'

'Bastards! Get me out.'

'Are you going to help him?' asked another of the women, who was starting to look a little worried.

'When we've got enough footage... maybe.'

'Bastards!' Wayne repeated, as a prelude to a fit of swearing and convulsive jerking.

It didn't work, and Razor, seeing potential disaster, ran forward, grabbed Wayne's head and levered it free. Dishevelled and red in the face, Wayne got to his feet, screaming abuse at his mates, before stopping mid-rant to turn around and thank Razor, who nodded and stepped back, half-expecting bloodshed. Yet, within seconds, Wayne had simmered down and was watching the video clips, laughing and play-punching with the rest of the gang as they drifted towards a bar.

Razor walked away, worrying that they'd caught him on their videos and that someone might recognise him when they shared them to social media—not that he could do anything about it. He hurried through the Wharves, not exactly lurking in the shadows, but using whatever cover was available, and with a strange sensation of being watched, though he was sure he was alone. He reached a plaza, feeling footsore, weary and bored, and noticed a squalid gap between an enormous wheelie bin and a shop wall. He slipped in and leant against the wall for a breather. His hidey-hole allowed a good view of a square where a few youngsters had gathered to drink cheap cider from cans and have a laugh. Though noisy, they weren't doing much they shouldn't. Time crawled, the youngsters drifted away, and The Wharves quietened. A scruffy, straggle-bearded old man, muttering nonsense, dragged a flattened cardboard box from the wheelie bin and lugged it into the shop's doorway, where he pulled a grubby sleeping bag from a muddy pack and prepared to bed down for the night. Razor was debating whether to give the poor old fellow a little cash when a quick movement on the edge of vision alerted him to a figure crossing the square. It was a burly young man in a dark grey hoodie and the way he kept looking around as he scurried into a passage opposite the shops made him appear furtive. Suspicious, Razor slipped from concealment and followed him on tip toe.

He sneaked down the passage, wishing the lamp above wasn't broken, and listened. To start with, there was no sound other than his own breathing. Then he heard water trickling. The moon peeped out between clouds. The young man was standing within an arm's length, his face to the wall. Razor jerked back and clattered a discarded drink can.

'Jesus!' yelped the young man and looked over his shoulder.

'Not quite,' said Razor. 'What are you doing?'

'What do you bloody think I'm doing?'

'You tell me.'

'I'm having a piss, and I prefer to do it in private. Get lost, pervert!'

'Oh. Sorry. I thought... never mind.' Razor walked away, embarrassed. A man sneaking into a dark passage after the pubs had shut—he might have guessed the reason, though there'd been something about him that had suggested worse. And, though he'd only glimpsed part of the guy's face, Razor felt he knew him.

He'd not quite made it back into the square when a muscular arm hooked his throat.

'Give me your money,' said the man, thrusting Razor against the wall.

'Eh?' said Razor, stunned and winded. A painful, cold sharpness pricked his neck and made him shiver.

'You heard. Hand it over. Now.'

'Why?' Although his body trembled with uncontrollable animal fear, Razor had recovered from the initial shock and decided to play along, hoping to goad the young thug.

'Because I've got a knife at your throat.'

'That's nice for you. I bet it's a big shiny one. I've got plenty of them at home.' Although he'd tried for sarcasm, Razor cringed, suspecting he'd sounded like an imbecile.

'They're no good to you there,' said the thug.

'But if I had them here, I could make you a salad.' Where had that come from? He'd never cut up a salad in his entire life.

'I'll make it simple for you, moron. Shut up and give me your money. If you don't, I'll slice you into rashers. Is that clear enough?'

Although his heart was pumping in overdrive and his body was shaking, Razor's brain was flicking through the options while trying to get a grip on the man's voice. Surely he'd heard it recently?

It was time to heat things up and fight back. With any luck he'd provoke the knifeman into administering the killing cut.

'Thank you for explaining so clearly. Let me go and I'll give you my wallet.'

'D'you think I'm going to fall for that? D'you think I'm stupid?'

'Now you mention it, yes I do. I bet you don't even realise you're on camera. Smile.' Razor pointed at a blank wall and the bad guy turned to look.

As the grip round his throat loosened, Razor thrust an elbow back into something soft and broke free, but before he could do anything else, his legs were swept from under him and the man was upon him, punching and kicking.

Dazed, Razor sprawled beside a stinking bin. There was a strange tearing sound that went on for a minute or so and then he sensed movement. A soft, cool hand touched his forehead, he shut his eyes and lay still for a minute or two.

'You are in the wars today, aren't you my lovely?' said a woman. 'How are you feeling now?' For a moment, Razor caught a whiff of scent and thought it was Flit, that he was at home and that the previous months had been a nightmare, but the rancid stink of the passage was all too real.

Though his mind was as thick and clear as week-old porridge, he felt he should answer her question. 'I'm... er... not too bad. I think. What happened? There was this guy... with a knife.'

'He was giving you a good beating, but he's gone now,' said the woman.

'Why?' Razor peered up, but her face was in shadow.

'He just had to go.'

'Did he take my money?' He checked inside his coat. His wallet was still there—not that he was much bothered.

'He took nothing,' said the woman.

'That's good, I suppose.' The world seemed very distant.

'What were you doing in this passage at such a late hour?' she asked.

'I was following the guy because he looked suspicious. Only it turned out he'd only gone for a... to take a... to urinate. That's what he said. Then he attacked me.'

'You shouldn't make a habit of following furtive folk down dark byways. You'll get yourself hurt or killed.'

'I was hoping there wouldn't be much pain.'

'Well, my lovely, you were lucky. As far as I can see you haven't picked up any serious injuries. Where are you staying?'

'I'm not. I was going for a walk... by the way, what are you doing down a dark alley at night on your own?'

'Looking after you.'

'Thank you. I'll be alright. I'll go home and get some rest.'

'You live in Willoton don't you?'

'Yes.'

'What's your address?'

Not knowing why, he told her.

'Good, are you alright to stand?' She helped him to his feet.

'Er... how did you know I lived in Willoton?'

'You told me.'

'You're the lady on the bus,' said Razor.

'I was. Let's get you a taxi.'

'There's no need, I'll be just fine,' said Razor as his leg muscles turned to mush.

Sometime later, he was homeward bound in the back seat of a taxi, but couldn't remember how he'd ended up there. He supposed the woman had something to do with it, but his thoughts were fuzzy with fatigue. He was grateful the taxi driver was of the rare silent breed.

When they reached Riverside Cottage, Razor

got out, paid the fare and stumbled down the path to the front door, fumbling through all his pockets for his keys. They weren't there! How could he have lost them? He'd certainly heard them jangling when he'd fled from the police in Ride Park. Memory returned—taking off his Parka, Kev. He cursed himself as a fool for not taking his keys back, even though he'd assumed he'd no longer need them. All he wanted was to sleep. Panic and self-pity vied for mastery of his brain.

The porch light came on.

The front door opened.

'You look terrible. What have you been up to?' asked Kev, who was standing in the doorway, wearing a pair of Razor's pyjamas. They were far too long for him.

Razor gaped.

'You'd better come in.'

Razor accepted the invitation into his own house as if in a dream. He wished it was a dream. His head thumped like a bastard, his legs were shaking and his brain couldn't cope anymore. For a moment he feared he might collapse, but Kev steadied him and led him upstairs and into the bathroom. 'You'd better clean yourself up if you can. I'll make the bed in the spare room while you're doing that. I'm in the big bedroom. You can tell me your misadventures in the morning.'

Razor closed the bathroom door, eased his bladder, washed and glanced in the mirror. His cheek was swollen like a hamster's, his nostrils were packed with congealed blood and there was a long graze down the side of his chin. When he took into account his shaved, but now bristly head, he looked like one of the grotesques carved into Glevchester Minster. Sick with fatigue and pain, he left the bathroom.

'This way,' said Kev, directing him to his own guest bedroom. 'Get undressed and into bed.'

Razor did as he was told.

'Drink this.' Kev handed him a glass of water.

It was cool and soothing, and it felt pleasant to be tucked into bed, but before he could express his thanks, sleep took him and held him in its soothing embrace until morning.

It was light when he woke. He drank a little more water and drifted back to sleep.

Next time he opened his eyes, the bedroom door was opening.

Kev stood there. 'I hope gentle sleep was nature's soft nurse?'

'What?' Razor sat up dreamily.

'I was asking if you felt better after a good sleep.'

'I think so, but I've still got a whale of a headache.'

'Do you have any painkillers?'

'I think there are some in the kitchen cupboard—the top drawer on the right.'

'I'll get them.'

Razor lay back, feeling as if someone had bludgeoned a rusty spike through his skull. A minute later, Kev reappeared with the tablets and a glass of water. Razor gulped them down, lay back and closed his eyes. Later he became aware of the scent of tea.

Kev pressed a mug into his hands as he sat up. 'Drink this. I got milk from the village shop. Outrageous prices, but the old girl running it is a sweetheart.'

'Thank you,' said Razor and sipped.

When he'd finished, Kev refilled his mug and when he'd drained that one he felt human again.

'You want something to eat?' Kev asked. 'I picked up a microwaveable shepherd's pie. It's not much but...'

It wasn't what Razor would have chosen for

breakfast, but he was in no position to negotiate and he was well acquainted with the limited choice at the shop. He wondered when he'd last been brought breakfast in bed.

Kev returned bearing food on a tray and though Razor found the meal bland and salty, it filled the hole. When Kev took his tray away, he dozed again, not waking until it was already growing dark. He got up, showered, dressed and headed downstairs.

'How are you?' asked Kev, sprawling on the Italian leather sofa, looking up from a book.

'Much better,' said Razor.

'Sleep is the balm of hurt minds.'

'Yeah, I guess it is,' said Razor vaguely. 'Look, thanks for everything you've done today, but... but... what are you doing here?'

'I brought your keys back. You weren't in, so I thought I'd hang around until you were.'

'Thanks. But... er... how did you know where I lived?'

'I used my detection skills.'

'I didn't know you had any.'

'Nor did I.'

'It was as easy as that?' Razor was worried.

'Yes, though I did have to make a few enquiries around the village. I must say you've found yourself a nice place.'

'Thanks.'

'And yet it doesn't feel like a home. There was barely any food in the fridge and most of that was furry.'

Razor fought to control a burst of anger. 'That's not your concern. I eat out.'

'Fair enough. Only you've got a smart modern kitchen that has just about everything.'

'So?'

'It's clear someone used to cook here. Was it you or the pretty woman in the photographs?'

'Don't interrogate me!' Razor's temper flared at being asked to justify himself in his own home. One more question and he might boil over and Kev was going to get scalded.

'Okay, mate, no problem. Are you hungry?'

Razor simmered down—some questions were acceptable after all. 'Yes, I am.'

'So am I. Sausage, egg and frozen chips alright? I hope so because it was all I could get. Or we could try the Watermill Inn—it looks nice.'

'What you've got will be fine. I'm not really up to going out at the moment... and, well, there's still the police...'

'I doubt they'll be too worried about hunting

for you after what happened in Glevchester last night.'

'What was that?'

Kev handed him that morning's *Glevchester Mirror* and headed for the kitchen. The headline read: Shocking Killing in The Wharves.

Razor's fears that the pretty young woman had become the victim abated when he read that the body of an unidentified man, or at least enough parts to identify him as a man, had been discovered in a passage between Wharf Six and the shopping centre. After skipping the more gruesome details, he read that the Glevchester Police wished to question a person seen following the victim by a rough sleeper. Razor turned cold, but the description was nothing like him—he had most definitely not been wearing a black cloak, nor had he wielded a silver-tipped cane.

Although it was clearly nothing to do with him, the coincidence of location was troubling, and despite the weird description, he wasn't entirely sure he was in the clear—there was a gap in his memory from falling until the woman spoke to him. What if he'd just blacked out the incident? A police spokesman had said the killer must have been covered in the victim's blood. Razor ran upstairs.

His clothes, though grimy, were blood-free. After the relief of knowing he'd not done it, misery returned. Had he missed out on becoming a murder victim? Was he that unlucky? He sat and brooded. Had the man who'd attacked him been the killer? Or was he the victim? He supposed that if someone had to die horribly, then it was better it was the bad man.

'Your supper will be ready in five minutes,' said Kev, emerging from the kitchen and handing Razor a mug of tea. 'Such a terrible thing to happen. Didn't you get onto the Glevchester bus?'

'Yes, but I never made it there,' Razor lied, bewildered by Kev's knowledge of his movements. 'It was delayed, so I decided to come back here. I... er... walked into a lamp post in the dark.' Razor pointed at a bump on his head to prove his lie. 'A woman had to put me into the taxi—a bit embarrassing now I think about it.'

Kev returned to the kitchen, leaving Razor to his thoughts and to his hunger.

'It's ready,' said Kev, sticking his head round

the kitchen door.

Razor sat down at the table without further ado and began to stuff his face. Although he had an idea the sausages weren't premium quality, they had been well fried and were tasty. The eggs were cooked to perfection and the pile of chips was pretty good too. 'Thanks,' he mumbled, his mouth full. 'It's great.' To start with, he thought there might not be enough, but the mound of chips defeated him. Afterwards, he felt good and full, and then guilty. Sausages, fried eggs and chips had definitely not been on Flit's healthy menu. He cheered up—it would not be bad eating that killed him.

He was on his third mug of tea when he caught a glimpse of the paper Alex had left and panic returned, despite Kev's assertion that the police would now be focused on the horrible murder. What if the forces of law and order still wanted to question him? Perhaps the net was already closing as he sat there. He sprang to his feet.

'What's up?' asked Kev.

'Nothing,' he said, unable to give a rational explanation.

'Then why are you leaping around like a

startled foal?'

'I'm not used to lying in bed all day. I need air.' Razor lurched towards the back door and jerked it open.

The garden was full of fog so dense he could barely see his hands, despite the kitchen lights. It was worrying and then reassuring—not even the police would drive out on such a thick night if they didn't have to. Besides, Riverside Cottage was out of sight of the village and it was probable no one realised anyone was home. He went back in and shut out the night.

Kev was sprawling on the sofa, reading his book. Razor turned on the TV. It was showing an old film. He slumped into his armchair, expecting boredom.

'Do you want a drink?' asked Kev.

'Don't mind if I do. What is there?'

'It's your house, mate, and I don't know what you've got, though having seen all the empty bottles, I doubt there's any whisky left. However, I bought beer.'

'A beer would be great.'

Razor's initial worry about the wisdom of consuming alcohol after getting stunned in an alleyway diminished as one beer turned into five. They watched the film, a naff comedy that grew mysteriously funnier with every emptied can. At the end, yawning like a tomb, Razor went to bed.

He felt relaxed. It was a sensation he'd assumed he'd lost.

7

The following morning, despite the shouty man having haunted his dreams again and waking with a beery head, Razor felt far better than he had any right to. His hangover was mild—and not worth a mention alongside the monsters he'd fought when he'd hit the whisky bottle after the funeral. He still planned to die, but for the time being it felt okay to be alive. However, though a little more sleep would have been great, he could not ignore the frantic signals from his bladder. He got up, yawning and wandered into the bathroom.

All the surfaces were gleaming and a fresh scent filled the air. Since he hadn't bothered to clean since Flit's death, or, to be more honest, ever, it must have been Kev, which was a mystery as the little guy's own bathroom had been such a stomach-turning disaster area.

A minute or two later, he examined his battered face in the mirror. The swelling had reduced and the grazes and lumps were less obvious. During a long, hot, relaxing shower, Razor's headache faded into the background and he caught himself humming a section of

Beethoven's Ode to Joy, a favourite when he'd been happy and a reminder of an old girlfriend at university who'd introduced him to classical music—among other things. He wondered what Jill was doing now, whether she was still as pretty and whether she'd ever married, but, as he stepped from the shower, memories of the young woman from the night before last nudged such thoughts aside. His conscience kicked back in. Cursing his unfaithful mind and needing to punish himself, he slapped his face hoping to put an end to thinking that way. When the pain had subsided, he dried, dressed and went downstairs.

Kev, engrossed in yet another book, looked up from the sofa. 'Your face looks like a slapped arse—what happened?'

'I slipped in the shower.'

Kev looked unconvinced. 'Would you like breakfast? There's bacon and eggs, or porridge, or toast and marmalade. Or a combination.'

'Just some porridge would be great, thanks… if there's any syrup?'

'There's a tin in the cupboard.'

'I didn't know that,' said Razor, feeling like a guest in his own home. Come to think of it, why was Kev still there? However, being hungry, he had no wish to press the point and followed him into the kitchen.

Kev set to work with oatmeal and water in a copper saucepan that Razor didn't know he owned. He felt inadequate—other than cheese on toast, he'd never got much beyond pouring semi-skimmed milk onto muesli and, since Flit's death, he'd regressed. His confidence as a cook, always fragile, had shattered after his brilliant timesaving idea for boiling eggs— weeks later, the microwave still exuded a faint eggy aroma. His incompetence was his own fault—both his mum and Flit had been fine cooks, albeit in very different ways, but he'd chosen to remain ignorant, adhering to the weird concept that cooking was only for women and girly men. Now he wondered if being as reliant on others as a newborn baby was anything to boast about.

Kev dished out a bowl of steaming porridge and Razor made the most of it, still enjoying the experience of eating something at home that was neither cold nor ruined by his failure to read the instructions.

'Thanks,' he said when he'd scraped the bowl clean. 'How do you make it like that?'

'One third good oats, two thirds fresh water

and just the right amount of salt. Then all I do is heat it up, stir like crazy and keep it on a simmer until it looks and tastes right.'

'Is that all?'

Kev nodded. 'Simple really.'

'And then you put in sugar and cream?'

'There's no cream—it's creamy enough on its own the way I make it and I left it to you to add sweetener.' Kev tapped the unopened tin of golden syrup.

'How did you learn to cook so well?' asked Razor.

'It's nice you think I do. I used to watch Aunt Elsie when I was a kid and the rest I learnt by trial and error.'

'I suppose I ought to try harder, but I was never much good. Everything turns out wrong because I don't know what I'm doing. Do you ever make mistakes?'

'Yeah, but not often,' said Kev, taking a seat opposite. 'Probably the worst was my incendiary disaster.'

'Go on.'

'It was years ago and I was cooking a pease pudding. A wasp got in and began buzzing around my head, so I chased it round until I could catch it in a bottle and evict it. Then the post arrived with a letter I'd long been expecting, so I sat down and started reading. It was a good one and it was only the burning smell that alerted me how long I'd been away.'

'And then what?' asked Razor, smiling at Kev's expression of woe.

'The pan was ablaze, so I opened the window and chucked it out. Unfortunately it was giving off so much smoke that I didn't notice my neighbour's moped out there. To cut a long story short, the moped caught fire, its petrol tank exploded and set his cat alight.'

'Poor cat! Was it hurt?'

'It died, but only after it had run into my neighbour's house and set fire to the bed.'

'That's awful.'

'Yes. Especially as my neighbour was taking a nap at the time. He didn't make it either.'

'Gosh,' said Razor, so appalled he couldn't think of a more appropriate reply.

'And do you know the worst part of the story?' Kev continued.

'No.'

'It didn't actually happen.'

'What do you mean?'

'It's true I did once set fire to a pease pudding when reading a letter, but the rest of the story was pure embellishment.'

'So the cat was alright? And the neighbour?'

'There never was a cat and my neighbour never had a moped.'

Razor clapped his hands to his head. 'So, why did you tell me all that bullshit?'

'I wanted to see your reaction.'

'Why? That wasn't very nice.'

'Sorry,' said Kev, a smirk belying the apology, 'but without invention life can be as tedious as a twice-told tale. But, to get back to your question, I do sometimes have culinary cock-ups, but not often, and I hope my worst mistakes were when I was learning. It sounds like you've never cooked.'

Razor shook his head. 'I never had to. Perhaps I should have made more effort, but I could never see the point when my wife was so excellent.'

'She's the lady in the photographs?'

Razor nodded. 'Felicity. I called her Flit. She died.' It was the first time he'd said it.

'I'm sorry to hear that,' said Kev. 'What happened?'

'I'd rather not talk about it.'

'Then I won't ask about it. Have you had enough to eat?'

'Yes,' said Razor, getting up and walking away, unwilling to let Kev see the tears in his eyes.

'I'll wash up,' said Kev.

Razor dashed to the bathroom, splashed cold water in his face and took deep, calming breaths. Although he'd revealed little, it was more than he'd wanted to, and although the horror of that awful evening had ebbed a little, his shame and guilt had reached the point where he feared he might explode. He'd have loved to have got it all off his chest, if he could only have borne the shame of explaining just how much he'd let her down, and how useless he'd been.

Ray had always been a coward. He hoped Razor was braver.

It must have taken half an hour before he'd tamed his tumult of self-loathing and could trust himself to keep a stiff upper lip. He drifted downstairs where the hall clock lied that it was one o'clock. It had stopped months ago—not, poetically, at the moment of Flit's death, but a few days later, and for a week he'd failed to understand why it always showed lunchtime. He thought he might have gone mad. He certainly would have done at the funeral, had it not been for Alex. It was sad how he'd once got the man so wrong, for since that terrible day, Alex had been the only one to visit, to ask after his well-being and to help out. All his other so-called friends had become strangers. Not that he blamed them—he suspected he'd have done the same had the situations been reversed. Other peoples' bereavements were so awkward.

Razor sat down in the armchair.

Kev was curled up on the sofa with his book. 'Alright, mate?'

'Not so bad,' said Razor.

'Have you any plans for today?'

'Why do you ask?'

'I was just wondering what to do about food.'

'Buy something if you want—there's money in my wallet. But first tell me why you're still here? I'm grateful, of course, for all your cooking and cleaning and tidying up and all that, but I don't understand why you're doing it.'

'You appear to be in need of help, and I have nothing on my schedule that I can't put off for a few days.'

'Thank you, but I'm going out now,' said

Razor. He needed the soothing routine of mindless walking to trample down the guilt.

'Will you be back for lunch?'

'I don't know.'

Razor put on his new coat and beanie, left via the back door, and marched, keeping well away from roads and houses, grateful for the few remaining fog pockets in which he could lose himself. After a while, he was squelching along a public footpath around the edge of a muddy field, but exercise and solitude weren't as comforting as usual. The waterlogged mud clinging to his boots made every step a feat of endurance, but did at least remind him how soon he'd be laid to rest deep in the earth—it was some comfort. After trudging for a couple of hours and his legs growing tired, he began to feel lunch might be advisable. Regretting his earlier terseness, he decided to head home and hope Kev was still there, so he could apologise and eat. And if it worked out as he hoped, after lunch he would say thank you and goodbye, and return to Glevchester.

His walk had taken him to near Willoton Manor, where Alex lived in one of the six luxury apartments. A rustle alerted him to a tall, plump man lurking in the hedge and peering through a gap. The cold gleam of a blade in the man's right hand gave Razor hope that a glorious death might have come closer to home than expected. The lurker, oblivious to being watched, took a deep breath, squeezed through the hedge and lumbered across the lawn, splashing as he went. As soon as he'd disappeared around the side of the manor, Razor followed, wondering what to do next.

A terrible scream made up his mind. He broke into a run, preparing for battle and trying to convince himself that it would be a good day to die. As he crossed the sodden lawn, chill water spattered up his trouser legs. Gravel scrunched when he reached the path. After a brief pause to gather his strength, he charged round to the front of the manor, screaming something he hoped sounded as fierce as a Viking war cry. He expected to do or to die and hoped to get transported to Valhalla, or wherever dead heroes ended up. The man he'd been following turned, white-faced and shocked.

It was Tom Talbot who lived next door to the manor in a once derelict cottage he and his wife, Serena, had done up. In Tom's right hand was a butcher's knife, in his left the scrawny neck of Launcelot, a cantankerous peacock whose penetrating cry had annoyed the villagers for years. Tom dropped both knife and bird and fled. Launcelot ruffled his feathers and launched a vicious counter-attack, a blur of flapping wings, slashing feet and jabbing beak.

The knife looked sharp and heavy. Razor stooped to pick it up.

'What the hell's going on out here?' A slim, elegant man was standing in the manor's doorway. 'Oh, it's you, Raymondo.'

'Hi, Alex.'

'Did you come here to slaughter our peacock?'

'No, it wasn't me.'

Although Alex looked and sounded relaxed, he was gripping the heavy studded oak door in one hand as if he feared he might need a shield. 'Okay, mate, I believe you—thousands wouldn't. To tell you the truth, I wouldn't blame you if you did. He's not to everyone's taste.'

Razor shook his head. 'Somebody was out to get him, but it wasn't me. All I did was pick up his knife... he dropped it when he ran.'

'Okay, if that's your story. But are you sure you're alright? It's not sensible to be out in public carrying a big knife—someone might get the wrong idea and call the police.' Alex paused. 'By the way, if you aren't here to murder Launcelot, what are you here for?'

'As I told you, I like to walk and I ended up passing here by chance.'

'Fair enough. And who's that little guy in your house?'

'Just a friend.'

Alex nodded, still keeping an eye on the knife. 'You should put that down.'

'No, I'll return it to… to its owner.'

'Alright, Raymondo, if you must. Did you know the police were round your place on Tuesday? Was it in connection with the incident on Bindover Bridge that the paper reported?'

Razor's throat felt dry, and he was aware of gulping air. 'I don't know what you're talking about. I've done nothing wrong.'

'Okay, but why that?' Alex nodded at the knife.

'It really isn't mine. Honest.'

'So whose is it?' asked Alex.

'The man who brought it here.'

'Did you recognise him?'

'Yes, or rather, no,' said Razor, 'because it was… a stranger. I'd never seen him before in my life.'

'And yet you seem to believe you can return it to him? Okay. Could you describe this... stranger? Because, if there is a maniac on the loose, I'd better inform the police—who knows what other weapons he might be carrying, and he might not stop at birds next time.'

Razor nodded, trying to exude sincerity. 'I got a reasonable look at him. He was about average height. Not fat. Nor thin. About average you might say. He wasn't young, or very old. And he was wearing a black leather jacket, and... er... shoes... and trousers.'

'That's it? An average man in shoes and trousers? That'll give the police something to go on.' Sarcasm and scepticism mingled in Alex's voice.

'That's right. They were ordinary ones. Nondescript.'

Though Alex shook his head, Razor couldn't help feeling proud that his, admittedly rather generic, description was nothing like Tom. He quite liked the man, having met him and his glamorous wife a few times at village events. He also sympathised with, if not quite condoned, the attack on Launcelot, whose frequent screams, even out of the usual breeding season, had vexed so many.

'In all seriousness, Raymondo, I'd feel much safer if you put your weapon down,' said Alex.

'Of course, though I say again that it's not mine.' Razor squatted and placed the knife on the edge of the lawn.

'That's better,' said Alex, smiling. 'Do you want to come in while I call the police?'

'You're really going to call them?'

'Of course, and since you are the only witness, you'd better stay here.'

Although Razor was certain he could clear up the misunderstanding on Bindover Bridge and the incident with Danny in minutes, he still couldn't bear the thought of answering questions, whether they came from the police now or whether they came later at Flit's approaching inquest. He feared what might emerge and what people would think of him. He glanced at his watch. 'Sorry, Alex, I'd love to, but I'm late for lunch already. See you.'

He turned away with what he hoped was a casual wave and strolled down the long gravelled driveway towards the road. As soon as he was out of sight of the manor, he bolted, taking the shortcut home. Yet again he intended to run away, but first he needed his things.

Heart pounding, he burst into the kitchen, startling Kev who was stirring something on the stove. The aroma was wonderful.

'What's up?' Kev asked.

'Just thought of something—got to rush over to Charnham. No time to explain—the taxi's waiting.' Razor grabbed his backpack, stuffed his wallet and a few essentials into it, and slung it on his back. 'Bye.'

'What about lunch?'

Razor shook his head and ran for the fields, hoping his mention of Charnham might throw the police off the track should they come looking for him and question Kev. It was a feeble ploy, but it was all he had.

8

Razor's pace slackened to a brisk sneak. He kept close to walls and hedges where possible, keeping his head down and trying not to leave a trail. When at last he reached a small copse, he flopped onto a mossy tree stump and rested, glad it provided a soft seat though damp spread up through his trousers, making him shiver. Although he doubted anyone would be near enough to notice him, he made a point of not moving and tried to think. Had he perhaps been a little paranoid in supposing the police would mount an immediate search for him? Probably, though it remained a possibility— assuming Alex had called them, as Razor suspected he'd done before. All things considered, he thought it best to keep out of sight until 'the heat was off', and despite everything, thinking such a corny expression made him laugh and wonder where he'd picked it up—from some TV cop show he assumed.

It was ironic that having nothing left to lose except his life, his life had become interesting again. He'd never envisaged becoming a desperado, but couldn't deny the thrill of his present situation—he'd done so much in the last few days he'd never have dreamt of. Maybe he'd become boring and complacent before Flit's death, but now he felt almost like he had as a boy, free of guilt, with few worries and responsibilities, and when the consequences of misdeeds had been slight, even if they hadn't always seemed so at the time. When had he allowed routine, order and work to dominate his life? Why had he allowed it?

He perched on the stump for over an hour, seeing no sign of anyone else. The only movements were birds flitting in the trees, a fox crossing the far field and the clouds rolling in. By the time he'd forced himself back into being comfortably miserable, the sun, a pale glow behind clouds, was getting low, and his stomach was growling about not being fed. He'd put a little food in his pack, but that was for emergencies only and for now, hunger was just another experience for a hero to endure without flinching.

The wind got up, raising a haze from the sodden soil. Razor put on his beanie. It helped a little, though to survive until morning he knew he'd either have to walk all night or find shelter. Since he was already yawning, the latter seemed best. But where? Farmer McGill's barn wasn't too far away, but he feared McGill might have dogs. He suspected all the garden sheds in the village would be padlocked after a spate of burglaries the previous summer, and the bus shelter was far too public. Then he remembered stumbling across a 'pillbox', a crumbling fortification from the Second World War, during one of his walks along Willoton Ridge. It was, perhaps, a mile away and though it was hardly *The Ritz*, it might keep the wind and rain off.

Chilled and stiff, he got to his feet and crept from the shelter of the trees, trudging upwards through the fields and seeing no one. Movement in the distance caused momentary alarm, but it was only a fat grey cat out hunting. A few minutes later, Razor reached a tumbledown Cotswold stone wall he hoped he recognised through the growing gloom and scrambled over into scrubby undergrowth. A mist, though still patchy, was thickening as the sun lowered and he feared getting lost until the hexagonal shape of the pillbox, half-hidden under ivy and moss, rose before him. Its pocked and rusting door was closed and refused to budge even when he put his shoulder to it.

Having failed to anticipate this possibility, he turned around to vent his frustrations in an outburst of swearing and shrub kicking, and had broken into an angry sweat by the time a thought came to him. Going back, he gave the door a tug. It swung open with a creak and crashed against the entrance wall.

He dug a torch from his pack, turned it on and looked inside the pillbox, finding it in better condition than he'd expected, although some bricks were crumbling, and green and black mould streaked the walls. However, the air did not stink of urine, or worse, as he'd feared, and held only a faint odour of damp and decay. It looked much smaller than it had appeared from the outside which puzzled him until he noticed a wall dividing it down the middle—to prevent ricochets he supposed. There was still enough space for a tired man to lie down, and the brick floor was puddle-free. A fierce cold breeze blowing through the embrasures on one side had swept dried leaves into deep drifts. He gathered up armfuls, carried them to the more sheltered side and heaped them into what he hoped would prove a comfortable mattress.

By the time he'd done all he could to make his bed, night was filling the room, though a glimmer on the west side suggested the sun was not yet fully down. Since he was unsure how much battery remained, he took his emergency supplies from his pack and turned the torch off. His evening meal was a bag of turkey jerky, a packet of digestive biscuits and a bottle of water. To start with, he resolved to leave half for breakfast and rationed himself. The jerky was chewy, the biscuits comforting. Just one more wouldn't hurt, but one wasn't enough. Soon he'd scoffed them all, and his stomach still growled for more. Unable to resist, he finished the jerky, but its saltiness made him thirsty. He drained the bottle and shrugged—morning was another day and would just have to take care of itself. He'd bet Kev had cooked something wonderful and tried not to feel sorry for himself.

Determined to make the best of things, he pulled up his coat, pulled down his beanie, shoved his hands into his pockets and lay back on the leaves, thrashing about like a landed fish as he struggled to find a comfortable position. The leaves compressed to the hardness of planks, providing far less insulation than he'd hoped for. They rustled every time he took a breath or wriggled, and despite yawns so vast he feared his jaw would crack, sleep felt a long way off.

He shivered and fretted about hypothermia until a memory popped up of the previous winter when The Cotswolds was expecting a fierce cold snap. Jeremy Pratt, an exceptionally smug and patronising local television presenter, had offered advice in case motorists became stranded in snow. Although most of it was obvious stuff about carrying a thermos of hot drink, food and a blanket, Jeremy had used computer graphics to show how heat sapped from a body's extremities and explained a technique for slowing the process.

Razor remembered the importance of maximising all available insulation. He sat up and rummaged in his backpack for the towel, spare t-shirt, underpants and large cotton handkerchief he'd stowed in there. He wrapped the towel around his thighs, fitted the underpants on his head beneath his beanie, twisted the handkerchief around his throat like a scarf, spread the t-shirt over his torso and pushed his feet inside the pack. Then, following a brief struggle, he released his arms from the coat sleeves and tucked them inside his coat. Soon afterwards, the shivering stopped, he relaxed, his eyes grew heavier and his head lolled as he dropped into a deep sleep.

Despite the familiar nightmare man screaming into his face, nothing disturbed his slumber until something began tickling his cheek. Barely conscious, he tried to scratch it away, only to find his arms pinioned as if in a straitjacket. It was completely dark and terror kicked in, but although he writhed and wriggled like an escapologist, he could not break free. He had a phobia of creepy crawlies, even harmless ones, and his memory thought it a good time to remind him of the venomous bugs the guides had warned against on some of their foreign treks. The tickle grew worse and his imagination suggested insect feet tap-dancing on his cheek, searching for a shortcut to his nostrils. Or might it be a leech?

Ignoring the cold stiffness of his back, he jerked into a sitting position with a scream that would have done credit to a teenage victim in a horror film. Sweating with frantic haste, he released his arms and scratched at his face, still expecting to find a massive centipede or a huge hairy spider, but as he became a little more with it, he laughed. His beanie had worked down over his eyes and a loose thread had caused the tickle.

He pulled the hat back. The heavy grey light showed night had passed and he stood up, shedding leaves like an autumn tree, before heading outside to relieve himself in a bramble bush. Steam rose, he looked around, shivering as he surveyed the land, blinking in the watery morning sunlight. Last night's mist had all but dispersed, except in a few deep hollows, the clouds were high and thin, scudding along in a brisk north-easterly wind.

He headed back inside, longing for a mug of hot tea and a big cooked breakfast. His eyes re-adjusted to the gloom, and he gasped—there was a stainless steel thermos and a small foil package on the floor right beside where he'd slept. Somebody had been in. Therefore somebody knew he was there! Panicking, he ran back outside. No one was in sight.

A second glance at the flask suggested a remarkable similarity to the one he'd taken on picnics when he'd still had time for fun. It brought to mind a glorious holiday on the Isle of Skye four summers ago when he'd made Flit laugh by slipping on a scree and splatting onto his flask. A dent in its base confirmed it as the same one. The mysterious visitor must have been Kev, but even that was a puzzle, for how had the little guy known where to look? How could he have followed Razor's trail? As far as Razor knew, he didn't even know the area. One thing at least was certain and comforting—Kev wouldn't tell the police.

Relaxing, Razor opened the flask, sniffed the coffee, poured a cup and sipped. It was strong, hot and sweet and although as a rule he took it without sugar, it was just what he needed. Even the cup warmed his chilled fingers. When he opened the foil package, he was delighted it contained four rounds of thick-cut bacon sandwiches, still slightly warm and fragrant. He ate and drank his fill.

Afterwards, a tremendous euphoria engulfed him, and he blamed Kev for making it so difficult to stay morbid. It required effort, but he forced himself to become angry and resentful. What gave the little guy the right to look after him? All the interference, whatever the reason, was unasked for and intolerable. He had to get away, leave Willoton forever this time, and take his chances somewhere with more chance of danger. Sorenchester was too quiet. Pigton, less than twenty miles away, had more than its share of trouble, but he'd never liked the place. It had to be Glevchester again. Perhaps it was not such a hot spot for crime as Pigton, but, having been a victim twice before, he hoped it might be third time lucky.

A gunshot made him jump. It had been close.

Had the police found him? Did they want him dead? It was too early—he was not yet in the right state of mind and was trembling like a wet kitten. Yet, why shouldn't this be his moment? He'd read something about the phenomenon of suicide by police, so perhaps if he charged forth, like a latter-day Sundance Kid, he could go out in a blaze of bullets and glory. The rational part of his brain kicked back in and overruled his paranoia. He was in Britain—the police tended not to shoot people without a strong reason.

Another shot followed, but no bullet smacked against the pillbox, and anyway he suspected the old reinforced walls would keep him safe. Razor calmed down and tried to think. There had to be another explanation. He sneaked outside, ducking behind a tangle of brambles and peeped over the top. About twenty yards away stood the sturdy frame of Farmer McGill, a double-barrelled shotgun resting across his chest, and a bloodied brace of wood pigeons limp at his belt. A pheasant, disturbed by Razor's unexpected appearance, took off in a flurry of wings and squawks.

As McGill turned, hoisted the gun to his shoulder, and fired, Razor hurled himself to the ground, hearing the retort as he was dropping, and the flying pellets as they shredded the bushes, littering him with old wood and thorns. He lay still, shaking, but unharmed. Damn his reflexes! His misery could already have ended.

Footsteps squelched towards him.

'I'm sorry. Are you alright? What are you doing here?' McGill's voice shook. 'I didn't see you… is that underwear on your head?'

Shaken, Razor stood up and removed the underpants. 'I'm okay. I was… er… Mr McGill?'

The old farmer looked troubled, his ruddy face turned as white as rice water and pearls of sweat glistened on his forehead. The shotgun dropped, McGill clutched his chest and fell to his knees.

'What's the matter?' said Razor.

Gasping for breath, the old farmer opened his

mouth as if about to speak, but fell on his side and lay still. Razor had only met the man twice and hadn't much liked him, but he felt obliged to do something—heroes didn't just leave people to die. He ran to the old man's side, squatted down and, forcing himself not to recoil at its clammy coldness, pressed two fingers against his neck. McGill's pulse was as fast and feeble as a baby bird's. His breathing was shallow and rapid.

Razor knew he ought to get medical help as soon as possible, but since he'd smashed his mobile in a drunken rage after Flit's funeral he wondered how. He considered the old-fashioned red phone box in the village which local worthies maintained for the sake of appearances, even though no one used it, but calculated that McGill's farmhouse might be closer. He reckoned he might run there in ten minutes and call for help—though this would mean leaving the old man alone in a muddy field.

Time was of the essence. If he made the wrong decision, there'd be one fewer farmer in the village.

Could he carry McGill? He made an attempt, but the stout old farmer seemed to weigh as much as a horse. Perhaps he could drag him. He grasped the farmer under his arms and around his chest and set off, though it wasn't long before his heart was thumping so hard he feared there'd soon be two casualties lying side by side in Cardiac, or more likely, in the morgue. McGill's face had turned a nasty shade of grey, though he still appeared to be breathing. It spurred Razor into a superhuman effort. Sweat rolled down his face and his head spun but still he toiled, step after step, his lungs bursting, his muscles burning. Had the farmhouse not been downhill, he would never have made it, but at last, a glance over his shoulder showed the stone walls of the farmyard. A final exertion took them up to the front door. It was open and he could hear someone moving inside.

Razor, gasping for breath, had none left to call for help, so sat McGill down with his back against the wall. The old man's wellington boots had come off and his heels poked through his green woollen socks. Razor pressed the doorbell and staggered away as fast as his knackered legs could carry him until he flopped down behind a wall to catch his breath. Reassured by faint voices from the house, he crept away, heading back towards the pillbox.

About halfway, he spotted McGill's boots side by side in a puddle. He carried on and, although it was still a climb, the distance felt like nothing without his heavy load. By the time he was approaching the top of the ridge, he no longer expected to keel over and die. On impulse, he picked up McGill's shotgun and cartridge bag, and stashed them out of harm's way under leaves in the pillbox. Then he grabbed his backpack, stuffed his things back into it and walked away, his back to the pale sun that was peeping from behind a thin film of cloud.

Hours later, muddied and tired, and far enough away that the chances of meeting anyone who might recognise him were remote, he turned onto a narrow rutted lane with a streak of grass down the middle like a Mohican haircut. Razor trusted it would at least take him to where he could find his bearings, and although it rambled like a drunkard, it appeared to be heading in roughly the right direction for Glevchester. At the back of his mind was a fear of delaying too long. He could not allow himself to live—it would be betraying Flit.

His mind in turmoil, he did what he always did—he walked and walked and kept on walking. Fatigue, thirst and hunger acted as sedatives to soothe his tortured soul.

Every step towards Glevchester took him closer to the end of his life.

The thought was invigorating.

9

Razor followed deserted lanes, forgotten paths over windswept hills, and steep muddy tracks into deep valleys until he emerged beside a wide road with traffic. The feeble sun, his only companion, dipped its head, leaving him to the care of sodium lights as they came on, though it wasn't yet too dark. The chill on his face suggested a possible frost though the exercise and his new coat and hat kept him toasty.

By the time he reached the outskirts of Glevchester, the turmoil in his head had trickled away, leaving only hunger. All the small cafes he passed were closed, a puzzle until the bells of Glevchester Minster reminded him that it was Sunday. He trudged on, trusting there'd be places to eat further into town.

His confidence was not misplaced and, before long, a whiff of curry drew him towards The Good Lucknow restaurant. His mouth was watering even before he entered the smart establishment where the fragrance of cooking spices almost made him cry. Although busy, one or two tables appeared free.

A skinny little waiter in a white shirt and neat

black trousers approached, his forehead rutted into a frown. 'Good evening, can I help you... sir?'

'I'd like a table for one, please.'

'You would like to reserve a table for one o'clock? Tomorrow?'

'No, for now, please, and for one person—me. If that's okay?'

As the waiter looked him up and down, shaking his head and his frown deepening, Razor realised what a horrible sight he must be. A man who'd spent the night on leaves, was encrusted in mud, had two days of stubble bristling on his head, and had a wealth of bruises decorating his face evidently did not reach the required standard for customers. He became aware of how clean and smart everybody else looked. They were staring at him: some with disapproval, as if a verminous beggar had barged in, others with amusement, and one or two with sympathy.

'I'm sorry, sir, but we are fully booked tonight.'

'Oh no,' said Razor, his spirits sinking to his boots. 'It's just that I haven't had a bite since breakfast. I will tidy myself up, first... and I can pay.'

'Sorry, sir.'

'Well, is there anywhere else around here I can get something to eat?'

The waiter looked more sympathetic, but shrugged. 'There's a burger place about half a mile down the road.'

After his previous experience, it was not at all what Razor wanted, but he thanked him and turned towards the door, sagging with disappointment and fatigue.

'Or, we could do you a takeaway, sir. If you'd care to sit over there and read through the menu, I'll be with you in a moment.'

'Thank you,' said Razor, 'that's most kind.' He took a seat in an alcove by the door, resting his weary legs.

He glanced at the menu and ordered chicken tikka masala with naan bread, like always. Flit had used to take the mickey, claiming it wasn't even a genuine Indian dish, but he liked it and didn't care. After paying, he absent-mindedly slipped his wallet into his backpack and picked up the *Glevchester Mirror* from the rack.

A paunchy middle-aged man and an ample woman of similar vintage were already eating at a nearby table. It took all of Razor's resolve not to watch every mouthful, as if he were a ravenous dog.

The last time hunger had hurt so much was after Flit's funeral and a four-day whisky binge. The resulting humongous hangover had left him too lethargic and indifferent to feed himself. In the end, Alex had turned up, made toast and marmalade, cajoled him into eating it and more or less forced him out of the house for a walk in the fresh air. Now, Razor could hardly wait. He flicked through the paper, but found little of interest—there was no mention of Bindover Bridge, of knife-wielding maniacs, or of anyone being injured in St Stephen's Park.

At last, the waiter brought over a bulging paper bag. Razor took it, said goodbye and walked from the restaurant.

A bench by the bus stop on the far side of the road offered a place to sit, and though it was not a scenic spot for a picnic, it would do. He crossed over, sat down and unpacked the bag, trying not to drool. Out came a box of curry, a white packet of naan bread, a polythene bag with a salad garnish, a paper napkin and a little packet containing a wet wipe. After cleaning his hands, he spread the empty bag across his lap and opened his meal, delighting in the blend of chicken, yogurt, coconut, tomatoes and spices, scooping mouthfuls up with chunks of naan, and it would not have taken much to persuade him it was the most delicious meal in the universe. After he'd hoovered up every last morsel, even the garnish, he sat back with a sigh, filled with gratitude for the waiter's kindness, the cook's skill and for the genius who'd created the dish in the first place.

Razor stretched out and watched life pass by, thinking how much Flit would have loved The Good Lucknow. Although the thought hurt, he felt almost cheerful and put it down to elevated blood sugar. Attempting to regain his happy state of misery, he considered likely places to meet his death, until distracted by two scruffy young men. One was lanky, the other short and rotund. Both were lurching down the road, shouting, swearing and swilling lager from cans—not the first they'd consumed that evening judging by their staggering gaits. Now and again they'd intimidate other pedestrians with sudden rushes, shoulder barges and slurred threats. Razor braced for trouble though it looked like being of the annoying rather than of the lethal variety. However, if they even noticed him, they ignored him, and lurched across the road, causing a car to screech to a halt inches away. They jeered and gesticulated when the driver sounded his horn.

Razor relaxed and considered his next move—he had intended to head straight to the perils of the Severn Wharves, but he was so damnably tired. Yet, why should that be a problem? He still had plenty of money and what would be the harm in checking into a hotel? A hot shower, a long sleep in a warm bed and a good breakfast would leave him much better prepared for whatever came next. Tomorrow would be just as good a day to die.

As he yawned, a prolonged outbreak of foul-mouthed shouting drew his attention back to the two drunken louts. Egged on by his big mate, the squat one was urinating on The Good Lucknow's window. As the skinny waiter rushed outside, imploring them to leave, the lanky one pulled a brick from under his jacket and hurled it. The waiter ducked back inside, the brick missed him, rebounded from the door frame and landed on the tall guy's foot. Bellowing and cursing, he dropped to the ground. The squat one, outraged by the poetic justice, barged into the restaurant, knocking the waiter to the floor.

It all happened so fast that Razor was still on

the bench. When his brain caught up, adrenaline flowed and he sprang into action. Dropping his napkin, he grabbed his backpack, sprinted across the road and roared, 'Stop that!'

Much to his surprise, Squatty stopped a kick aimed at the fallen waiter's face. The lanky one, hopping on his good foot, retrieved the brick and launched it at Razor, who was so fired up he barely noticed it bounce off his chest. The two thugs exchanged a glance and fled. Razor took off after them, fatigue forgotten in the exhilaration of the chase, though he wasn't sure what he'd do if he caught up. At first this seemed unlikely—Squatty showed a surprising turn of speed and the tall one, despite his flattened foot, was a born runner.

Razor, puffing like a chain-smoking dragon, came close to admitting defeat, but something impelled him to make a valiant effort. Gritting his teeth, he put on a spurt. It soon became clear that, despite his initial speed, Squatty didn't have much in the way of staying power. Razor was closing the gap, though the lanky one was already out of sight. They were heading towards the Severn Wharves.

Pent-up rage boiling over into blood lust,

Razor maintained the pursuit down a narrow passage between old warehouses until he was within spitting distance of Squatty, whose breathing was erupting in loud, strained gasps. Just as Razor reached out to collar him, Squatty reached the end of the passage and made an abrupt left turn.

Ahead, a dock reflected street lights like a dark mirror. Razor's momentum carried him onward. He put the brakes on and came to a stop, teetering on the brink, looking down into the water. A noise made him glance over his shoulder.

The lanky thug was on the charge, using a supermarket trolley as a battering ram. Razor had no time to react.

It hit him.

He fell.

The shock of icy water took away any remaining breath, and although he gasped in desperation, his lungs just wouldn't fill with air. When he tried to swim, his new coat puffed up and stopped his arms moving. The cold hurt. Panic took over. Foul water flooded his mouth as he screamed, and he knew he would sink. Although his body kept up the fight for precious life, his brain accepted death. His last sight was an ornamental rowan tree, its berries glowing like blood beneath a street light. As he slipped below the surface, there was a moment of exhilaration that he'd achieved what he'd set out to do.

All was cold. Blackness engulfed him.

Then there was nothing.

The water was nice and warm, but he didn't like the pain. He tried to retreat to the comfort of oblivion, but had to come to terms with one incontrovertible fact—he was still alive. This was impossible. He must have drowned. So why could he smell flowers? He opened his eyes. His naked body lay in a white bath, in a white bathroom.

'Welcome back, my lovely,' said a woman with a soft lilt to her voice.

'Where am I and what am I doing here?'

'You're in the bath, taking a bath.'

She was in the doorway, a small, pretty woman with eyes as blue as forget-me-nots and a strange air of sadness. Her lips twitched into a half smile, and it took a moment before he knew her. Without her coat or cloak she looked tiny and fragile, and the shapeless black dress she wore accentuated the paleness of her skin.

'You're the lady who looked after me on the bus,' he said, intensely aware of his nakedness. He covered up as well as possible, feeling ridiculously vulnerable.

'I know,' she said.

'Who are you?'

'People call me Miranda.'

'Pleased to meet you, Miranda. I'm Ray... Razor.'

'I know.'

'How?'

She shrugged.

'How did I get here?'

'We carried you.'

'And how did I get out of the water?'

'You're still in the water, my lovely.'

'But at the Wharves?'

'We pulled you out as you were on the way down.'

'Who did?'

'We did.'

'We?'

'My companion and I.'

'Thank you, I suppose... both of you.'

'You are most welcome.'

Her answers weren't entirely satisfactory and

Razor wondered if she was hiding something. Then again, her accent might hint she was a foreigner and was answering as well as she could, though her words were clear and concise without undue pauses for thought. Her half smile disconcerted him.

'Are you warm enough?' she asked. 'You were icy when you arrived.'

He nodded. 'I think so, thank you, but where is here?'

'In my house.'

'Then thank you for taking me in, Miranda.'

'My pleasure.'

Razor's head was so full of questions he couldn't concentrate on any one in particular, and when he thought he had something to say and opened his mouth, the words wouldn't come out. He feared he was doing a fine goldfish impression.

'Are you ready to get out?' asked Miranda.

Razor nodded. She stepped towards him, picking up a vast white towel.

'Can you leave it on the edge?' he said, unwilling to stand up and expose himself. He blushed.

'I'll fetch a robe,' she said putting the towel down and walking away.

'Thank you,' he managed, regretting her departure though relieved to be alone. He pulled the plug, stood up and dried himself.

All sorts of feelings needed resolution. While part of him resented still being alive, another part was grateful he'd been spared. A large part found Miranda intriguing. Who was she? Where did she come from? How was he still alive and in her bath? Despite this, and though he tried to persuade himself that he wasn't interested in her in the way a man is normally interested in a pretty woman, another part condemned him for disloyalty to Flit.

His emotions still unresolved, he got out the bath and glimpsed his reflection in the mirror. Something didn't look right, but it was only when he scratched his chin that he put his finger on it—he'd been shaved. The thought of Miranda's cool little hands touching his face caused a shiver of excitement and allowed in another thought—had she washed him? Had her hands been all over him? He broke into a sweat, trying to unthink it and to ignore the guilt it brought, though one thing was clear— he'd missed a woman's touch.

It was wrong! He would not allow such thoughts. Nothing she could do would deflect him from his mission. He was determined to die and she couldn't keep on rescuing him, but he would have felt more heroic and resolute had he been dressed. The bathroom door opened and she handed him a soft white bathrobe.

'Thank you,' he said as she left.

Her scent was alluring and her face looked angelic and calm, but Razor experienced a deep unease, way beyond his normal background level.

He put on the robe, making sure to tie it in a double knot, before stepping out onto a landing lit only by two flickering gas lights. The ceiling was high, the walls were covered in dark wooden panels and the floor with time-dulled red and white patterned tiles. There were three closed doors to his right and two to his left. Just ahead was a wooden staircase, with a strip of threadbare maroon carpet held in place by stair rods. Razor hadn't seen such things since his grandparents moved—about the time he first went to school.

The house was cold and as quiet as the grave. He shivered, wondering what had put that thought into his head.

'Hello,' he said.

There was no response. He shrugged and headed downstairs. This too was gas lit and dim.

'Miranda,' he shouted on reaching a hallway, much like the upstairs landing, but with an immense grandfather clock standing to one side. 'Where are you?'

She didn't answer. Even the old clock was silent. It looked well cared for and smelled of beeswax, but both hands pointed straight down, though his watch told him it was approaching two o'clock. The door opposite was ajar, which he took as an invitation. He entered a large room with four maroon-leather chairs huddling around a wide stone fireplace in which a pile of hefty logs blazed, scenting the air with apples and a hint of smoke. Shelves sagged beneath a library of old books on three sides, and heavy curtains concealed a window on the other. A rich, deep red carpet covered the floor.

Razor checked the next room, finding it cool, damp and dark, with mysterious shapes covered by white dust sheets, like the ghosts of old furniture. The next two rooms looked empty, though one was huge, with French windows at the far end boarded up with heavy planks. He tried the last door, not expecting an electric strip light to come on as it opened. He'd reached the kitchen. It was compact, clean and modern, like the bathroom. A sheet of cream paper lay on the table in the middle.

It was a short message written with a fountain pen. The handwriting was small and neat.

Dear Mr Razor,

I apologise that we had to go out and leave you alone in a strange house. The fire in the drawing room is made up and should last, but feel free to add more logs should the need arise—there are plenty in the basket. The fridge is well stocked, so please help yourself to any food and drink you require. In addition, should you fancy a nip, there are alcoholic beverages in the globe in the drawing room.

Your clothes have been laundered, but are still drying, and I regret my wardrobe has nothing that would fit you, or, indeed, suit you in the meantime.

I have prepared a bed for you in the bedroom

with the blue door. Toiletries are on the chest. Please make yourself as comfortable as you can.

Don't wait up for us. We will probably be late, but should be back before first light,

Miranda

P.S. Go anywhere you want to, but, please, avoid the cellars as the staircase is rotten and there is no lighting.

Razor dropped the note back onto the table, struggling to understand his disappointment. He wondered who the 'we' was, and hoped it wasn't her boyfriend or husband, though it was none of his business—or so he told himself. Something about her intrigued him even though it had no right to.

Trying to divert himself, he thought he'd make a pot of tea—everything he needed was on a side table. He took a delicate china dessert plate from a selection on a pine dresser and piled it with biscuits from a tin although he wasn't hungry. After making tea, he loaded his bits and pieces onto a richly decorated enamel tray, carried it through to the drawing room and took a seat by the fire, trying not to feel like an intruder.

Everything in that room would have looked at home there a century ago—there was no television, phone, radio, or computer. He didn't mind—as far as he was concerned the outside world could stay there until he was ready for it again. The house, with its assortment of ancient and modern, neglected old rooms, smart modern ones, and its mix of gas and electric lights, fascinated him and added to the mystery of Miranda.

After drinking the whole pot of tea and clearing the plate of biscuits, he no longer felt at all like sleeping and was unsure what to do. There were plenty of books—it had been an age since he'd read one for pleasure. He examined the shelves, hoping for a light novel, but found mostly leather-bound volumes that were either financial records or medical tomes. The few novels scattered through the shelves at random looked old, and he'd never heard of most of the authors or titles. He did recognise Defoe, Bronte, Dickens, and Austen, but none of them suited his mood.

After slumping back into his chair, twiddling

his thumbs and sighing, he got up, dropped another log on the fire and decided to explore—she'd said it would be okay. Being a methodical man, he thought he'd start at the top and work his way down, avoiding the cellars, of course. He strolled upstairs, and looked inside the room with the blue door, which was his to use, should he feel the need of sleep. A faint gas light cast dim shadows.

It was a small, cosy bedroom with an iron-framed single bed covered in thick blankets and a colourful counterpane. There was a small oak wardrobe, a matching chest of drawers and a round bedside table supporting a silver candlestick with a long white candle. On top of the chest was a soft white towel, a toothbrush, a bar of plain soap, a shaving brush and a safety razor like his granddad had used. On impulse, he opened the drawers. There was nothing in them. Nor was there in the wardrobe.

The next room, slightly larger, was empty, with an uncurtained sash window and a bare wooden floor. The boards creaked as he walked across and looked out. All he could see were tall evergreen trees, a sliver of pale grey sky and a ragged string of dark cloud. Perhaps there was a hint of moonlight though it might have been a distant street light.

The second room was much the same and had a similar view, while the third faced a blank wall. After that there was only the bathroom, and two closets with a selection of cleaning materials. He wished he'd found some clues to help him work out where the house was. Not that it mattered—he'd find out sooner or later.

He hadn't seen his clothes anywhere, which was a puzzle. Could he have missed a room? Impossible. Even more puzzling, was that he'd found no sign of Miranda's bedroom. Surely, she and her mysterious companion slept somewhere. He just hoped it wasn't together.

10

A perverse fascination with Miranda's sleeping arrangements had rooted in Razor's brain, and there seemed no way of grubbing it out. Perhaps she'd had the cellar converted into a comfortable basement apartment? Perhaps her warning to keep out had only been to protect her privacy? If he opened the door and peeped inside, he could satisfy his curiosity and what harm would there be? He returned to the kitchen.

The cellar door, contorted with age, gave a hideous creak as it opened to a hefty shove. A musty, dusty odour rolled out. There was no lighting and nothing suggested it was anything more than an old-fashioned, neglected cellar. Those few wooden steps lit by the kitchen lights looked solid enough, but further down where it became as dark as a mine, there was no way of knowing. He needed the torch from his backpack—except he didn't have his pack and had not come across it during his exploration. Maybe this was for the best since he had no intention of blundering around in the darkness, which was an excellent excuse for ignoring the urge to explore. The cellar would just have to remain a mystery. He might as well give up and go to his bedroom—but he'd noticed a candle and matches up there.

He fetched them down, lit the candle in the cellar doorway and peeped through.

The flickering flame made the shadows shift, giving an impression of movement, but revealed little more than previously. The coward in him suggested it would be a good time to call it quits and sleep, but something inside rebelled—he'd just been spooked by light and shadow, and it was vital he re-asserted his heroic status. Darkness should hold no fear for a man of courage.

Stiffening his upper lip in the approved manner of Victorian adventurers, he stepped into the cellar. The old stairs seemed robust enough, despite the occasional creak, but still he took care, descending one tentative foot at a time. Some steps flexed under his weight, but held up. Miranda, he concluded, was being excessively careful with her guest.

Though further down than he'd expected, he reached the bottom without mishap and stepped onto the hard brick floor, a shock to his bare feet. The echoes of his footsteps suggested a chamber of some size. He raised the candle higher, his breath smoking. The cellar, brick-lined and vaulted, appeared larger in area than the house, but other than spiders' webs, shadows and the dank reek of history, it looked empty. A little less nervous, he approached the far end. What he'd assumed were deeper shadows turned out to be large wooden boxes resting on trestles. His timorous mind returned and suggested coffins and that he was intruding. It took all of his resolve not to rush back to the kitchen.

The candle flickered even more with the trembling of his hand though he tried to persuade himself that he wasn't scared—it was just the cold air down there. Conspicuously courageous, he approached the nearest box and nudged its lid. It stayed put. He might have walked away, but curiosity intervened. After setting the candle on the ground, he had another go, shoving with both hands and grunting until the lid slid free and dropped with a heart-stopping clatter. Dust swirled, raising the stink of damp and mildew, and the light went out. Razor turned away, covering his face, coughing and gagging. Although primeval instincts prompted blind panic and flight, he'd lost his bearings. Only a thread of sense held him back—in such a blackout he would almost certainly run straight into a wall. He forced himself into a phony calmness and looked around, hoping for a glimmer of light from the kitchen. There was only blackness—and a faint rustling sound. If he had a buyer, he'd have sold his soul for a good torch. Instead, impressing himself with his own fortitude and quickness of mind, he remembered the matches in his pocket. Despite breaking the first three in his urgency, the fourth flared and allowed him to find and relight the candle.

Inexplicably afraid, he looked into the box... and laughed.

It contained a mess of faded, mildewed cloth and a number of rotting wooden poles—some sort of large tent he assumed. The rustling came from a family of mice distressed by the disturbance of their little world. Razor exhaled, took a moment to regain composure and replaced the heavy lid—no easy feat. Peace and quiet returned.

He opened the second box.

More mice scurried for cover and distracted him for a moment. They were nesting in an old-fashioned lounge suit, faded, blotched and mouldy. It was still being worn by the skeleton of a man who must have been quite short in life, and who, to judge by his tie, had attended Eton College. Razor gulped. His head spun like a frisbee, his muscles might have been disconnected from his bones and he swayed, close to collapse. All he could see, all he could sense, was death, just like it had been at the ICU of Glevchester Hospital with Flit unrecognisable beneath bandages, tubes and wires as she passed away. He'd felt then, as he did now… numb, confused, lost. Was Miranda a murderer? Why else would she conceal a body down there? What did she have in store for him?

Time stopped. Part of his shocked brain registered the candle burning low and sputtering out.

A woman's voice called to him through the blackness. He might have been standing there for minutes, hours, or eons.

'Mr Razor?'

For a millisecond he thought he might be waking from a nightmare and hoped the voice was Flit's, but as his senses returned and he became aware of his frozen feet, he knew he wasn't in their nice clean bedroom at Riverside Cottage—he was in a dark place of horror, with the odour of damp and decay in his nostrils.

'Where are you?' It was Miranda.

Embarrassed at being discovered where he shouldn't have been, and filled with dread, he pulled himself together and struck a match. Sheltering the flame with one hand, he used its scant light to reach the steps. The match burnt out as he started upwards and something cracked. There was no step where there should have been one. His left leg dropped into the void, and momentum carried his upper body forward. Most of his bodyweight fell onto his arms and left hip, but there was enough left for his head to deliver a fierce butt to the edge of a step. Dazed, he was still able to fully appreciate his collection of pains. Where hurt most was the question that consumed him. He groaned.

The cellar door opened.

'Mr Razor? What are you doing down there?' Miranda sounded worried.

'I... got lost. A step broke.'

'Which was why I asked you not to come down here. Are you alright? You're bleeding.'

'I'm not sure... ' A trickle of blood ran down

his face.

Miranda shouted over her shoulder. 'Our guest has had an accident!'

Razor grimaced as a new twinge in his shin drew attention to itself.

'Can you get up?' she asked.

'I think so.' He pulled up his dangling leg and crawled towards the light, battered in mind and body.

'What bloody man is this?' asked Kev, sauntering into the kitchen as Miranda helped Razor to a chair.

Razor's mouth opened and shut and opened again. Only a weird, confused whine emerged.

'Brain damage?' asked Miranda, frowning.

'Probably not. He's always just as articulate.'

Razor shook his head.

'My mistake,' said Kev with a grin. 'He's not always so articulate. He is, however, a prize chump.'

Miranda smiled at Razor. 'We'd better patch you up.'

'Are you going to murder me?'

'Why would you even think such a thing?' asked Kev, screwing up his face.

'Because of what I saw.'

'What exactly did you see?' asked Miranda,

taking a first aid kit from a drawer.

'A body,' said Razor, trying to look brave, but not feeling it. He wanted to be killed in action, not to be murdered by a pretty woman, even if the result was the same.

'What body?' asked Miranda.

'The one in the box.'

'Oh, you mean the skeleton.' She laughed.

She looked amazing when she laughed. Razor forced his mind back on track. 'Of course!'

'Skeleton?' said Kev.

'Uncle Bob's,' said Miranda.

'I wondered what had become of that,' said Kev.

'Your uncle's skeleton?' said Razor, shocked. 'Isn't that illegal?'

'I don't think so,' said Miranda.

For Razor it was as if a ton of flummox had been heaped onto a pile of confusion. A thought popped up. He seized it. 'Are you saying Bob's your uncle?'

'He was,' said Miranda.

'But Bob's his uncle too,' said Razor, pointing at Kev, who was grinning and chuckling like a maniac.

'Many people have an Uncle Bob,' said Miranda. 'It's quite a common name.'

'I suppose… but it's still a bit of a coincidence, isn't it?'

Kev chuckled. 'Cousins have some relatives in common.'

'What have cousins got to do with it?' asked Razor, his brain floundering and clutching at straws. 'You mean you two?'

Miranda nodded and opened the first aid kit.

'In that case, it's amazing I've met both of you. What are the chances?'

'Not as unlikely as you might think,' said Kev, watching Miranda sit down and pour a smelly yellow liquid onto a wad of cotton wool.

'What do you mean?' Razor asked and flinched as she dabbed his forehead.

'Sorry,' she said. 'This might sting a little.'

As far as Razor was concerned, it stung more than a little, but he wasn't going to let on, not to her. 'Are you two really cousins?' He tried not to yelp as she dabbed again.

They nodded.

Miranda leaned towards him and examined the graze. Her closeness, her fragrance and the touch of her fingertips as she probed his injuries sent primeval, almost-forgotten signals around Razor's body. He stayed as still as possible, willing her to continue, but too soon she nodded and slapped a big plaster onto his head.

With some reluctance, Razor turned to Kev while she returned the first aid kit. 'Why aren't the odds of meeting both of you as high as I might think? There must be a million people in the Cotswolds—how come I just happened to get rescued by your cousin?'

'Because we talked and decided to look out for you,' said Kev. 'We believed you were showing a reckless disregard for your well-being.'

'Thank you for your concern,' said Razor, 'but you should let me go about my life as I want to. I didn't ask to be rescued.'

'But you have been,' said Miranda, 'and, by the way, you're welcome.'

'Sorry,' said Razor. 'I am grateful... but Kev, and I apologise if this sounds sexist, but why would you let her look after me? You're just putting her in the way of danger.'

Kev shrugged. 'Though she be but little, she is fierce.'

'Yeah right.' Razor shook his head.

'I can take care of myself,' said Miranda. 'Sometimes I have to, and it's no problem looking after you as well.'

'Yeah, maybe you can look after yourself, but you shouldn't be putting yourself in harm's way—especially on my account.'

'She's stronger than she looks,' said Kev.

Miranda sat down next to Razor and smiled. She looked so vulnerable.

'What if some guy hit you?' Razor demanded. 'I've been bashed and it hurts—and don't think a thug would let you off because you're a girl. There's precious little chivalry these days.'

'That has always been the case in my experience,' said Miranda. 'However, I wouldn't let it happen.'

Razor scoffed.

'Are your arms alright?' asked Kev.

'Yeah,' said Razor, puzzled by the question. 'The left one's bruised, but the right one's fine. Why?'

'I wondered if you might care to arm wrestle her.'

Miranda shook her head. 'I don't think that's a good idea. He's had a bad time already.'

'Good point,' said Kev.

'I wouldn't want to hurt her,' said Razor, torn between manly pride and reluctance to humiliate her. 'I'm fitter and stronger than I look, and she's got no more muscle than a kitten. Sorry.'

'Are you sure you don't want to respond?' asked Kev.

Miranda shrugged. 'Okay. I'll go easy.'

'You don't have to do this,' said Razor, as she positioned her chair and placed her right elbow on the table.

'It might be best if I do,' she said.

'If you must. Just be gentle with me.' Razor chuckled.

'I will be.'

'Are you both ready?' asked Kev.

'As ready as I'll ever be,' said Razor, casual in his confidence.

Miranda nodded.

'Good. Lean in, square off and take a grip,' said Kev. 'The bout begins on the count of three.'

Razor's fist engulfed Miranda's cool little hand. The touch took his breath away.

'One... two...'

Razor tensed his muscles.

'... three!'

Although he was expecting a swift and overwhelming victory, Razor's hand stayed put. He upped the effort but nothing happened except that his male ego stirred. Miranda smiled and showed no signs of effort.

Desperate, he applied full power, straining and sweating, only to see his hand being forced back and down, slowly and gently. There was nothing he could do about it, and though his muscles burned, she looked as if she'd done no more than turn the page of a book.

'How did you do that?' he asked, crestfallen and humiliated, hoping it had been some sort of trick.

'Incredibly easily by the looks of it,' Kev answered for her. 'Would you like her to pick you up and spin you around? She could you know.'

'That's enough,' said Miranda.

Confused and belittled, Razor wanted answers, but so many questions kept whirling around in his head that he was incapable of asking any. At last one emerged. 'What are you going to do with me now I know about your uncle's skeleton?'

'Nothing. Why?' said Miranda.

'But how do you know I won't go to the police if you let me go?'

'Let you go?' Kev laughed. 'What do you mean, let you go? You can leave whenever you want, mate.'

'But you've got my clothes.'

'You can have them now,' said Miranda. 'They're dry.'

'Why are you hiding them?'

'We're not hiding them.'

'But I searched everywhere! Where are they?'

Miranda pointed. 'Over there—Kev took them to the all-night launderette. They're in that hemp sack.'

'All clean and dry,' said Kev, 'though not pressed yet.'

'Thank you.' Razor lowered his eyes and hoped he wasn't blushing. 'And my backpack?'

Miranda shook her head. 'I know nothing of that.' She looked at Kev.

'He did have one.' Kev nodded.

'I know I did,' said Razor. 'All my money was in it.'

'I'm sorry,' said Miranda, 'but you weren't wearing it when I pulled you out.'

Her blue eyes looked innocent, and Razor wanted to trust her, but...

'It must have come off in the water,' said Kev.

Razor was devastated, but, though suspicious, he was inclined to believe Kev, for he had only the woolliest of memories from going into the cold, dark canal to surfacing again in the bath. It wasn't the loss of the money that bothered him as such, but the fact that it had been his only means of living beneath the radar until he'd found someone to kill him. Now, despite owning a nice house in a sought after village and having oodles of cash in the bank, he'd have to live like a penniless tramp.

He yawned, tried to apologise and yawned again.

'You look tired, mate,' said Kev.

Razor nodded. 'All of a sudden I am. I need sleep.'

'Sleep that knits up the ravell'd sleave of care,' said Kev.

'You don't half say the weirdest things,' said Razor.

'Get up those stairs and into bed,' Miranda commanded, like the strict mother of a naughty toddler.

Razor was in no mood to argue.

'Do you want a drink or anything?' she asked as he stood up.

'Yes, please.'

'I'll bring you a chamomile tea in a minute. Now, move!'

He was happy to oblige. As soon as he reached his bedroom, his head fuzzy with sleep, he put on the large-waisted, short-legged, stripy flannelette pyjamas left for him and crawled into bed. It was comfortable and cosy, and despite lingering worries about Miranda and Kev and a host of questions that kept surfacing, he felt safe.

Miranda brought him his drink and set it down on the bedside table. 'Drink it while it's warm,' she said.

Razor nodded as well as he could with his head resting on a soft pillow. She smiled and turned away. As soon as she'd closed the door behind her, he plunged headlong into a dark pool of sleep. At some point, he finished his drink. It was cold.

Then he dozed off again.

11

Despite nightmares involving icy waters, dead uncles in boxes and a blurry figure screaming into his face, Razor did not wake until the night was long passed. His left side was sore, his forehead tender and there was an unfamiliar smell, an exotic blend of mustiness and wax polish, topped off with a hint of Miranda's delicate fragrance. On opening his eyes, he saw his clothes, all clean, pressed and folded, atop the chest of drawers. He could hardly believe that he'd ended up in Miranda's house. Even more amazing, Kev was her cousin. The two of them shared the blame for Razor still being alive, though why they kept bothering with him was a mystery—he deserved no kindness.

When conscious enough to move, he got up and walked out onto the landing, clutching at his pyjama bottoms, several sizes too large around the waist and far too short in the leg, as they attempted to drop around his ankles. He pulled them up and held them, hoping she was not around to see, but the house sounded quiet, as if no one else was yet up. Out of nowhere came a horrific thought—he'd bet he was wearing Uncle Bob's pyjamas.

His skin crawled at the idea of a dead man's garments. With a shudder, he hurried back to his room, stripped and flung on his own clothes. Released from the horror, he tried to think about his mission. It would be difficult to live without money or possessions though this should spur him towards a quick end.

First, he told himself, he'd have to ditch Kev and Miranda.

He tiptoed downstairs, trying to convince himself he wasn't sneaking, and was being considerate in not disturbing his friends. After all, they'd had at least as long a night as him and were, no doubt, still fast asleep, wherever they were. Why their sleeping arrangements should bother him was a conundrum—they were both adults, even if they were cousins, and there was no reason for jealousy, which was fortunate. He definitely wasn't jealous.

Another note lay on the kitchen table.

Dear Mr Razor,

Help yourself to breakfast. There is food and milk in the fridge and cereals in the cupboard by the back door.

Breakfast struck him as an excellent suggestion. He made tea, poured out a vast bowl of Frosties and picked up a carton of milk. It was full-fat and Flit had always insisted on skimmed. Since her death, without thinking too much, he had more or less stuck to the rules, but what was the point now? He opened the carton, splashed milk onto his Frosties and sat down to eat.

Afterwards, still peckish, he toasted two slices of bread, slapped on butter and plum jam, and stuffed his face to fullness. When he arose, he was unhealthily and happily full of carbs, as Flit had called them—a sensation he hadn't enjoyed since his bachelor days. Back then, he'd been a little on the podgy side. She'd helped him stay healthy and slim, but with no time left to get fat, he was determined to enjoy any remaining meals.

He washed his dishes, set them to dry on the draining board and prepared to leave, although his body was more inclined to slump into an armchair and digest his breakfast.

Putting aside such weakness, he scribbled a polite thank you note, picked up his coat and opened the huge, heavy front door, briefly wondering why it had no lock.

He stepped out into bright autumn sunshine. Ahead, was an impressive gravelled driveway, lined with tall evergreen trees and scrubby looking grass that had presumably once been a lawn but could not have been cut in years. He walked along it for a minute or two before stopping to look back at the house. It was far bigger than he'd imagined, with two gabled wings and an outhouse. He realised he'd only explored one side and had unaccountably failed to find the other wing and the top floor. It was perplexing, but comforting since it could explain where Miranda and Kev had slept. Observation had never been one of Razor's strengths—Flit had often called him Sherlock in jest when he'd yet again missed something obvious.

He turned away. A few minutes later, he approached a massive iron-studded wooden gate set in a high stone wall and with wicked-looking spikes on top. The formidable chain and padlock securing the gate made him wonder if he might be a prisoner after all, but on drawing closer, he noticed a small door in the big gate. It was just tall enough for a short person to step through without ducking and swung open easily. He stooped, stepped over the frame and felt the sudden exhilaration of freedom. The door swung back into place and clicked. There was no handle on the outside, and no way for him to get back in—not that he wanted to.

Razor had come out into a puddle-strewn, rutted back lane, carpeted in damp brown leaves. The tall walls along either side made it appear even narrower. At first, he wasn't sure which way to turn, but the muted sound of heavy traffic indicated a main road to his left. He set off, his shadow suggesting he was heading roughly southward, though the lane twisted and turned like an eel. It came as a shock when he rounded a bend and came out on a busy dual-carriageway, with cars, vans and lorries flashing by almost within touching distance. He was back in the modern world, with all its pollution, smells, noise, dirt and people, though he still wasn't sure which bit of it.

Turning in a random direction, he strode

along a wide pavement until a sign indicated he was on Osric Way, a major road through Glevchester. However, it wasn't until the imposing tower of the Minster came into view that he finally got his bearings. Soon, tiring of the noise and exhaust fumes, he turned onto a quiet side road, lined with banks of large older houses, all with gardens and mature trees. It appeared to run parallel to Osric Way and would take him towards the peace of Glevchester Park—a good place to sit and think.

'Help!'

The cry made him start like a dog that had just spotted a squirrel. A damsel was in distress—a perfect opportunity. Thoughts of chivalry and glorious death filled his head. Adrenalin surged in his veins. He broke into a run.

A little, white-haired older lady was facing a tall young man with cropped black hair and a bushy beard.

'Alright, what's going on here then?' Razor demanded because, although mentally prepared for battle, he'd learned a lesson and had no intention of rushing in without knowing what was happening.

The woman looked startled, but pointed at

the young man. 'It's all his fault.'

'What's he done?' asked Razor, slowing to a walk.

'Nothing. It was an accident,' said the man, 'and I said I'm sorry.'

'Accident, my arse!' The woman shook a bony finger. 'You shouldn't have let it happen.'

'I didn't let it happen. The damn thing escaped when…'

'… when you weren't looking. So you said. How many times have I told you to be more careful?'

The old woman appeared more angry than frightened, the young man apologetic rather than threatening. Razor struggled to stay in hero mode. 'What's escaped?' he asked.

The woman pointed.

'The tree?'

'No, you idiot.' The old woman rolled her eyes. 'Elsa.'

'Elsa?'

'Gran's stupid cat,' the young man explained.

'You're the stupid one, my lad. I keep telling you to be careful, but you never listen, do you?'

'Never what?' said the grandson.

'Listen… and you can wipe that silly grin off your face.'

Razor cut in. 'Your cat escaped and is in the tree?'

Gran nodded.

'Is it stuck?'

'She's meowing.'

'I'm sure she'll come down when she wants to,' said the grandson. 'After all, you never see cat skeletons in trees, do you?'

'True,' said Razor.

'You never see any squirrel skeletons either,' Gran pointed out.

'That's also true,' said Razor. 'I guess they fall out when they're dead.'

Gran wailed. 'I don't want her to die. Go and fetch her down.'

Grandson shook his head. 'I'm no good with heights, but if you're still worried I'll call the fire brigade. They might be willing to help.'

His hour had come.

'No need,' said Razor, stepping forward. 'I'll do it.'

'You're a kind man,' said Gran. 'Not like him.'

Razor squinted into the tree. 'Where is she?'

Gran pointed. 'There… at the top.'

His gaze followed the direction of her finger, and his stomach lurched. A small, fluffy white cat was clinging to a swaying branch a heart-stopping way up. Still, he'd said he'd do it and he would—if he could.

'How do you intend getting up there?' asked the grandson, his expression suggesting interested scepticism.

It was a good point. The trunk was too broad to grasp, and its lower branches were way above jumping range. Razor looked around for inspiration and found it in the shape of a green plastic wheelie bin standing next to the house. If he positioned it with care and jumped from it, he should reach the first branch.

'Watch and learn,' he said, and fetched the bin, trying to look nonchalant, despite his lily-livered body trembling. It wasn't heights that terrified him as such, more the idea of plummeting from them. Although trying to convince himself that death would be welcome, the process of dying terrified, and what if he survived but was left with grotesque injuries, or paralysed? However, it would be too embarrassing to walk away now. This was the time to do or die.

Squaring his jaw, assuming a careless attitude, he scrambled onto the bin and stood up.

'Be careful,' said Gran as he wobbled.

'Of course,' said Razor, and jumped.

But he'd failed to take into account one important factor—wheelie bins move easily on their wheels. Instead of a graceful leap into the branches, he performed a graceless dive onto the ground.

'I wondered if that might happen,' the helpful grandson remarked as Razor sprawled in the dirt like a defeated gun slinger. 'I'll hold it steady next time, shall I?'

Razor could only nod as he got back to his feet.

With the bin secure, his next attempt was a little more successful. A light leap skyward and both hands got a firm grip on the lowest branch. He dangled a moment before swinging up his legs, hooking them over the branch and hanging like a sloth. It was exhilarating to have accomplished the most difficult part, for he could see the rest of the climb would be relatively easy—at least until the tiny topmost branches where the cat was still hanging out, making piteous cries. He shuffled along to where he could reach the next branch and steadied himself. It was time to get cracking.

Something cracked.

He plunged and splatted onto his back, still

grasping the broken branch between hands and knees, and with all the wind knocked from his lungs. As he sprawled there, dazed, in pain and struggling for breath, the cat ran straight down the trunk, hissed at him and minced towards Gran.

'There you go,' said the grandson, as she bent to stroke the beast. 'I told you she'd make it down alright.'

'And you were correct,' said Gran. 'She's a clever kitty, and I'm just a silly old fusspot, but I do worry about her. She's all I've got.'

'Nonsense, Gran. You've got a big family… and three other cats. Let's go in, it's time for lunch.'

Grandson picked the cat up and led Gran back to the house. Razor had just managed to reinflate his lungs and was in the process of sitting up, groaning and checking himself for injury. Nothing seemed to have broken, but it shocked him that they'd just walked away, ignoring his accident and his pain. It was no way to treat a fallen hero, though, thinking about it, all he had achieved was the fall. Battered and bruised, crestfallen, he struggled to his feet and hobbled away.

Yet the failure had not knocked all the optimism from him. He set course for the massive bulk of the Minster.

Next time, he might do better.

Next time happened sooner than expected. As he passed a Chinese restaurant, crockery shattered and a woman screamed. He ran inside.

A tubby, bald man with tomato-red cheeks and streaming eyes was staggering around, clutching his throat, gurgling and wheezing. Two smart women, a mother and daughter by their looks, were trying to catch up as he crashed into tables and chairs.

'Somebody help him!' the older woman cried.

Razor grabbed the choking man from behind as he slumped onto a table, one hand in a dish of Mu Shu pork, the other making frantic gestures. The elderly couple sitting there were gape-mouthed, chopsticks loaded for action. Razor thumped the casualty between the shoulder blades with the heel of his hand. Nothing happened. He repeated the procedure with the same result.

The younger woman began crying.

Razor, an island of calm in a sea of panic, tried the Heimlich.

On the third attempt, a mess of semimasticated pak choi flew from the casualty's mouth and splashed down in the old man's lager.

'Are you alright, Dad?' asked the younger woman, pushing past Razor.

Dad nodded and wiped his eyes, the redness draining from his face, breathing returning to normal.

'I told you not to wolf it,' said his wife. 'Why do you never listen?'

Without waiting for thanks, if any were going, Razor ambled away, playing the silent hero, modest, but pleased to have helped. Although the incident had not offered him a chance of death, it had been an encouraging sign of the opportunities in Glevchester. If he remained alert, his chance would come.

Razor entered the ancient part of the city where a multitude of medieval and Tudor buildings clustered in the Minster's shadow, attracting tourists as a picnic attracts wasps. A party of elderly Americans stopped to pose for photos in front of the fifteenth-century timber-framed Pilgrim Inn.

'Holey Moley!' exclaimed a petite, grey-haired lady who was reading a booklet. 'They reckon

William Shakespeare performed here and...'

A massively muscled man in tattered khaki trousers and shabby sweatshirt darted from the shadows, snatched her bag and ran.

'My purse!'

People stared. Some took photos, others gathered around to comfort the robbed woman, but Razor took off in pursuit.

The bag-snatcher was threading a twisting path through the crowds, occasionally barging people aside. Razor, more careful of other people, lost ground. By the time the crowds had thinned a little, he'd lost sight of the man and thought he'd failed. Disappointed, he was about to walk on when he heard a groan from a narrow alley just in front. Exhilarated, Razor charged in, hoping he was heading for glory, but only found his quarry lying face down on the litter-strewn slabs, the handbag still gripped in one hand and blood trickling down his face.

Half suspecting a trick, Razor approached with caution. He noticed a loop of nylon strapping, the sort used for holding parcels together, was wrapped around the robber's ankles. The fleeing man must have run into it, tripped and knocked himself out as he crashed to the ground. Disappointed, though victorious, Razor took the handbag, and went to find its owner. The woman, surrounded by her friends and a larger group of gawpers, was quietly having hysterics.

Enjoying his big moment, Razor squeezed through the crowd. 'I believe this is yours, ma'am,' he said.

She took the bag with amazed thanks, but Razor had glimpsed two police officers approaching. 'Tell them they'll find their man in the alley opposite the tea shop.' He slipped back into the crowd and marched away.

He was heading nowhere in particular, except away from the Minster, but after a few minutes, he noticed he'd come out near Glevchester railway station, where he and Flit used to wait for trains after nights out in town. That had all ceased when he started working for Burke and Coe, enjoyed the privilege of a company car and had to become responsible. He wondered what had happened to his car. All he could remember was parking it near the Severn Wharves, walking to and from the cinema, and the attack. Was it still there waiting for him? Probably not. He guessed someone had reclaimed it—there'd been letters from work that he'd never got round to reading. He still had no recollection of getting home from the hospital, though he remembered Alex had been there, tidying up. Even though Razor would have preferred to have been alone, he'd appreciated the gesture of support.

Tired and thirsty, he headed for the station. There were a few coins left in his coat pocket, enough for a drink at the cafe. He went in, bought himself a large coffee and carried it to an empty plastic-covered table in the corner.

'Well done, mate,' said Kev, sliding into the seat opposite. 'You've had a busy day. Action makes the hours seem short.'

Razor spluttered and gaped.

12

It took a moment for Razor to accept that Kev, sitting within touching range and with a rift valley grin splitting his face, was real. 'What the hell are you doing here?'

'Getting a cup of tea before my train,' said Kev. 'How about you?'

'Coffee.'

'I thought you'd lost all your money.'

'Other than a little loose change, I had', said Razor. 'After buying this, I have precisely six pennies left.'

'Six pennies may form a basis from which to remake your fortune,' said Kev, 'but it won't be easy.'

'I have no intention of remaking my fortune,' said Razor.

'How will you live?'

'By my wits.'

'Then I fear you won't last long, mate.'

'I'll be fine. I have money in the bank if I get desperate, but I won't.'

Kev gave him a long, hard stare. 'You worry me, and I fear you'll do something foolish... or do I mean reckless?'

'Don't waste your time on me. I'm grateful, really, for everything you and Miranda have done—please tell her next time you see her. However, from now on I'd appreciate being left alone.'

'So you can throw your life away?'

'How would you know my intentions?'

'Well, mate, it's clear you keep putting yourself into dangerous situations. At first, I suspected you were an arrogant prat who believed himself immune to injury or death, but Miranda reckons you are actively trying to get yourself killed.'

'It's none of your business,' said Razor, wishing he could get away, but unwilling to leave his drink.

'Sorry, but I've made it my business.'

'Please leave me alone.'

'It's because of your wife, isn't it? You blame yourself for her death and can't live with the guilt. Am I right?'

Razor took a sip of coffee. It was still too hot to gulp. 'Get lost,' he suggested.

Kev nodded towards the counter and the girl carried over a mug of tea and two slices of cake. 'Thanks, Kylie.'

'You're welcome, as always,' she said, giving a

smile and a wink as she turned away.

'You're still here,' Razor observed as Kev picked up his tea.

'I am, because I want my drink and I thought we might chat. Have a piece of cake.'

'I'd rather be alone. You can't understand what it feels like to lose someone you love. People say it gets easier, but it doesn't.'

Kev nodded. 'I do understand. Everyone thinks they can master grief until it strikes them.' He pushed the plate of cake towards Razor.

Razor sighed, lacking the energy to stay angry. He picked up a slice and took a nibble. It was dry, with an artificial taste—probably an attempt at an almond cake. When he'd finished it, his coffee was cool enough for cautious sipping.

'Help yourself to the other one as well,' said Kev.

'I'm alright,' Razor lied, 'You can have it.'

'I know I can, but I'm offering it to you, since your need would appear to be greater than mine.'

'Then I thank you,' said Razor. This one was carrot cake, bland and too sweet, but better than the first. When he'd finished, he washed it down with the remains of his coffee and made as if to get up.

'Linger here with a fool,' said Kev. 'I have a question.'

'What?'

'Can you think of a reason why one of your neighbours should try to enter your house? That is the question.'

Razor shrugged. 'No. Who was it?'

'I don't know, but he didn't look like an average burglar.'

'What makes you think he's a neighbour?'

'I've seen him around your village. He's tall, smartly dressed, well-groomed and I'd guess in his early thirties. He drives a flashy car and lives, I think, in that big hall place.'

'Sounds like Alex,' said Razor with a laugh. 'He's no burglar. He comes round from time to time to check on me.'

'In that case, why did he run as soon as he saw someone was home?'

'I don't know... I think I worried him last time we met, though it was all a misunderstanding. He's a friend... well, sort of.'

'Sort of?'

'He used to work with Flit. I'd only met him once or twice before the accident, but since then he's been very helpful. Sometimes, he comes round to check I've got food and suchlike, and I've even caught him cleaning when I've come back from walks.'

'But there was precious little in your fridge, mate, and your house, and I apologise for saying this, is a tip—and I know a tip when I see one.'

Razor shrugged. 'The mess is probably my fault—I've never done much about the house. Alex does come round to see me and sometimes makes me drinks and sandwiches and things. To be honest, I don't think I've ever shown much gratitude. Perhaps I should have, but, well, he's not someone I'd choose to be friends with. Still, I'm sure he means well, and he is the only one who's bothered with me since...' He swallowed and closed his eyes. '... Flit died.'

'I see,' said Kev, frowning, 'but I'm worried.'

'What's the matter?'

'You know the feeling you get when you think something wicked this way comes? Well, I got it.'

Razor laughed. 'He's harmless.'

'Then why was he trying to get into your house? And why does he have a key?'

'Because I gave him one.' Razor thought for a moment. 'Actually, I don't remember doing that—he must have picked up a spare so he could look in on me. I never minded too much.'

'Don't you have any family to take care of you?'

'A sister in Texas. Kate and I don't communicate much. Maybe a card at Christmas.'

'Friends?'

'I thought so, but I haven't seen any of them since the funeral. Mind you, I'd have probably told them where to go if any had turned up.'

'But maybe you really wanted to see them? Maybe their neglect is what makes you so sad.'

'Losing Flit makes me sad.' Razor scowled, wondering why he was wasting time talking to this irritating little guy, and fearing to say something he shouldn't.

He became aware of a growing commotion on the platform. A woman screamed.

Kev leapt to his feet, but Razor, already up, shoved him out the way and sprinted to the rescue. A shouting crowd had formed on the platform around a young woman holding a baby in a pouch. 'Darren!' she shrieked, staring past the end of the platform.

A small boy in a red anorak was running along the tracks, looking back with a cheeky grin.

'The train now arriving at Platform Four is the delayed three twenty-three from London Paddington,' announced the station tannoy.

The train came into view, a long way off as yet, but on the same track as the kid. Although people gasped, yelled and pointed, only Razor did anything. He pushed through, leapt onto the tracks and ran towards the kid, as fast as a hare. The train, despite slowing for the station was too fast, even though its brakes were screeching and its horn was blaring. The gormless child, oblivious, stopped running and waved.

Razor went hell for leather, racing faster than ever before, though he doubted he'd make it in time. The train loomed larger. At the last millisecond, Razor launched himself into a desperate dive. His outstretched hands made contact, the kid screamed, and a blast of noise and hot metallic air swirled around them.

Infuriatingly still alive, Razor sprawled on the gravel, too puffed and winded to do much more than gasp for air. The train came to a standstill. The kid, face down on the track, screamed for his mum. Razor struggled to his feet, taking the kid's raucous yelling as a sign of nothing much being wrong.

Still fighting for breath, he tottered down the track away from the station and flung himself into the undergrowth at the side. As he crawled away, he peeped back. Two railway workers were running towards the child who'd sat up and was howling. Razor cursed the misfortune that had kept him alive again, but was happy to have got away before anyone could thank him or ask questions. Furthermore, he'd given Kev the slip.

He pushed through rank grass and dead weed stalks, heading towards the top of the embankment where he crouched beneath a leggy gorse bush and looked back. A railway man was handing the boy up to his frantic, tearful mother, and the useless crowd was cheering and whooping. Razor turned away, creeping down a steep slope towards a small road.

On the way, his feet slipped. He slid and bounced, gaining momentum until the slope levelled off, when he cannoned into the steel perimeter fence. It was one way of getting down, though not the most painless. After a muted groan and deep breaths, he pulled himself to his feet and looked up at the razor-sharp edges of the spikes topping the fence. They would deter anybody except the terminally insane.

The evening shadows were deepening as he stomped through the brittle undergrowth, heading away from the station and hoping to chance on a way out. He tripped and stumbled once or twice and was then ambushed by the abandoned wreckage of a bike. Swearing and sore of shin, he hobbled past on his second attempt. There was no sound of anyone following, which was for the best, though it felt ridiculous to be running like a hunted criminal after doing something he considered a true act of heroism.

Amazed and proud of his own courage, he couldn't stop a grin developing, and he might even have started humming had he not noticed the light of a small fire casting weird flickering shadows against the walls of a rail bridge through the gloom ahead. Razor approached with caution, watching as an old man hobbled from under one of the arches, chucked a log onto the blaze and slouched against the brickwork.

'Good evening,' said Razor, wood smoke

curling around him.

'What do you want?' asked the old man, his voice cracked and hoarse.

'Nothing, I'm just passing through,' said Razor, raising his hands in a gesture of peace and harmlessness.

'Who are you?' asked the man. His snaggly beard and face looked sooty, but his eyes were round and white. He took a pull from a gin bottle and shuddered.

'Just a peaceful passer-by out for a walk,' said Razor, slowing to dawdle pace.

'Leave me alone and take your black-cloaked demon with you!' shouted the man as he stared over Razor's shoulder.

Razor shivered and glanced behind, but there was nothing but smoke.

'Take it away,' the old man screamed, waving his arms as if swatting flies. 'I know you, and I've seen what it does.'

'You don't know me,' said Razor.

'I do. I saw you and that thing by the Wharves. Take it away!'

The penny dropped. 'You're the homeless guy,' said Razor.

'Well I wouldn't be lying under this bloody bridge if I wasn't homeless, would I? And I wouldn't be here if you and that thing of yours hadn't brought all the cops into town. Leave me in peace. Please.'

'I will,' said Razor, 'but you'd better lay off the booze. You're seeing things.'

'That's what the cops said,' the man roared, 'but I don't drink alcohol.'

'Really?' said Razor with a glance at the bottle.

'It's water—no one's going to bring me a mug of cocoa out here are they? You're just stereotyping me because of my appearance and that's not right. I have a medical condition, you know.'

'Sorry,' said Razor. 'But you are the guy who was sleeping in the shop doorway the other night, aren't you?'

'So what?'

'Did you see what happened?' asked Razor, though he wasn't hopeful—the evidence suggesting the old man was not all there.

'I was trying to sleep. That was my spot until you and your thing messed it up.'

'I did nothing—I was the one who got attacked.'

'I don't know about that, but your demon was there. Don't set it on me, please. I'm trying to be helpful.' The man's gaze fixed on a point behind Razor's right ear.

'I won't,' said Razor, humouring the old fool. 'As long as you continue to be cooperative.'

'I will be.'

'Good. Tell me what you saw that night.'

'Like I told the cops, a bloke went down an alley and another bloke—you—followed him in. There was a scuffle, your demon swooped in and there was screaming. Then you came out with the demon.'

Razor sighed.

'Where did you get it?' asked the old man

'The demon? There's no such thing.'

'Everyone says that, but I know what I see… I've done what you asked, now, please, take it away.'

'What does it look like?'

The man frowned. 'Like a demon, of course, and it's black as night. Go away!'

Since the poor old chap was becoming even more agitated, Razor thought he'd best leave him to his madness. 'Thank you for all your help, sir. I'm going now… that is we're going. Come along, be a good demon and stop bothering the nice gentleman.'

A rough path pounded into the mud made his

route easier, and a few minutes' walk took him to a break in the fence, just wide enough to squeeze through into a narrow backstreet, a rift between tumbledown red-brick buildings. When something moved in the shadows, visions of black-clad demons filled Razor's mind, along with some half-remembered line about walking through the valley of the shadow of death, but it turned out to be nothing scarier than a foraging rat.

Razor followed the backstreet until it joined a broader road, lined with derelict buildings and desperate-looking shops—either triumphs of wishful thinking or symbols of continuing failure. He continued, turning into another street of similar bleakness and then into another, before reaching a concrete multistorey car park. He was searching for a name or any other clue about his location when he heard a yell from above. It was followed by more shouts and a burst of harsh laughter.

Razor took it as a call to arms. After a deep breath, he jogged up the ramp as it twisted into semi-darkness in the bowels of the foetid-smelling car park. Several young men were standing around a large guy with cropped blond hair. His back was to Razor and he held a wodge of bank notes in one hand. Assuming a mugging was in progress, Razor prepared to charge to the rescue, but the big guy said something that made the others laugh and pushed the cash into his pocket. Razor hung back in the shadows, keeping an eye on things, convinced something was wrong. The big guy glanced at his mobile, said he'd got to go, turned around and walked towards a gleaming black car.

Razor gasped and stared—it was the man who'd thrown him off Bindover Bridge.

The car started and sped down the ramp. Instinct made Razor squeeze against the wall. The car missed him by inches.

A few seconds later, the rest of the mob ran towards him, though they didn't appear to notice until a lanky guy with matted hair ran into him and went down in a tangle of arms and legs. The others stopped and stared. Their eyes were dark, like sharks' and their mouths snarled and swore. To Razor's untutored eye, they appeared high on something. It had not had a mellowing effect. The fallen one lay groaning.

'The bastard's done Baz,' said one, whose head was as smooth and white as a hard-boiled egg.

'Sorry,' said Razor. 'But he ran into me.'

'You were inadequately lit, and your flagrant disregard for safety has caused an injury to our companion,' Egghead continued. 'He's, therefore, entitled to compensation. In addition, the rest of us will seek financial reparation for the trauma of witnessing the incident.'

'You what?' asked Razor, baffled by the unexpected legalese.

A huge, flabby youth with a flat nose and rotten teeth translated. 'Give us your money.'

As the youth stepped forward and shoved him in the chest, making him crash into the wall behind, Razor smiled—perhaps his luck was changing at last. 'This is all I've got,' he said, reaching into his pocket and showing them his remaining six pennies.

They did not appear impressed. He'd not expected they would be.

'Shake him down,' said Egghead.

Razor reacted first and flung the coins into the flabby one's face, making him shy away and yelp. Seeing an opportunity, Razor darted forward, swinging a fist that connected with the young man's jaw, felling him like a rotten tree.

'Now he's done Deano,' said Egghead. 'It behoves us to seek revenge for our fallen companions in arms.'

'Yeah,' said another. 'Let's do him!'

Razor drew himself into what he hoped was a fighting stance, hoping to provoke them. 'Come on then, if you think there are enough of you. Prepare to die... horribly.' Although his voice came out stronger than he'd hoped, his heart raced. He expected battle and hopefully death—his assailants looked the sort he imagined carried knives. Whatever happened, he wished they'd be quick about it, but they hung back, apparently put off by his bogus bravado. He almost pitied them—there was something in their blank expressions and dead eyes that reminded him of the hopelessness of derelict buildings.

And then they attacked, fists and feet breaking through his defences, and though he landed many a punch, knowing there was no way he could win felt good. When a lump-hammer fist slammed into his belly, he doubled up, a knee caught him on the chin and he went down, gasping, clutching his guts and helpless. It was only a matter of time before they finished him and, despite the pain, he smiled, hoping for the coup de grâce.

It didn't come. Hearing a revving engine, tyres screeching and his assailants panicked yelling, he opened his eyes. A misshapen, rusty little car was juddering up the ramp towards them, emitting smoke like a dragon. Razor's assailants fled or scrambled over the wall in their panic to get away.

The car stopped next to him. The door opened. Someone emerged. Hands dragged him up and pushed him onto the back seat. Doors slammed, the car reversed down the ramp, performed a handbrake turn at the bottom and drove away.

Razor lay still, fighting for breath, and whispering curses to the guardian angel who had saved him—it wasn't fair. A few minutes later, he sat up, still clutching his stomach and trying not to moan so much.

'What ails you to complain and groan so?'

'Bloody hell, Kev!' said Razor. 'Why do you keep popping up like that?'

'It looked like you needed rescue, my Lord.'

'And why the hell do you talk like that?'

'For my amusement,' said Kev. 'Seriously though, you looked in big trouble.'

'I can take care of myself.'

'It didn't look like it from where I was. Anyone would think you wanted to get hurt... or worse.'

'I've told you before that it's none of your business. Please leave me alone. I mean it.'

'I can't do that.'

'Yes you can.'

Kev shook his head. 'No, you're a friend.'

'You don't know me,' said Razor, touched despite himself. He fought to regain control. 'Stop the car and let me out. It is my right to live or die as I choose.'

Kev drove on.

'Stop.'

'Not yet.'

'When?'

'When you're home.'

'I don't want to go home,' Razor heard echoes of the petulant teenager he'd once been.

'Nevertheless, that's where we're going.'

'Stop the bloody car. Now!'

Kev turned on the radio, filling the air with classical music.

'Okay, I'm getting out, whether you stop or not.'

'Go on then.'

'I will... Thank you for being a friend. Goodbye.'

Razor tried the door handle. Nothing happened. 'Let me out.'

'I can't.'

'Turn off the child locks.'

'There aren't any, mate. The doors are somewhat temperamental, like the rest of the car.'

Razor considered clambering into the front and forcing Kev to stop, but that might cause a crash, and he had no wish to hurt the innocent. 'Damn you! Why are you doing this?'

'Because life is important and not for throwing away on a whim.'

'I thought the same once, but you're wrong. Life is meaningless. It can be taken away just like that. It's not worth the hassle.'

'It's always worth it,' said Kev. 'It's all we've got.'

'I don't care. Let me out.'

'I will...'

'About time.'

'... when I'm ready. We should talk first.'

'Talking won't bring her back.'

'Of course not, mate, but I don't want to talk about that. It's about your house...'

'You can have it. It's got too many bad memories.'

'And plenty of good ones, I expect, but I don't want it... I've got enough.'

Razor sighed. 'Then what do you want?'

'I want to know about that mate of yours that keeps showing up. Miranda thinks there's something odd about his behaviour and I agree.'

'Alex? He's not really a mate, and I've already told you about him.'

'Yeah, but you haven't explained what he wants.'

'I expect he wants to make sure I'm alright,' said Razor. 'Why can't people just leave me alone?'

Kev ignored the question. 'Why would he do that if he's not your mate? And why would he try to get into your house when he knew you weren't there?'

'How the hell would I know?'

'We think he's looking for something,' Kev continued. 'Do you own anything of value?'

'I expect some stuff is worth a bit, but I don't think there's anything amazing and, anyway, Alex is already wealthy. To be fair to the man, he's done incredibly well in the last couple of years. Flit said she didn't know how he did it.'

Kev shrugged. 'That doesn't change my opinion. He wants something and thinks it is in your house.'

'Don't be so daft,' said Razor. 'He has his faults, but he's no burglar, whatever you think you saw.'

'Fair enough,' said Kev, although he didn't sound convinced.

Razor was not convinced either. Old worries, long since buried, had resurrected themselves. He hadn't much liked Alex from the moment Flit had first introduced him at a work social. There had been a time when he'd feared they were having an affair, but if they had, it had cooled in the months before her death.

13

Razor sat in a silent sulk, enduring the rattling and creaking, and barely conscious of time until he felt the car slowing. He looked up as Kev pulled into a lay-by on an unlit road. Two vehicles were already there—a smart black car and a battered pickup truck.

'Why stop here?' asked Razor, leaning between the seats.

'Because of that,' said Kev, pointing at the gleaming black BMW. 'I thought I recognised it—it's Kane Cullum's. What's he doing out here?'

Razor had seen it before too—it was the one from the car park. He was about to say something when bright flashes in the fields distracted him. 'What are those?'

'Poachers' lamps,' said Kev.

'What are they used for?'

'Poaching.'

'Don't they scare everything away?'

'No, they use them to dazzle targets, so they're easy to pick off.'

A not-too-distant crack made them both jump.

'What was that?' asked Razor, though he could guess.

'A rifle shot, mate. We'd better get out of here.'

'But they wouldn't shoot at us, would they? At least not on purpose.'

'I wouldn't put it past them. Cousin Gary may be a swine, but he's a pussycat compared to Kane and Liam Cullum. They are psychos.'

'Liam from the park? But he turned out to be a pushover,' said Razor, with a cold laugh. 'And I've had a couple of run-ins with Kane too, though I didn't know his name until now. He was in the multistorey before the fight—I suspect he'd been selling drugs to those lads.'

Kev pulled out of the lay-by. Distant street lights glowed in the direction they were heading. 'The pair of them are dangerous—I once saw Kane use an arm torn from a mannequin to knock out a shop assistant who wouldn't stop serving someone else.'

'Sounds like a right charmer.'

'That's the strange thing, mate. Both of them could be when it suited them. They'd lull you into thinking they were friendly and harmless, but then something would set them off. Kane has more in the way of brains and usually gets away with it, but Liam's police record was as long as your inside leg.'

'Was?'

'He came to a sticky end in Glevchester.'

'The bloke in the newspapers?'

'The same. Malignant death took him, and although I cannot rejoice when such a man dies, neither will I grieve. The world is a safer place without him.'

'It's strange him being killed so soon after we ran into him,' said Razor trying to feel jealous of the deceased. 'Have they found out who did it yet?'

'Not so far as I know. There is a rumour of a mysterious black-cloaked demon being spotted near the crime scene, but the source of that is somewhat dubious.'

'The homeless man?'

'Yeah… how do you know?' asked Kev, but before Razor could reply, he made a strange sound, one part exasperation, two parts fear. 'There's a car following us.'

'So what?' said Razor. 'That's what cars do.'

'This one's coming fast and the road's been almost empty.'

'Still…'

'I know,' said Kev, 'it may be a false alarm, but there's something about the headlights… I've a feeling it's...'

'Kane?' Razor suggested.

Kev nodded, changed gear and floored the accelerator, making the engine shriek as if it were being tortured. Although the car rumbled and rattled, its speed barely increased.

'Can't you make this thing go any faster... or smoother?' asked Razor, his teeth chattering.

'I'm trying, but age with his stealing steps hath clawed it in his clutch.'

Razor screwed up his face, bewildered by Kev's way of talking. 'Are you saying there's a problem with the clutch?'

'No, it's you that's clutching at straws, mate. I mean this poor old car is too set in its ways to speed.'

'And the clutch?'

'It is somewhat knackered, to tell the truth,' said Kev. 'Hang on.' He pulled the handbrake and turned the steering wheel, forcing the car into a convulsive skidding turn that took them into a tight gap on the far side of the road. It was the entrance to a twisting lane between high stone walls. Razor felt as if they were plunging through a tunnel with ever-narrowing sides. A growing claustrophobia gripped him, taking him close to panic. Kev twisted the steering wheel, the car skidded into a gateway and juddered to a halt. He killed the lights.

Seconds later the black BMW flashed past followed by the pickup. Kev pulled back out and reversed up the lane at full speed, but didn't turn the lights back on until they'd reached the main road and he'd spun the car back on course. They rattled away at what Razor guessed was maximum speed. He glanced at the speedometer—there wasn't one. In fact, there was no dashboard at all, just a square of plywood with a few switches over bare metal and a mess of wiring. The seats were also different shapes and colours, and the windows were unmatched—he couldn't even work out the basic model. They reached Fenderton, a well-heeled village on the edge of Sorenchester, where he and Flit had looked at several houses before settling in Willoton.

'Now do you think they were after us?' asked Kev.

'I guess so,' said Razor, shaken and embarrassed by the tremor of his voice. 'But why?'

'Perhaps because they don't want witnesses to their poaching. Maybe something else. Best not to find out.'

'And if they'd caught us?'

Kev shrugged. 'I'd rather not guess.'

'Why?'

'Kane is a violent man with contempt for others and a total disregard for the law. It's strange because he doesn't normally operate round here. He's scared of one of the local cops, though, come to think of it, I've heard that one's not around at the moment.'

'But there must be more of them.'

Kev nodded. 'Sure, and no doubt they'd do their best, but they don't worry Kane.'

'It's lucky we got away then,' said Razor.

'Yes, but it's likely he knows where I live.'

'That's not so good, but I doubt they even recognised you—we were some distance away.'

'Unfortunately, Kane would recognise my car at once.'

'Not necessarily—there are probably hundreds of old cars like it. By the way, what sort is it? I can't make it out.'

'It's not exactly a sort, mate. You might call it a Frankenstein car as it's made from bits and pieces from any number of old vehicles. Old Man Cullum, Kane and Liam's dad owned a breakers yard and enjoyed creating monstrosities with leftover parts. He called this one "The hatchback of Notre Dame". When he died, the boys sold everything, and I got this. It was cheap.'

'It would have to be,' said Razor.

Kev chuckled and continued driving until a red traffic light stopped them on the edge of Sorenchester.

'What are we going to do?' Razor demanded.

'Methinks there are terrors ahead, but be of good cheer, you have a man's heart.'

Razor clicked his tongue. 'I wish you'd stop talking like that.'

'Like what?'

'All the weird stuff.'

''tis but my mode of speech, nuncle.'

'Stop it!'

'I'll try to change if it offends you,' said Kev, 'but I can't always help myself.'

'Sorry,' said Razor, ashamed of his testiness, 'but it annoys me.'

'I shall endeavour to speak differently,' said Kev.

'Thank you. So, what are we going to do?'

'I'm not sure. I could drop you off here.'

Razor shook his head and tried to look

relaxed. 'No, I'm not leaving you in danger. We're in this together.'

'Thank you. A possible refuge does come to mind,' said Kev just as the lights changed. He turned left, heading up The Green Way towards farmland.

'Wouldn't you be safer in town?' said Razor. 'I doubt they'd do anything with witnesses about and we could go to the police.'

'I thought you wanted to avoid the police,' said Kev.

'I do... did. But now I think about it, I'd rather be questioned by them than get shot. I admit that I'm scared—and for you as well.'

'But aren't you searching for death?' asked Kev.

Razor didn't reply. Although he still hoped to die bravely and in a noble cause, the idea of a bullet tearing through his skin, bone and flesh gave him the shudders. What if it only left him wounded, his lifeblood dripping away while he writhed in unspeakable agony? Worse, what if it left him a helpless prisoner in his own body? The idea of spending the rest of his days in a hospital bed, unable to do anything except dwell on his follies and guilt was intolerable.

The look on Flit's face as they fled from the

mugger popped into his head again, almost obliterating the real world. Despite all the weeks of practice, he struggled to force himself back. By the time he'd recovered, the town had given way to countryside and trees had replaced the lamp posts. Kev drove at little more than walking pace, frowning and peering at the stone wall bracketing the lane.

'Are you looking for something?' Razor asked.

'There should be a turning around here,' said Kev. 'Aha!'

He swung the wheel and for a moment Razor thought he was steering them straight into the wall, but a narrow gap opened up allowing access to a rutted track barely wider than the car. Sticks from unkempt bushes scratched the sides.

A sign showed up in the headlights:

Private

No admittance

YOU HAVE BEEN WARNED!

'Hadn't we better turn around?' asked Razor, concerned his friend might get into even more trouble.

'Not till we get there,' said Kev, concentrating on keeping to the track.

'Get where?'

'Miranda's country pile.'

'Really?' Razor perked up. 'Will she be home?'

'I doubt it, but I know where the key is.'

'Won't she mind?' asked Razor. 'After all, I did leave rather abruptly last time.' He wished he'd at least said thank you to her in person.

'She won't mind...'

'Good,' said Razor.

'... as long as she doesn't find out,' Kev continued.

'Right. I assume she's rich?'

'Why?'

'Because she's got that big house in town and a country residence.'

'Poor and content is rich enough,' said Kev. 'You haven't seen the pile yet. It's just around the next bend. I don't think Kane knows about it—I hope he doesn't.'

They rounded the bend, but there was no country house.

'Perhaps I meant the next one,' said Kev. 'It's been a while. Yes, here it is.'

In a small clearing in a bleak copse stood a

dilapidated caravan. Kev stopped the car. 'It's not much,' he admitted.

'Not much?' said Razor. 'It's a dump on wheels.'

'It's got no wheels, mate. They fell off years ago. It's propped up on bricks.'

'I guess it's somewhere to hide,' said Razor with a grimace as Kev got out.

He'd only once, aged about ten, been in a caravan. It had been when money was tight following his dad's redundancy and his parents felt in need of a holiday. Despite rain battering the car during the long drive, and his sister Kate's bouts of car sickness, young Ray's head had filled with memories of sunny family holidays in Greece, Spain and Turkey. He could still recall the shock of his first glimpse of the tiny metal box adrift in a sea of mud at the bottom of a windswept field. They weren't going to stay there, were they? It was a joke wasn't it? How could they all fit? What about the beach? The cafes? The arcades?

Getting there had been the best part of the holiday.

Once his parents had dragged their mutinous offspring inside, and Ray was moaning about the nasty smell, his mum struck a match to light the stove. The resulting explosion had destroyed the caravan and sent the family to Accident and Emergency in the nearest town. Their injuries had been superficial though embarrassing—the flash had singed most of the hair from their heads and faces. They'd returned home as soon as they'd been discharged.

Since then, Razor had enjoyed amazing holidays with Flit: scuba diving in the Maldives, safaris in east Africa, treks in Nepal, skiing in fashionable alpine resorts, city breaks, relaxing beach holidays in the Caribbean—and all without entering a single caravan.

Kev used the headlights to illuminate what appeared to be an old rubbish tip and left the car for a rummage. After a few moments, he pulled out a filthy old jar, unscrewed it, tipped out a key, released Razor from the back of the car, turned off the headlights and approached the caravan by the light of a match. Razor kept his distance until Kev was inside and had lit an oil lamp. Since nothing went bang, he followed. It wasn't as awful as he'd feared, for although the inside was tiny and the prevailing colour was beige, it looked neat and well thought out. Despite it feeling like no one had been there for some time, he wondered if he could detect a faint whiff of Miranda's scent.

'Could be worse,' said Kev.

Razor nodded, comforted by thoughts of Miranda until he caught himself doing it and resorted to being practical. 'Is there food or water? A fridge?'

'There's no fridge, and no running water,' said Kev, opening a wall cupboard, 'but there are tins: baked beans, tuna, mushy peas.'

'Hardly gourmet fare and they appear to have been there some time to judge from all the mildew,' said Razor, pulling a face, 'but I'm too hungry to care. Let's get the stove on.'

'Stove?' Kev sat on a narrow bench along one side.

'But how can she cook?' asked Razor. 'Or heat the place?'

'She can't and nor can we. I'm the one who stowed the tins in case I had to get away for a few days.'

'And how did you plan to heat them?'

'I didn't, mate. If ever I had to come here, I suspected that would be the last thing on my mind.'

Razor shrugged. 'That sounds desperate, but I suppose stuff tastes the same cold. Is there a tin opener?'

Kev nodded. 'I believe I left one somewhere.'

'Cutlery?'

Kev scratched his head. 'I didn't think about eating irons. I'll have a look—and I'll do it now, because you are developing a lean and hungry look.' He got up, opened a few drawers and found the tin opener, but no knives, forks or even plates. 'I guess we'll have to make do. It is an ill cook that cannot lick his own fingers.'

'I guess so,' said Razor, 'but before anything else, I need the bathroom.'

'There isn't one. What you see is what there is. Either piss in the hedge, or do what a bear does—the woods are that way.' Kev pointed. 'There's a shovel behind the step.'

'But it's dark out there... and what about toilet paper? And how do I wash?'

'You'll get used to the dark and there are plenty of fallen leaves around—use the big ones and improvise. You can wash in the brook on the far side of the wood.'

'And I suppose that's where the drinking water comes from too?'

'You suppose right.'

'I guess soap is out of the question? Forget it, I've got to go.' Razor rushed outside.

He was reduced to groping for the shovel until his eyes adjusted and located the rusty implement. Grabbing it, he trotted towards the dark line he assumed was trees. Memories of trekking in Nepal flooded back as he made a rapid search for somewhere suitable.

Razor returned to the caravan, soaked, shivering and swearing.

'I see you found the brook,' said Kev.

'Found it. Fell in. Lost the shovel.'

'Well at least you're clean. What about your head?'

'I walked into a tree.'

'Nice graze. Take this.' Kev tossed him a rather inadequate towel.

'There's a towel, but no soap or toilet paper?' Razor shook his head, stripped off all his clothes except his underpants, dried himself and wrapped the damp towel around his waist. 'I'm cold—it's bloody freezing in here, and even more freezing out there, and what's most freezing of all is that damned brook. I don't suppose there's any heating?'

'Once again, you suppose right, mate. However, there should be blankets.' Kev hung Razor's dripping clothes on the door handle.

While Razor shivered, Kev tunnelled beneath the bench's lid and dug out a pile of rough grey blankets. They were folded neatly, but stank of dust and mustiness. When he shook one out, he showered Razor in a confetti of little lumps.

'Mouse shit! Sorry about that,' said Kev. 'The little devils have nested here and chewed it up. There's more hole than blanket.'

'What about the others?'

Kev checked. There were six in all, each chewed to uselessness, except for the last which had only one hole in the middle, though it was bigger than Razor's head.

'Poncho?' said Kev, handing it to Razor.

It stank of what Razor guessed must be mice, and the coarse cloth was scratchy, but there was no other option.

'Better?' asked Kev.

'Not really. I don't suppose there's any chance of a hot drink?'

'Sorry. There's brook water, or there might be beer.'

'I don't fancy water. You never know what's been in it.'

'You've been in it,' said Kev. 'I'll get you a beer, if I can find them.' After a scrabble through a cupboard, he pulled out two dusty cans.

'Sorenside Best Bitter Ale? I haven't heard of that one,' said Razor through the clattering of his teeth. 'How long have you had them?'

Kev nodded. 'Since the brewery burned down. Uncle Bob died in the fire, though they never found a trace of his body.'

'Then why tell me it was his skeleton at Miranda's?' asked Razor. 'Another of your daft stories?'

'Look, mate, the skeleton did belong to Uncle Bob, but the bones aren't his, if you see what I mean.'

'I haven't the faintest idea.'

'I'll explain. Uncle Bob was a doctor. In his day, medical students needed a skeleton for their studies.'

'I see… but if he was a doctor, what was he doing at the brewery?'

'Treating injured people. I was there to salvage beer. Then the roof fell in.'

'Sorry to hear that—but how come you've still got the beer?'

'No one else seemed to want it.'

'Is it still any good?'

Kev smiled. 'There's only one way to find out.' He handed a can to Razor and sat down with another.

Razor pulled the ring and took a sip. 'Not bad. Cheers!'

They sipped and drank in companionable silence for a few moments, listening as heavy raindrops started drumming on the roof.

Kev picked up a tin of beans and the tin opener. He dropped it and sprang to his feet. 'What's that?'

Razor heard a car's engine.

14

Kev pulled back the dusty curtain and peeped out. 'Shit, it's them!'

Car doors slammed outside.

Terror filled Razor. He couldn't stop trembling and though it might be his perfect opportunity for death and glory, he didn't feel up to an encounter with violent thugs—he was too cold and too undressed. Despite these handicaps, he resolved to do whatever necessary, no matter what the personal cost, to ensure Kev came through this in one piece. It was, he thought, a noble plan to lay down his life for a friend.

Razor nudged Kev aside and looked out at the battered pickup truck. A large ugly man who appeared to have outgrown his hair, was staring back at him, a rifle in his hand and another man was holding a baseball bat.

'Hell is empty and all the devils are here,' Kev wailed.

'I'll sort them out,' said Razor, getting to his feet and trying to square his chattering jaw. 'You get away while I do what I'm going to do.'

'A man's gotta do what a man's gotta do?' said

Kev. 'I first heard the expression years ago, and it was a cliché even then.'

'Maybe so, but I can't see another way out of this, if they are what you say.'

'They are,' Kev whispered, 'but there is another way. Follow me if you want to live—and you'll only be able to find out what Alex is up to if you do. Hurry!' He tiptoed to the end of the caravan, pulled back the threadbare rug, opened a hatch in the floor and slid down. 'Keep up and keep quiet.'

Razor hesitated, torn between heroism, terror and curiosity. When, to his amazement, curiosity won, he dropped through the hole, following Kev into a swampy hollow beneath the caravan. Outside, another vehicle drew up, a door slammed and Kane cursed the overgrown hedgerow that had scratched the sides of his flashy car.

'Over there,' Kev whispered as he reached up to shut the hatch, submerging them in darkness.

'I can't.'

'Why not?'

'I can't see.'

'Follow my voice… and take care. Uneasy lies the head that doesn't stay low.'

Razor crawled towards him, wondering what the little guy was on about until a sudden pounding on the side of the caravan made him start. He cracked his skull on some unseen projection and groaned.

'Shut up.' Kev hissed.

'Open up, Crumb!' Kane demanded.

The men thumped on the caravan yelling lurid threats. Razor followed Kev as best he could, heading for a faint glimmer and squeezing through a tiny cleft into the open, where he was relieved to see the caravan shielded them. He caught up with Kev who was creeping towards the trees.

'Micky, don't just stand there like a big muppet, get the wrecking bar,' said Kane.

'That'll be Micky Dunn,' Kev murmured. 'He's fat, stupid and amiable most of the time—he'd be quite harmless if Kane and his mates left him alone.

'Now, run for it while they're busy.'

Heads low, Kev and Razor were zigzagging through the trees when they heard a creaking, groaning sound followed by a loud crack.

'They've broken in already,' said Kev, 'and it won't take them long to figure out where we went. We'd better shift.'

'Where to?' asked Razor. 'It's alright for you, but I'm not dressed for this.'

'You're barely dressed at all, mate, but we'll worry about clothes when we're safe from these violent delights.'

'Release Simba,' Kane roared.

'What's Simba?' asked Razor.

A deep growl and a burst of excited barking answered him.

'Get him on the scent and let him loose,' said Kane.

Razor and Kev fled, heedless of brambles and holly and other obstacles that would have daunted less-desperate men. A projecting twig snagged Razor's towel. He did not bother retrieving it.

'If we make it to the brook, we might just stand a chance,' said Razor, gasping. 'They can't track you through water… can they?'

'Not in films, but I'm not so sure about real life.' Kev was panting like a dog.

They plunged on, not wasting any more breath, intent on getting as far away as possible, though Simba's barks were growing louder. Then it changed to a repetitive yip.

Kane's harsh voice carried on the breeze. 'What you got, boy? Have you found 'em?'

A burst of swearing followed. 'Stupid bloody dog. That's just an old towel! Drop it.'

Despite his terror, Razor chuckled, but although the distraction had led the dog astray, it didn't fool Kane. The pursuit continued. Razor and Kev plunged into the brook, gasping at its icy touch, stumbled out on the far bank and kept running. It wasn't long before they'd left the trees behind. A scramble over a stone wall and a leap across a muddy ditch took them into a field.

'There they are—over there,' shouted Kane. 'Sic 'em, boy.'

A lamp's glare lit them up like a spotlight on fleeing convicts, and Simba's howl sounded terrifyingly close. They fled like hunted hares, but Razor knew they'd never outpace the dog or a bullet. He forced himself to slow down and looked back. Simba, huge and hairy, his white teeth gleaming, was coming. Razor, though shaking, prepared for the ultimate sacrifice.

'Right you lot, what's your game?' asked a guttural voice.

As Kev gasped and stopped, Razor just avoided crashing into his back.

A plump man, tall, broad, bald and clean-shaven stepped from the shadows into the lamp's glare. Despite the rain and the cold he was wearing only baggy corduroy trousers and a checked shirt. He glanced at Razor. 'Forgive me for making an observation, but you're 'ardly dressed for jogging. Are you in trouble?'

Razor, too short of breath to speak, pointed at Simba, all teeth, hair and muscle, who was on the final charge.

'Sit!' said the man, taking a step forward and raising a hand the size of a shovel.

Simba sat. So did Kev and Razor.

'I meant the dog, but what the 'eck. Now 'oo are these likely lads with the big stick and the popgun?'

'Kane Cullum and Micky Dunn, sir,' said Kev, getting back up.

'And what 'ave you done that they feel the need to pursue you across my field at night?'

'We saw them poaching and...' said Kev.

'Poachers, eh?' The man frowned. 'I don't care for the likes of them. Especially when they're on my turf.'

Razor, bemused to realise he was sitting in mud, wearing only damp underpants and a smelly and inadequate poncho, looked back. Kane and Micky were galloping towards them. Micky, the rifle slung over his shoulder, kept the lamp shining into the man's face, which looked as pale and round as the full moon before age had cratered its surface. It was smiling.

'If you've done anything to my bloody dog,' said Kane, 'you're going to get your fat head kicked in.'

'I asked him to sit,' said the man. 'It appears there is truth in the ancient saying.'

'What?' asked Kane, slowing to a walk.

'There's no such thing as a bad dog. Just a bad master.'

'I don't like what you're getting at,' said Kane with an ugly sneer, 'but I do like teaching people who say things I don't like a lesson. Know what I mean?'

'I 'aven't a clue, lad,' said the man placidly, 'but I do know it's 'igh time you got out of my field.'

'We're not going anywhere until we're done,' said Micky, swinging the rifle into his hand.

'Done what?' asked the man.

'Done them,' said Micky, pointing a stubby finger at Kev and Razor. 'You too if you don't hop it.'

'I never 'op, laddie, and I don't appreciate being threatened when I'm out standing in my

232

own field. I assume that's what you were trying to do?'

Micky's face was a mess of confusion, as if his tiny brain was trying to work out what had just been said and was failing badly.

'Hand me the lamp,' said Kane. 'Shoot him if he doesn't behave.'

'If you say so.' Micky passed it over.

'I think you'd better run, sir,' said Kev.

'Run from my own field?' The man looked shocked at the suggestion. 'I ain't gonna do that, just because laddie 'ere has a popgun.'

'My name's not Laddie, it's Micky, and it's not a popgun—it's real and it's loaded. Put your hands up.'

'I think you'd better do as he says,' said Razor, who found the whole hero scenario more troublesome now another person was involved. No one except him was supposed to die, so why wouldn't the man back down and walk away?

'I'll do as I like, young man,' said the man, giving no impression of being at all concerned by the presence of two armed thugs and their thuggish dog, though in fairness, Simba was sitting and wagging his tail, like the top student in an obedience class.

'You'll do as you're told,' said Micky, looking to Kane for support.

'And be quick about it,' said Kane, anger distorting his features.

'I most certainly will not. This is my field, and if anyone is going to order folk about 'ere it will be me. Understand? I strongly advise you to go 'ome and get some sleep and think about changing your ways. Otherwise, you might get 'urt.'

'I'm not joking,' said Micky, waving the rifle.

'I can tell that, laddie,' said the man. 'If you were, we'd all be laughing.'

Micky looked at Kane. 'What should I do, boss?'

'Keep him covered,' said Kane. 'Blow him away if he tries anything.'

Micky stumbled as he raised the rifle and it went off. 'Ugh!' he said and fell backward.

'Ouch,' said the plump man, investigating a hole in his shirt with a huge finger.

Razor gaped, his ears ringing.

Kane turned the lamp on Micky, who was thrashing about in the mud, moaning and clutching his paunch, blood seeping between his fingers.

'I warned 'im to be careful,' said the man,

shaking his head.

'But he shot you!' said Razor.

The man nodded.

'And you're not hurt!'

'Well, it stung a bit.'

'But you should be dead.'

'Should I? Then it's lucky for me I'm not,' said the man, taking a step towards Micky.

'Back off,' yelled Kane, lunging and swinging the baseball bat in a downward arc.

It clunked against the man's head and snapped in two. The lower half rebounded and splatted Kane's nose.

'Why can't people be sensible?' asked the man, shaking his head as Kane fell back, groaning and covering his bloodied face with his hands. 'It would make their lives so much less painful. I suppose I'd better sort out the laddie with the bullet in 'im, but my old joints are turning to chalk and I ain't up to squatting these days. You two lads 'ad better give me an 'and. Get 'im to 'is feet, and I'll do the rest.'

'Yes, of course,' said Kev, his eyes wide. 'Come on Razor, do as he says.'

They pulled moaning Micky upright.

'What about Kane?' asked Kev.

'The lad with the stick? 'e can look after

'imself, though 'e'll 'ave a sore 'ooter. Serves 'im right I reckon.'

'And the gun?' asked Razor.

'I was forgettin' that.' The plump man turned and stamped on the barrel, bending it. 'That'll put an end to 'is mischief, unless 'e wants to shoot round corners. Reckon 'e'll be able to sniff round 'em too when 'is 'ooter stops spouting claret. Now come along.'

'Where to?' asked Kev,

'With me,' said the man, slinging the corpulent frame of Micky over his shoulder as if about to burp a monstrous baby.

Razor and Kev exchanged confused glances and followed. Razor shook with cold and hoped they were heading to a warm place where he might borrow some clothes, or at least a better blanket.

The plump man led them into the porch of a small Cotswold stone house. A stout walking stick leaned casually against the wall alongside an empty boot stand. A note on the bright red front door said:

I'm out, standing in my field.

'Take your muddy footwear off—those that 'ave any—and go inside,' said the man, turning a massive cast iron knob to open the door before removing Micky's boots and taking off his own with the help of a cast iron boot jack.

The procedure involved bending and resulted in a cacophony of cracks and creaks that made Razor gag and squirm. As he fought to stay in control of his squeamishness, his head light and dizzy, he clutched a heavy chain for support. A deep resonance thrilled through his feet into his bones.

'No need to ring the bell when the door's already open, lad,' said the man, straightening up with a repeat of the racket.

'Sorry,' said Razor through chattering teeth. As he rubbed his filthy bare feet on the mat, he yelped in pain—they were scratched and bleeding.

'I'll clean those for you when I've finished with this one,' said the man, ensuring all the boots were neat on the rack. 'Get inside and warm up by the fire.'

He guided Razor into a tidy little sitting room with a beaming log fire that made the shadows dance, and eased Micky onto a plain wooden table, before lighting a spill at the fire and applying it to a pair of oil lamps. When seen in the light, their benefactor didn't appear plump. Rather, he looked solid. Razor guessed he might be in his mid-sixties, though the smoothness of his face could almost have been that of a child, and there was something in the way he moved that wasn't right, as if his arms and legs didn't bend as they ought. His huge, pale hands were hairless and alarming yellow knitted socks encased his colossal feet.

'You,' said the man, with a nod at Kev, 'go through there.' He pointed towards a door in the corner, 'And put the kettle on. You'll need this.' He lit another oil lamp and handed it to Kev.

'What should I do?' asked Razor, more embarrassed by his unconventional costume now he could see himself.

'Nothing until you're warm. When you are, I might need some assistance with this idiot.'

Micky groaned as if on cue.

'Shouldn't we call an ambulance?' Razor asked. Now the prospect of taking a bullet had passed, he was fretting about the likelihood of the police arriving, and was unsure whether to stay or run. The list of things they might question him about kept lengthening.

'No phone,' said the man, pulling Micky's hands from the wound, tearing the bloodied clothing away and examining the oozing midriff.

'I could run for help,' said Razor.

'Like that? You'd catch your death.' said the man.

'Could you lend me some clothes?' asked Razor, his teeth chattering.

Weird creaks and the sound of water splashing into a kettle emerged from the kitchen.

'Later,' said the man, moving Micky into position, his movements firm but gentle. 'And now, please, shut your face—there's doctorin' to be done.'

Micky lay still, his skin as pale as the whites of his eyes. 'Am I going to die?'

'Yes...'

Micky bit his lip.

'... but not today.'

'He's bleeding a lot,' said Razor, grimacing and turning his head away.

'It looks worse than it is—'is shirt is wet and a little blood goes a long way.'

Micky raised his head, glanced at the oozing hole in his fat belly and slumped back, limp.

'Excellent,' said the man. 'An unconscious patient is easier to treat than a conscious one.' He headed into the kitchen, allowing Razor a glimpse of Kev, crouched on a wooden stool like a hobgoblin in a fairy tale. He was staring at a fire over which a blackened kettle dangled from a rusty chain. An old-fashioned water pump occupied one corner. The door swung back and Razor's attention returned to Micky who, in his dormant state, and with his big, almost bald head, resembled a grotesque sleeping baby.

Something cold pressed into the back of Razor's leg. It was Simba's nose. Razor backed away and gasped.

'What's 'appening?' said the man bursting back in, rubbing his shovel-hands on a threadbare towel. 'Oh, it's you, doggy. 'ow can I 'elp?'

Simba whined and licked his lips.

'Thirsty, eh?' He glanced at Razor. 'If you still want to be useful, fetch 'im a bowl of water. Your pal knows where stuff is.'

Razor hobbled out, keeping his back to the wall, his eyes on Simba, though the brute appeared placid and relaxed. He'd never trusted dogs since a big brown one saw him off when he'd trespassed onto a building site in looking for a lost cricket ball. He must have been twelve or thirteen at the time and the incident had put him off canines for life.

'I need a bowl of water for Simba,' he said as the kitchen door shut behind him. Kev's face was paler than normal. 'Are you alright?'

'I'm okay,' Kev whispered, 'but he just washed his hands in boiling water!'

'What?'

'As soon as the kettle had boiled, he filled the basin and washed his hands in it.'

'There was probably some cold water in there already.'

'No, there wasn't—I'd just taken it from the cupboard to fill. His hands didn't even turn red.'

'Weird,' said Razor. 'Who is he?'

'He's the guy who lives here. Miranda said he stands out in his field.'

'What field is that?'

'The one he was in when we bumped into him.'

'You mean he just stands outside... in a field?'

'Apparently.'

'But why?'

'On that I suffer the common curse of

mankind: ignorance.'

'Well, I stand by what I said—he is weird. I think I like him though.'

Kev nodded. 'So do I, and I feel safe here... but there's something about him that makes me suspect he could be dangerous.'

'Yeah, rather like the difference between an old cat dozing by the fire and a raging tiger,' said Razor. 'Mind you, the way he tamed Simba was incredible, though I fear the dog will turn bad again if I don't give him his drink soon.'

Kev nodded. 'There are bowls in the cupboard in the corner. Grab one and I'll work the pump.'

Razor fetched one. 'It's bone china—isn't that too fragile for dogs?'

'That's all there is, mate. Just be careful. Hold it under the spout and keep clear—it's freezing and splashes.'

Kev pumped the handle, water sluiced into the bowl and despite Razor's best efforts, icy drops splashed his bare feet, making him dance and gasp.

'I don't think you need to fear Simba anymore,' said Kev. 'The dog's been won and will fawn on any man—at least while our host is present.'

Razor was unconvinced, but after his

crushing defeat at the tiny hands of Miranda, had no wish to lose any more face—though there was a chance of losing all of his face and more if Simba reverted to the savage. 'Could you hold the door for me?'

To his surprise, the dog behaved in a most civilised fashion, sitting and waiting for the bowl to be placed in front of him, before standing, wagging his tail and lapping up the contents. Razor retreated to a hard chair by the fire and kept a wary eye on him.

Their host leant over Micky, probing with a pair of forceps, and occasionally grunting and making strange expostulations. 'Got it,' he said at last and straightened up, gripping a bloodied lump of metal in the forceps' jaws.

Micky moaned, but showed no other signs of consciousness.

'Is he alright?' asked Kev walking back in.

'I reckon 'e will be. 'ell be a lot 'appier without this lump o' lead rattling around 'is guts. It was a small calibre, low-powered bullet and barely poked through 'is peritoneum—'e was lucky— I've seen too many die of gut shots in my time, but I reckon nothing vital was 'it. Pass the iodine, would you? Then I'll plug him up.'

Kev handed a glass phial to him. The man

snapped off the end, poured the contents over a pad of lint and swabbed the wound. Razor watched with repulsed fascination until the stitching began.

'All done,' said the man. 'Maybe it'll teach the silly bugger not to mess with firearms.'

'Maybe,' said Kev, 'but I doubt it. Micky's not such a bad guy, but he is always getting into bad company—like Kane's'

The man nodded and glanced at Razor. 'I'll look at your feet now. Put 'em up on the chair.'

Razor did as he was told. There was a long cut across one sole and the other had several small gashes. The man gently probed and squeezed. 'Barely more than scratches, young man. I'll wash 'em and patch 'em, and rub in some ointment a friend makes—it's good stuff. Your feet won't cause you any problems afterwards, as long as you keep 'em dry and clean and don't do anything silly.'

Razor could only nod since the icy smoothness of the man's huge hands had taken his breath away. Despite this, he felt secure and relaxed. 'Are you a doctor?' he asked as the man dressed his feet.

'No.'

'You appear to know a lot about tending

wounds.'

'I 'ad to learn 'ow to patch blokes up when I was in the army.'

'You were a soldier?'

'Aye, lad, I was… many years ago.'

'I didn't catch your name.'

'I never dropped it. It's Rock, Leroy Rock. Some call me Rocky. You may.'

'Thank you er… Rocky. They call me Razor, and my friend is Kev.'

Rocky nodded. 'Aye, I recognised 'im. I used to 'elp 'is Uncle Bob back in the day, and young Kev sometimes came along.'

'I can't summon up any remembrance of such things past,' said Kev.

'Well, you were a young 'un back then and more interested in messing with my marbles than anything else.'

'Do you know Miranda?' Razor asked.

'I did. Nice lass, but I reckon what we need to do now is to find you something to wear.'

'That would be most helpful,' said Razor, 'but I'm not your size.'

'Reckon you're right. 'owever, I 'ave a store of garments in the attic. Some might fit you—if the moths 'aven't eaten 'em. Stay 'ere and keep an eye on Micky. 'e might feel a little discombobulated when 'e wakes up.'

Rocky left them with Micky, who was still out, breathing peacefully as if fast asleep. Simba, having lapped up the water, had curled up on the rug by the fire, yawning and showing off a magnificent set of sharp white teeth. Kev returned the empty bowl to the kitchen to wash and Razor, warming up at last, nodded on his chair.

Simba growled and leapt to his feet, bristling.

The front door juddered and burst open.

15

As Razor sprang to his feet, he was struck first by a chunk of wood flying from the door frame and then by the size of the figure in the doorway.

'What are you doing to Micky?' demanded the newcomer, barging his way in. Kane, his nose bent and swollen, and with blood staining the front of his hoodie, followed.

Razor rubbed his shin and gaped. Simba backed into a corner, snarling and cringing.

'You'd better answer, if you know what's good for you,' said Kane, his voice nasal, murder in his eyes. 'And when you've told him, you can tell me why you're still alive—didn't I chuck you in the river?'

'I... er,' said Razor, breathing hard. An acrid smoky taint blew in on the breeze and made his nose wrinkle.

The kitchen door opened and Rocky marched in carrying a pair of blue and white flannelette pyjamas, a grey dressing gown and a pair of tatty slippers. 'Why 'ave you busted my front door?' he demanded, stone-faced. 'You never 'eard of doorbells?'

'I'm sorry, Mr Rock, I di'n't know this was your place,' said the big man. ''ow is Micky? Is 'e 'urt bad?'

''e'll be fine, Winston. I've done some doctoring and patched 'im up,' said Rocky.

'You know this geezer?' said Kane. 'That is... unfortunate.'

'Why's that?' asked Winston.

'Because I was intending to make sure there were no witnesses.'

'What do you mean?' asked Razor, trying to look tough which wasn't easy in a poncho designed by mice.

''e means dead men tell no tales,' said Rocky.

'Got it in one,' said Kane. 'Perhaps you're not as stupid as you look.'

'But you definitely are,' said Kev, peering around Rocky.

'You little...'

'Dead men?' said Winston. ''oo's dead?'

'No one... yet,' said Kane with a bloody sneer.

'No one at all,' said Razor, hyperventilating. With his heart going like the clappers, he surprised himself by springing forward and swinging wildly. He yelped as his fist crashed into Kane's chin. Kane swayed, staggered and stretched his length on the rug.

'Nice one, mate,' Kev murmured, as Simba emerged from the corner, wagging his tail and nuzzling up to Winston.

'There was no need for that, young man,' said Rocky. 'We could 'ave sorted this all out amicably—we are supposed to be civilised. You could start to look the part by putting these on—they're a little on the large side, but you can roll up the arms and legs and tighten the draw string.' He handed the pyjamas to Razor.

'Although we might be civilised, Kane isn't,' said Kev. 'He'd have done something nasty.'

'What with?' asked Rocky. 'I'd already broke 'is popgun and 'is stick. I reckon 'e was mostly 'armless.'

'He's very handy with his fists,' said Kev.

''oo is, Kane or your pal?' Rocky smiled.

'Not me,' said Razor, and pulled up the pyjama bottoms, wincing as a raw knuckle brushed the cloth. 'I don't normally go around hitting people. I got lucky, but from what I've seen Kev's right—Kane is dangerous.'

'Not now 'e ain't.'

'True,' said Kev, 'but he is, when conscious, a murderous nutter who hates me.'

'Why?' asked Rocky.

'Maybe because he's a mate of my cousin, Gary, and Gary thinks I took something that should have been his. I didn't though—Uncle Bob bequeathed it to me because of all the bad stuff Gary had done.' Kev paused and looked guilty. 'Though, thinking about it, I suppose I never actually got round to paying the Cullums for my car.'

'What do you make of 'im?' Rocky asked Winston, nodding at Kane who lay as still as a toppled statue.

'Mr Cullum is violent, and 'e's getting violenter.'

'Why are you 'anging around with 'im then?'

''cause 'e pays, and a job's a job. Guys like me can't be too choosy.'

'You'll get yourself into trouble,' said Rocky.

'I 'ope not. I don't mostly do much except knock doors over and stand next to Mr Kane when 'e needs a bit o' muscle to back 'im up.'

'So you don't hurt people?' asked Razor.

'Not unless they 'it me first or try to 'it 'im.'

'You're like his bodyguard?'

Winston nodded, looking at Micky who'd started twitching and moaning. 'Kind of... only it's not easy when you're trying to protect a nutter.'

Micky opened his eyes, attempted to sit up, clutched his belly and whimpered. 'What have you done to me?'

'He's removed a bullet from your belly and stitched you up,' said Kev.

'A bullet? Tell me, 'oo shot you and why?' asked Winston.

'I think he shot himself,' said Razor. 'Or rather, the gun went off and the bullet bounced off Rocky and hit him. I don't understand how.'

'I expect Mr Rock 'as a thick skin, like what I've got.'

'Yeah, right,' said Razor.

'Sometimes it's just the way things are,' said Kev. 'People get lucky.'

'But...'

'Best to leave the subject,' said Kev, 'and be grateful no one was hurt.'

'I'm hurt,' Micky pointed out.

'And so is 'e.' Winston nodded at Kane, 'but it serves 'im right—'e's been going too far recently, and I don't think I want to work for 'im no more.'

'Good for you, Mr Flint', said Rocky, leaning over Kane, with a repeat of the medley of pops and creaks. 'I reckon our unconscious friend here will be fine, more's the pity.' Rocky glanced back at Razor and grinned. 'You clobbered 'im right and good.'

'I know,' said Razor, grimacing at his grazed and swollen knuckles, and flexing his fingers.

'You knocked out two of 'is gnashers.' Rocky picked the gory trophies from the rug and unbent. 'I'll keep 'em for a friend.'

Razor, though shocked to have caused such damage, couldn't deny a glow of pride.

'That's a risk you run when you're a thug,' said Kev with a glance at Razor. 'The same sort of thing happened to him before—or so I heard. Apparently, some hero smacked him in the mouth on Bindover Bridge when the bastard attacked a former girlfriend.'

Razor said nothing, but put on a modest smile as he tried on the dressing gown. It was thick, warm and comforting.

'Where am I?' asked Kane, choosing that moment to come round.

'You're in my 'ouse, on my rug and in disgrace after breaking my nice front door, what I'd only just painted.'

Kane sat up, holding his jaw. He put a finger into the bloody gap in his mouth and glared at Razor. 'He hit me!'

''e did that,' Winston confirmed.

'So, why is he still in one piece? Why haven't you messed him up like you should have?'

'Why should I 'ave?' asked Winston.

'Because I pay you to look after me.'

'But you was already out, boss, and 'e wasn't threatening you anymore.'

'Fine. But now I'm ordering you to take him out.'

'Are you asking me to kill 'im? I don't do that.'

'You obey me—it's what I pay you for. Do it. Now!'

'No, boss.'

'Damn you! Why not?'

'I don't do that sort of thing.'

'Since when?'

'Since always. I've 'it blokes for you, but only 'cause I 'ad to. I ain't never killed no one, and I ain't starting now.'

Kane's fury came to the boil. Spitting blood, he sprang to his feet, his face plum red, his eyes fierce. He charged at Razor but Winston stepped in his way. Kane, though bulky and strong, might just as well have run headlong into a brick wall. He went down again, eyes glazed.

'I apologise for the unpleasantness,' said Winston, 'and especially for busting your door,

Mr Rock.' He reached into Kane's jacket pocket, pulled out a leather wallet and removed a wad of banknotes. "e should pay for it. I 'ope this'll cover the cost.'

Rocky waved it away. 'No need for that, Mr Flint. I'll fix my door in the morning.'

'Very good,' said Winston, pocketing the cash and hoisting the limp figure of Kane over his shoulder. 'I think I should take my friends away now. Can you walk, Micky?'

Micky, though pale and wobbly, stood up, one hand pressed to his wound. 'Thank you for doctoring me, sir.'

'You're welcome, young fellow,' said Rocky. 'Take it easy for a few days and you'll be just fine. I would also advise you to give up on the crime and be good—and if you can't be good, be careful.'

Winston raised a hand in farewell, called Simba to heel and helped Micky stagger away.

As Rocky waved them off, Kev exhaled and slumped into a chair by the fire.

Razor joined him. 'Your cousin does indeed keep bad company.'

Kev nodded. 'Kane is the worst.'

'What about Winston? He's scary, but he seemed almost reasonable.'

'That's 'cause 'e's a mercenary,' said Rocky, examining the door frame. ''e 'as no personal gripe with you two, but, you're correct, 'e could be dangerous.'

'How do you know him?' said Razor.

Rocky sighed. 'It's more like I know of 'im. 'is old dad, Ebenezer, was in my regiment. 'e was a good sort, if a bit dim, until a mortar shell 'it 'im.'

'Was he killed?' asked Razor.

'That's usually what 'appens when a bloke sticks his 'ead in a trench mortar to see why it ain't gone off and it goes off.'

'Nasty... when was that?'

'In the war.'

'The Gulf War?'

Rocky shook his head and smiled. 'Years before that. I was unaware any of the Flints still lived around these parts.'

'I've bumped into Winston a few times,' said Kev, 'though not like Kane did. He doesn't normally talk so much.'

'I believe I've seen him too,' said Razor. 'I thought there was something familiar about him—I saw him leaving my local pub a couple of days ago... and I'm almost sure Kane was with him. What would they be doing there?'

Kev shrugged. 'I dunno. Kane normally only leaves town to engage in rural mischief.'

'I suppose that's likely.'

'What are we going to do now?' asked Kev.

'I don't know,' said Razor. 'I suppose we should go back to the caravan.'

'What's that?' asked Rocky who was examining his front door. He pointed towards a flickering orange glow behind trees.

The stench of smoke was strong.

'It's the caravan!' Kev clutched his head and sprang from his chair.

'Now what?' asked Razor.

'Put it out,' said Kev.

'I doubt we 'ave the means,' said Rocky, 'but we should look.'

Kev pushed past Razor and ran towards the glow. Razor followed, though the painful cuts on his feet made him slow and his baggy pyjama bottoms kept coming down and dragging in the mud. By the time he reached the caravan, billows of oily grey smoke were gushing from the door and the shattered windows. He caught up with Kev as the entire structure collapsed in on itself. A fireball rolled out.

It set Kev's car alight.

The fuel tank ruptured and flames speared the sky. Kev shrugged. 'Oh well, it wasn't much of a car.'

'We'd better call the fire brigade,' said Razor.

'I still don't 'ave a telephone,' said Rocky who had just joined them. ''ow you gonna do that?'

'Well, somebody round here must have one,' said Razor.

'I don't know. I've never 'ad cause to ask. Besides, no one lives nearby at the moment.'

Razor clutched his head. 'Well what are we going to do?'

'Return to my 'ouse and get some kip,' said Rocky. 'I 'ave a spare room with two beds. There's no point fussing, 'cause the caravan and the car 'ave 'ad it, and there's nothing else around 'ere that'll burn—not after all that rain.'

'But...' Razor began and stopped. What else was there to do? The fire would burn itself out, they knew who'd done it, and they could inform the police just as well in the morning if they wanted to.

Kev nodded, though his expression was glum. 'What am I going to tell Miranda? We shouldn't really have been using it, though she wouldn't have minded if we'd left it as we found it. Damn Kane! A burning devil take him.'

Following a hot drink and a quick, though substantial, snack of fresh bread and nutty Sorenchester cheese, Rocky guided Razor and Kev to a plain but clean attic room. Razor collapsed into an old wooden bed in the corner and made himself comfortable and cosy between lavender-scented sheets. Despite Kev's snores from the other corner, he slept well and awoke in daylight, delighted not to have been disturbed by the usual nightmare. After a long stretch and a longer yawn, he got up and headed downstairs. Kev was already at the table, dressed, wide awake and spooning porridge down his throat.

'Morning,' said Razor.

'It still is,' said Kev. 'You slept well.'

'Where's our host?'

'He's out standing in his field again.'

'Why?'

'I suppose he likes it. Hungry?'

Razor nodded.

'There's porridge in the cauldron. Rocky said to help ourselves. There's a bowl out in the kitchen—it's the one Simba used, but I've washed it.'

Despite Kev's assurance, Razor scrubbed the bowl again before ladling a mass of steaming oats into it and carrying it to the table. He ate in silence, his brain marking time until his belly was full of the thick, gloopy mess. Kev appeared deep in thought.

'I need clothes,' said Razor and pushed his well-scraped bowl aside. 'I can't go out like this and, anyway, Rocky will want his pyjamas back.'

'No problem,' said Kev, 'though it will take time. I'll have to go into town and buy something—none of my stuff will fit you and your place is too far away.'

'I can't ask you to do that,' said Razor, shaking his head. 'I've got no cash to pay you back and you've already lost your car. Anyway, it's a long walk.'

'Don't worry,' said Kev. 'A friend in need is...'

'... a bloody nuisance,' Razor interrupted. 'Don't worry about me, I'll be fine.'

'Sure you will. What are you thinking of doing? Staying here forever? Or would you rather catch your death by walking into town like that?'

'I don't know, but I still think we ought to leave here soon. It was kind of Rocky to put us up for the night, and I'm grateful, but I'm sure he'll be glad to see the back of us. And there's another thing—I like him, but he worries me. There's something not right about him.'

Kev nodded. 'You mean the way bullets bounce off him, and how he can wash his hands in boiling water?'

'That's not normal, is it?' said Razor.

'Normal enough for these parts.'

'I can't make him out at all.'

'You need to switch off your preconceptions and trust your own senses,' said Kev, smiling. 'You saw what happened when Micky shot him.'

'Yes, but...'

'Bullets don't bounce off people, do they?'

'Of course not, so there must be another simple explanation. Perhaps it hit his cigarette case?'

'Does he look the sort to have a cigarette case?'

Razor said nothing. He'd not been thinking right for days, maybe not for months, and whatever Kev was saying made as much sense as anything else at this point in his life.

'However, what might or might not have happened is irrelevant,' said Kev, 'because it does not solve your sartorial dilemma.'

'My what?'

'Your lack of suitable clothing.'

'Why didn't you just say so?'

'I did but you couldn't hear it.'

The front door creaked and juddered open and Rocky entered. 'Good noontide,' he said. 'I trust you 'ave eaten?'

'We have, sir,' said Kev.

'Excellent. Is there anything else I can 'elp you with? If not I intend to fix this door.'

'My friend could do with some clothes,' said Kev. 'I don't suppose you have anything suitable?'

Rocky stared at Razor, who found the intensity of the gaze worrying and embarrassing. 'Let me see.' Rocky closed his eyes.

A minute or two later, wondering if Rocky had fallen asleep on his feet, Razor coughed.

Rocky jerked. 'I believe I might 'ave something that may be of use, though it won't be what a young gentleman would consider fashionable.'

'Fashion is the least of my worries,' said Razor. 'Anything would be better than nothing.'

'Stay 'ere. I'll be right back when I get back.' Rocky headed for the stairs.

Whoever… whatever their host was, he was a decent sort and Razor decided to accept his oddness until there was time to think—assuming death didn't find him before then. For some reason, the idea of dying, no matter how heroically, held less appeal. He recognised that he now wanted to live—at least until he'd worked out what Alex was up to. Kev's insinuations had brought back old, barely acknowledged suspicions and he needed answers. He was also itching to find out more about Miranda, not to mention Kev and Rocky. Were they really so weird? Or could it be that he was the odd one?

Rocky returned with a huge wooden trunk and placed it on the rug. 'Is any of this of use?'

It contained folded clothes in all shades of sombre. Razor picked out a grey tweed jacket from the top and shook it out, recoiling at the stink of mothballs, a scent that took him back to his grandparents' cottage, where he'd stayed after his parents' death and before university. The jacket looked like one his grandfather might have worn. He held it against himself. It was a little too broad in the chest, and a tad short in the sleeves, but not bad in the circumstances.

'You're welcome to anything you want,' said Rocky. 'I 'ave no need for it.'

'That's most kind of you,' said Razor.

'It belonged to my old friend, Nenea. When 'e died, 'is lady wife chucked 'em all out. I suppose I only keep 'em as keepsakes.'

Razor selected the essentials and dressed, trying not to think about the days when he'd made a point of keeping smart and fashionable for Flit rather than for work.

There was another thing—the last person to put on these clothes was dead! Razor forced himself to be rational. After all, Riverside Cottage must have witnessed many a deathbed over the three centuries of its existence, but it had never felt spooky. Nor had it seemed to belong to the dead until after Flit's accident— she had done so much more than him to make it a home. Had she already become a stranger to him even before then? Had she and Alex been having an affair after all? It was a terrible possibility. Instead of dwelling on it, he pulled on a soft cotton checked shirt and forced himself to become practical and logical, which had always been his way.

He tried on a pair of baggy trousers and pulled out the front. 'I could stick a watermelon down here.'

'You could, but why would you?' asked Kev.

'Just what I was thinking,' said Rocky.

'I meant a figurative watermelon.'

'Don't reckon I ever ate a figurative watermelon,' said Rocky. 'I 'ave 'ad fig rolls, though.'

'No… I mean these trousers are so big I could stick a watermelon down there if I wished. Clearly, I never would.'

Rocky was reluctant to give up the thread. 'I'd like to taste a figurative watermelon. Where can I get 'em from?'

Razor shook his head. 'Forget it—I'm sorry I even mentioned watermelons. The problem is that these trousers are too big. Do you have a belt?'

'No,' said Rocky.

'Oh well, I'll just have to hold them up, unless you've got any string.'

'I do 'ave string.'

'Great.'

''owever, you may find these braces suit you better. Nenea used to swear by 'em. 'e said belts cut off the circulation to 'is privates, and 'e didn't want that, 'cause 'e 'ad a young wife to attend to. I've 'ad no such problem with belts myself.'

Razor stared as Rocky pulled the braces from the chest. 'How do they work?'

'Like this,' said Kev. He slung them over Razor's shoulders and made a few adjustments around his middle. 'How's that?'

'Comfortable.' Razor bent and stretched.

'Good. What's your foot size?'

'Ten, I think.'

Kev searched through the shoes. 'These are elevens, but they'll be okay with a thick pair of socks.'

Razor tried on some woollen socks and a neat pair of black leather lace-ups. He took a few steps and broke into a jig. 'Not a bad fit at all. Yeah, these'll do well. Thank you.'

'You're wearing dancing shoes with nimble soles,' said Kev with a grin.

'Aye, lad, 'e is,' said Rocky, 'and I 'ave a soul of lead—I ain't 'eard those words for an age.'

'What?' said Razor, annoyed that Kev's inane jabbering seemed to mean something to Rocky.

'You know Romeo and Juliet?' asked Rocky.

'The night club?' said Razor.

'The play by the immortal Shakespeare.' Rocky shook his head as if appalled by such ignorance.

Razor scowled, feeling left out and stupid. How dare they talk of things that were beyond all understanding, particularly his understanding? Noticing his annoyance bubbling towards rage, and remembering how much the weird old guy had done for him, he forced an expression of calm interest onto his face. 'Oh yes? Is it any good?'

Rocky nodded. 'With the right players it is. Now I need to fix my door before the badgers get in again. Is there anything further you require?'

'No, I don't think so.'

'Thank you so much for your hospitality and for your help last night,' said Kev. 'We must be away.'

'Pleased to 'elp. Farewell, friends.'

'We wish you well and so we take our leave,' said Kev with a bow.

Taking Razor by a tweedy sleeve, he led him out beneath a bright autumn sky.

16

The footpath took Razor and Kev towards Sorenchester. Despite mud and some puddles, the way was clear and easy for the most part. Unseasonal sunshine beamed down, making the fields steam, and Razor could have enjoyed the warmth and the exercise had he been able to forget the treks and rambles he'd enjoyed with Flit before work had gnawed away so much of his life. He'd now accepted that he'd gone home tired, grumpy and preoccupied far too often, and that he'd been reluctant to waste any remaining energy on leisure or culture. It was awful that he'd scoffed at Flit's attempts to explain the work-time balance, and had taken her love for granted. What a fool he'd been to waste so much time getting rich. What use was money now?

Such recriminations pointed back to his usual swamp of guilt and despair, though thoughts of Miranda, Kev and Rocky prevented him from wallowing in its familiar, comfortable misery. Kev, trudging by his side, stayed glum and silent until they were long past the blackened carcasses of the car and caravan.

'I liked Rocky, but I don't know what to make of him,' said Razor after a few minutes of futile musing on the man's weirdness.

'I have an idea,' said Kev, 'though I'm not sure I should tell you.'

'Why not?'

'Because I don't think you'll believe it, and you'll get all red-faced and cross like you do when you don't understand something.'

'I don't,' said Razor, getting angry, which was not helped by Kev's smile. 'Well, if I do it's only because someone is withholding information.'

'Alright then,' said Kev, 'I will concede that you are the most even-tempered bloke I know.'

'That's more like it. Now tell me what you mean.'

'I really don't think you'll like it.'

'Spit it out, man.'

'I will not, but can you see the sign over there?'

'The old wooden one?'

Kev nodded. 'Take a look. It might give you a clue.'

Razor looked. 'The Olde Toll House. So what?'

'What do you think it means?' asked Kev.

'That's easy—Rocky's place is where the toll keeper lived in the olden days.'

Kev nodded. 'That would be a plausible explanation, if his house was situated by an important road. However, this little track could never have been one.'

'True,' Razor admitted, 'but I fail to see the significance—it's just a name.'

'But names can mutate over the years. Letters get changed or missed out entirely as folk forget their original significance. There's a possibility it was originally called something that looked and sounded similar but had a completely different meaning, like the Olde Troll House. There are more things in heaven and earth, Horatio, than are dreamt of in your philosophy.'

Although Razor's annoyance flared up at Kev taking him for a fool, he shook his head and calmed down. 'I take it you're as much in the dark as I am. Let's get out of here.'

They continued along the track until it joined The Green Way. Razor, lost in a maze of disconnected thoughts, took off his heavy tweed jacket and slung it over his shoulder.

'Warm today,' Kev remarked.

'Makes a change,' said Razor.

Conversation exhausted, they trudged on, pleased when a cooling breeze sprang up. The

Green Way became a suburban road, leading them to the busy crossroads before the centre of Sorenchester.

While they were waiting for a break in the traffic, Kev pointed to a wall of lead-grey cloud building on the horizon. 'The tempest growls. I imagine any threat from Kane has diminished considerably so you're welcome to come back to my place.'

'Thanks for the offer,' said Razor, 'but I intend to head back home—there are things I need to check, and I'd rather be alone.'

Kev shrugged. 'If that's what you want, but you'll need your keys.'

'True.' Razor held out his hand.

'I don't have them,' said Kev.

'You've lost them?'

'I didn't lose them—I gave them away.'

'Why would you do that?' Razor felt like punching the little guy and restrained himself with some effort.

'Because you said you didn't want them.'

'So I did,' said Razor. 'Who did you give them to?'

'Miranda.'

'Why?'

'Why not?' asked Kev. 'She was available.

Should I have given them to someone else?'

The question stumped Razor. 'It doesn't matter. I'll get them later… if I need them.'

'How?'

'I'll take the bus to Glevchester and see her.'

'You don't have the bus fare, mate.'

'Perhaps I'll walk then.' Razor found the idea of seeing her attractive. He wouldn't allow himself to understand why.

'You may have visited her house, but could you find it again?'

The lights changed and the traffic came to a stop. Razor and Kev stayed put.

'I reckon so—more or less,' said Razor, though details of its location were hazy.

'I don't reckon you could.'

'Well, tell me her address.'

'There isn't one as such—I just know how to find it. Anyway, you'd never get past the gate.'

'What about her phone number?'

'She doesn't have one—you must have noticed when you were exploring.'

'Everybody has a phone these days.'

'She doesn't,' Kev pointed out, 'I don't, Rocky doesn't, and neither do you.'

'I used to have a nice one,' said Razor, his position as an authority on the subject undermined.

'But you don't now. Why not?'

'I smashed it.'

'Why?'

'I was drunk and upset.' Remembering how he'd felt at the time, Razor was unwilling to say more. He didn't want to leave Kev with a bad impression.

'Fair enough,' said Kev. 'We all have our guilty secrets.'

'I didn't say it was a secret, and why would you think it was a guilty one?'

'Fair enough. It was just a feeling.'

'I'm interested why you'd suggest such a thing,' said Razor. 'Does that mean you have a guilty secret? What is it?'

'It wouldn't be secret if I told you.'

'No, I suppose not, but I bet yours is not as bad as mine.'

'Aha! So you admit to having one,' said Kev. 'Is that why you've been trying to snuff out your life?'

'Was I so obvious?' asked Razor.

Kev nodded 'Guiltiness will speak, though tongues were out of use.'

'What?'

'Actions speak louder than words.'

Razor pondered a moment. 'Was that Shakespeare?'

'Abraham Lincoln this time.'

'How do you know all this stuff? Did you go to a good school?'

'It was approved. No, the truth is I didn't get much schooling, but I read a lot,' said Kev.

'I've never had much time for books,' said Razor. 'I was always too busy trying to pass exams or making a living.'

'It shows,' said Kev with a grin.

'An insult?'

'An observation. I may have had little formal education, but Uncle Bob said if I read, watched, listened and thought I'd get more enjoyment from life. He also reckoned a few beers judiciously applied enhanced the happiness.'

'Are you happy?' asked Razor. 'From my point of view, you've got little and achieved less.'

'I wouldn't say that, mate. I've got what I need, and I achieve what I must.'

'Sounds lame,' Razor insisted, although without the conviction he'd have once had. He knew he'd lost sight of the enjoyment of life. Even worse, he'd neglected the one person who'd made him happy.

'So,' said Kev after a while, when the traffic lights had changed colour several times, 'what are you going to do?'

Razor decided. 'I'm going home. I need to talk to Alex and I should be able to get my key back from him. If not, I'll break in if I must. Thanks for all your help. Goodbye.'

He walked away, a little disappointed Kev had not offered to come with him, for although he didn't dare admit it, he'd found it pleasant to have someone to talk to, despite the infuriating way the little guy spoke in idiotic quotes and stuck his nose in where it wasn't wanted. For the first time in what felt like forever, he had a friend and was finding life almost tolerable.

Nevertheless, Kev's question about Alex had made him curious. He needed an answer. Furthermore, old worries about Flit's fidelity had been rekindled. He hated suspecting her and needed to find out the truth—it was the only thing that would set his mind at rest.

Unless it didn't.

Willoton lay seven or eight-miles along the winding main road from Sorenchester, though he knew of shortcuts across the fields that would cut the journey to about five miles—a two-hour walk or thereabouts. No doubt his belly would be empty when he got there. It would have to stay that way, unless he could get into his house and Kev had left something in the fridge.

At first, he had no option except to walk along the main road, with cars and lorries hurtling past, blasting noise and dirt, but after about fifteen minutes he reached a stile and climbed onto a public footpath signposted to Willoton. The traffic rumble was soon muted.

A rising wind buffeted him and the neglected footpath was deep with mud. He re-estimated his journey time to about three hours as dark clouds blotted out the sunshine. Soon, the first heavy raindrops spattered down. He put his jacket back on, buttoned it up and turned up the collar. Within minutes a full-on downpour engulfed him, washing away all the pleasure of walking, turning the mud to glue. The naked trees and tumbledown stone walls along the way provided little shelter. He feared three hours had been over-optimistic.

The clinging mud sapped energy and willpower and his old-fashioned tweed jacket, though warm enough, retained water like a sponge, weighing him down like a suit of armour. Razor had hoped to use the journey time for thinking, but the storm blew everything away, except his determination to keep going.

His mud-slick dancing shoes slipped halfway down a slope. He crashed onto his back, knocking the wind from his lungs. Unable to stop, he slithered into a hollow filled with icy water. If not for the torment of Flit's death, this would have been a contender for the most miserable moment of his life—even worse than a horrific incident in the Himalayas when he'd sat down to rest after a long trek and had squished a succulent blood-engorged leech between his buttocks. A day or two earlier, he might just have closed his eyes and allowed hypothermia to take him, but something inside had shifted. He had no wish to die until he'd sorted things out. After that, maybe he might even build on his friendship with Kev... and with Miranda.

Dripping wet and chilled, he dragged himself from the puddle and resumed his yomp, as the army called a trek over tricky terrain. The word reminded him that for a short time between university and Flit, he'd considered joining up after an invitation to a mess dinner by an old school-friend. In the end, despite having enjoyed great food and copious wine and the sense of comradeship, the thought of being ordered into some pointless war in a place he'd never heard of, where people wanted to kill him, had dissuaded him. It had been early evidence of his cowardice. If he'd only had a teaspoon of courage, Flit might still be alive.

Trying to muffle the morbid horrors in his head, he counted steps which helped avoid thinking, though it made the tedious trudge seem even longer. Hours later, energy flagging, worrying he'd lost his way, he emerged from a bare brown, hedge-lined field and recognised the outline of Willoton Ridge ahead. How long was it since he'd holed up in the old pillbox? It felt an age, though it was only a few days. He wondered how McGill was doing and a new dagger of guilt stabbed his conscience—he hadn't even thought about the old farmer since that morning. Still, knowing he was approaching the end of the journey gave him a boost, and he found he was marching again, humming snatches of tunes with beats to match his increased pace as he began the climb. The rain diminished to an annoying drizzle as he started back down the slope, the afternoon darkened towards evening and hunger gnawed. At last, he left the fields and turned onto the lane into Willoton.

He trudged into the village, its emptiness suggesting it had reached the quiet time between school pickups and executives driving home from Sorenchester or Pigton. A sign outside the Watermill stated tonight was curry night, and the aroma of hot spice and onions wafting from the kitchen tormented Razor's growling belly. If only he had some money.

A male voice came from the small wooden shed where exiled smokers topped up on nicotine.

'What are you doing here? And what the hell have you been doing to yourself?'

Without a doubt it was Alex.

Shivering, Razor leaned against the car park's dry stone wall and waited.

'I had some bother last night,' said a rough voice that Razor knew but couldn't quite place.

'Your battered face would back that up,' said Alex. 'No wonder you wished to meet out here, though I fail to understand why it should concern me. Just because I have occasionally employed you does not mean I have any interest in what you get up to in your own time. I did not summon you, and have no immediate need of your services, so explain why you are here.'

'Because, Al, the bother might interest you.'

'Kindly refrain from addressing me as Al.'

'Sorry, Mr Bond.'

Razor barely smothered a gasp. The second voice belonged to Kane Cullum.

'That's better,' said Alex. 'Explain what you mean.'

'Well, Mr Bond, the boys and me were out lamping…'

'Get on with it,' said Alex.

'Well, it was like this—you remember that job I did for you in Glevchester?'

'The one you messed up? Of course I remember.'

'It wasn't my fault. I couldn't have known she'd…'

A BMW, its headlights blazing in the gloom, pulled into the car park, its engine drowning out the conversation. Razor ducked out of sight and kept his head down. The driver was Tom Talbot, the failed peacock murderer. Tom parked before escorting his wife, Serena, towards the Watermill's entrance.

'Did you see the fellow lurking by the smokers' bothy?' Serena asked. 'For a moment, I thought it was the poor chap whose wife got killed.'

'He looked more like a tramp, dear. I bet he was looking for something to steal. We ought to mention it to Ron,' said Tom.

Serena nodded and stepped inside.

Razor was dismayed and a little amused that anyone could mistake him for a tramp—not so long ago, he used to pride himself on his smart appearance. Still, he'd enjoyed hearing sympathy in Serena's voice and seeing her again—she still looked incredibly beautiful. It came as a shock to realise that he'd admired her before, and still did—so much for his conviction that he'd only had eyes for Flit. But there was no time to wallow in recrimination—he had to look after himself first. Now he'd stopped walking, his teeth were chattering and his legs had stiffened.

Without heat he knew he'd soon be in big trouble, and trying to get his key back from Alex was out of the question for the moment—he had no desire to run into Kane again.

He remembered the gents' toilets being just

inside the pub's porch. They would provide warmth and, with care and luck, he'd reach them without being seen. He scrambled over the wall into the car park and sneaked towards the front door, though he needn't have bothered—the smokers' sanctuary was now empty. He slipped inside unnoticed, delighted to find the gents unoccupied. After filling a basin with hot water, he immersed his hands before they could freeze into permanent claws. As the mud washed away, warmth spread, making his fingers ache and tingle. He kept his hands in the water as long as he could bear it and dried them under the blower. An idea entered his befuddled brain. Unbuttoning his sodden jacket, he squeezed against the hot air nozzle and luxuriated as warm air circulated around his chilled body. After ten minutes of heat treatment, he was approaching normal body temperature, his face glowing.

Hearing footsteps, he darted into a cubicle and bolted it.

The door of the gent's opened and clicked shut. Razor used a hand to muffle his mouth.

There was a pause, a series of mobile phone beeps and Kane spoke. 'That you, Winston? Yeah, it's me... Have you come to your senses yet? Not even if I pay double? Give us a break, mate... That's your last word is it? Sure you won't reconsider? Right then, I suppose I'll have to do it myself. How's Micky? Good... Bye then.' Kane indulged in a bout of lurid and imaginative swearing.

Metal screeched. Glass shattered. The door opened and shut. Razor waited a moment and emerged from the cubicle as Ron, the landlord, and a barman entered.

Ron looked at where the hand-drier had been. Then he looked at the shattered window. Finally, he looked at Razor. 'Call the police,' he said.

Barging Ron aside, ducking beneath the barman's lunge, Razor legged it.

17

'I didn't do it,' Razor yelled and rammed through a cluster of customers who'd hurried from the bar to see what all the fuss was about. He dodged a half-hearted grab and made it into the car park.

A woman shouted, 'Look out!'

Distracted by the voice, Razor didn't see the reversing Mercedes until it knocked him to the ground. Before it had stopped, he was up and running. He kept going until his already depleted muscles ran completely out of fuel. No one had followed him and with any luck, no one had recognised him—Tom and Serena hadn't been sure and the regulars wouldn't— he'd not visited the Watermill since long before Flit's death.

As he caught his breath behind an old tree, blood dripped from a graze on his forehead and pain caught up with him. Dizzy and with the world feeling distant, it took a few minutes to realise that primeval instinct had directed his feet to the lane outside Riverside Cottage. He hobbled up the path to the front door, desperate to escape the cold wind nipping at his ears and nose, his hands automatically searching pockets for keys his brain already knew weren't there.

Ingenuity was needed. It was the one thing he lacked. Other than the key.

Not expecting anything, he jiggled the front door. It was locked. So were the windows. Perhaps he'd have more luck at the rear, but the back garden gate was bolted. Although this might have daunted a lesser man, Razor took a short run up, jumped, grabbed the top of the gate and hauled himself over. He dropped into the back garden with all the finesse of a sack of bricks and might have hurt himself had he not landed on the stinking pile of rubbish bags he'd still not carried out for collection. It was no surprise to find the back door and windows were also locked.

No cunning plan formed in his tired brain. Putting his hope in brute force, he prised a lump of limestone from Flit's ornamental rockery. Staggering under the weight, he lugged it towards the cottage and launched it at the kitchen window.

It bounced off and only a desperate hop saved him from a crushed foot. The window, other than a circle of white crazing, remained intact and he blamed Flit for insisting they had triple-glazed security glass fitted after a spate of burglaries in the village. With night falling, the temperature dropping and the wind getting up, his situation was becoming critical. Picking up the rock in both hands, he pounded at the windows and door, but his efforts caused only superficial damage.

He saw red. Blood was dripping into his eyes.

Defeated by his own home, his exhausted body collapsed onto the lawn and sought refuge in oblivion.

The sheets smelled clean and fresh, and the bedside light cast a soft glow. A mug of cocoa steamed on the night table at his side. He was in his own bed, wearing fresh pyjamas—the silk ones Flit had bought him in Thailand. It felt good to be home again. He raised a hand to a painful area on his head and touched a large sticking plaster. The clock radio indicated the time was approaching nine o'clock in the evening. Razor suspected Kev of coming to his rescue again, which raised the question of who was the real hero, as well as why the little guy kept turning up. It also increased Razor's chance of eating.

He returned to full wakefulness, sat up and sipped the cocoa. It was warm and perhaps a little too sweet, but it dulled the edge of his hunger even as he failed to fill a void in his memory between trying to break in and ending up in bed. When he'd finished his drink, he checked his feet and was amazed to see little evidence of the cuts—Rocky's treatment of them had been little short of miraculous. Razor got out of bed, wrapped his battered carcass in a bath robe and limped downstairs to look for food and answers.

There were no cooking aromas, just a lingering reminder of decay and dust that made him resolve to look after the place—after he'd sorted things out with Alex. Perhaps he'd get the decorators in and make the house his own, rather than it being a constant reminder of his dead wife. In the shadows at the back of his mind lurked a shocking question—could he build a new relationship with a woman, and could that woman be Miranda?

On reaching the bottom of the stairs, he could almost believe he'd caught a faint whiff of her sweet flowery scent, though that was impossible. Or was it? After all, she had his keys, though how would she have known he'd be in trouble again? How had she known before? How had Kev known? Neither she nor Kev even had mobiles. Perhaps there was a psychic link—Razor had heard of such things, but had always dismissed such fancies as poppycock.

Another thought came to mind—might there be a chance that she really was interested in him? He shook his head—he was nothing special. Besides, she already knew what a bad husband he'd been. Still, just thinking about her made him smile and there was no longer any guilt. Only hope.

The kitchen was empty though a saucepan and teaspoon draining by the sink was evidence of recent occupation. 'Hello,' he called, 'is anybody here?'

Silence.

Though he went from room to room, it soon became clear that he was alone and that the front and back doors were locked. Was he a prisoner in his own home? The idea didn't make him panic though—he lacked the energy.

Returning to the kitchen, he opened the fridge. It contained a loaf of sliced bread, cheese and butter, as well as a carton of milk. At least he wouldn't starve and, luckily, he could rise to making grilled cheese on toast. He put his knowledge into action and had soon wolfed down two slices. When he'd finished, he repeated the procedure twice more until hunger was defeated and he felt human again.

As his energy reserves replenished, his brain resumed normal operations and he remembered Flit insisting on placing duplicate keys close to all the burglar-proof doors and windows in case of fire. They were still in place, except for the one for the back door. Was that the one Alex had taken?

Of course, Razor's reason for returning to Willoton had been to learn about Alex—about Flit and Alex. But was ten o'clock in the evening too late for a social call? Did it matter? What if Kane was still around? In fact, why had Kane been in the village in the first place? How did Alex know such a thug and for what had he used him? Despite his need for answers, Razor dithered.

At last, he dragged himself upstairs and put on one of the sharp suits he used to wear at work, when he'd hoped they would give him an air of authority and professionalism—it had appeared to work for many of the other team managers at Burke and Coe, no matter how incompetent they'd been. Once dressed, a glance in the mirror made him wish he'd thought to shave first—the stubble on his chin and scalp, not to mention the collection of bumps, bruises and scrapes, gave him a thuggish look not quite in keeping with his suit. Would it be better to question Alex in the morning when he'd had time to think, or was delay just another symptom of his cowardice? He didn't need Kev to remind him that he who hesitates is lost. It was time to go.

After heading downstairs, he put on an old coat and a pair of wellington boots and stuck his nose out the front door. A chill wind was wuthering round the house and, although the rain had stopped, a heaviness in the air suggested it might kick off again at the slightest provocation. The moonless night was as dark as a cavern, other than a faint glimmer from the village. Once upon a time, he'd delighted in the lack of light pollution, enjoying the clear nights when myriad stars glittered in a black desert only disturbed by passing aircraft, orbiting satellites and the occasional shooting star. Now the darkness was a curse—reaching Alex's would be tricky and dangerous, without a torch, and his was rolling in the murky depths of the Severn Wharves.

But a hero is not easily deterred and, despite a residual headache, a solution came to mind—Flit had always loved candles. He looked in the kitchen cupboard and found hundreds of them in all sizes, colours and scents beneath a bag of garden cable ties. Much better, though, was an old-fashioned rubber torch. It gave out a bright beam as he set out for the confrontation.

Despite stiffness and aching muscles, he marched at a brisk pace, heading down the lane and turning into the shortcut, a narrow path like a tunnel beneath a dense canopy of conifers. It was squelchy and puddled underfoot, but no problem to a man such as him. Mud spattered up his expensive trousers with every step and it was a surprise how little it bothered him. He had no plan for when he confronted Alex, only a vague hope that the right questions would spring to mind and that Alex would give him the answers he craved.

The path took him out onto the road next to Willoton Hall. Letting himself into the grounds via the gate, he strode down the long gravel driveway, pleased to see Alex's white Lexus in its allocated spot. The hall's front door was locked as he'd expected, but all the doorbells in the porch were lit and labelled. Mr Alexander Bond lived in Apartment 3. Razor pressed the button and waited. There was no response. He rang again and again. It was only just past ten o'clock. Had Alex turned in for the night so early? Or was he still at the Watermill? Plenty of other options crossed his mind, but only one thing mattered—Razor's mission had failed. He might as well go home.

As he retraced his steps, frustration and anger boiled through his veins. Halfway along the shortcut, seeing an empty cola can lying in his path, he swung a furious kick at it. His standing foot skidded, he flung his arms out for balance and the torch broke from his hand. It flew like a low-flying comet and smashed into a tree trunk. The light went out, leaving him in utter darkness. He stood still, not daring to move, hoping his vision would adjust. It didn't, so with no other option, he shuffled forward, arms outstretched like a zombie in a bad horror film, feeling his way. The first few steps went well, and his confidence and speed rose together. Perhaps it wouldn't be too bad after all. Next step, took him calf-deep into oozing mud, with a stagnant stench rising and making him gag. He'd stumbled into the ditch.

As he flailed around for solid ground, thorny branches tore his hands until he found the bank and dragged himself free of the sucking ooze. His boots stayed where they were, and unable to find them, he crawled along the path until it joined the lane where he could just about see enough to walk.

As Razor reached the path to his front door, a light came on upstairs. His spirits leapt. Kev was back... or Miranda. The burly silhouette of a man appearing in the window disappointed him. A burglary was in process and, although a few days earlier it might not have bothered him much, knowing an intruder was violating space that had been sacred to Flit caused his rage to erupt.

Heedless of his unshod feet, he raced to the front door. It was open though he knew he'd locked it. He paused a moment, channelling feelings of outrage into righteous fury. Somebody was going to get hurt. He even considered taking a big knife from the kitchen until the squeamish part of his nature revolted. Instead, treading softly, every step squelching, he sneaked into the sitting room and grabbed the poker from the fireplace. The solid, heavy iron was the perfect implement for whacking burglars.

As he started up the staircase, a step creaked.

'What was that?' asked the voice of Kane Cullum.

Someone replied. Razor didn't catch the words, but it meant there were two burglars—or at least two, and he knew the type of thug Kane hung out with.

'I'll look,' said Kane.

Although Razor considered a tactical withdrawal, his blood was up. Besides, there was no time. He charged, brandishing the poker like a mace, intending to crack skulls and extract bloody revenge for the invasion. His damp socks slipped on the varnished wood as he reached the landing. Losing his footing, his momentum launched him into a forward dive just as Kane emerged from the spare room. Razor's head smacked into Kane's shins. Then came blackness.

When Razor came to, his head was thumping

and covered by a hood. He couldn't move his arms and legs, but it took a few moments to realise someone had tied him to the chair. He struggled.

'I'm glad you're back,' said a muffled male voice. 'It's about time.'

'Where am I?' asked Razor.

'You're in your house.'

'What happened?'

'I was rather hoping you might enlighten me.'

'Right... er,' said Razor, trying to piece together events in his head.

'Who are you with?' the man asked.

'No one,' said Razor, shaking his head and feeling sick.

'Are you sure? I thought for a moment... but never mind. Perhaps you'd be so good as to tell me how you came to be lying unconscious on the landing while my... assistant is at the bottom of the stairs with a poker through his neck.'

'Is he alright?'

'He's fine—other than being dead.'

'Oh,' said Razor, barely containing his stomach. 'Did I do that? I don't remember. I'm sorry he's dead, but he was burgling my house. Presumably that's why you're here.'

'Possibly.'

'What are you going to do with me?' asked Razor.

'Now, there you have me. I only came here to pick up something I need. I never intended anyone to get hurt, let alone killed, but you've put me in a rather delicate situation and I'm yet to decide what to do.'

'How's that?' Razor's nose was tickling. He would have given anything for a free finger to scratch it. 'Why can't you release me and walk away?'

The man laughed. 'You're joking, right? You think I'm going to give you an opportunity to kill me too?'

'I wouldn't do that.'

'Possibly not, but I don't trust you. Why should I? After all, it's not the first time you've been responsible for a death, is it?'

'What do you mean?' asked Razor, panic shooting through his nerves.

'I think you know.'

'No.' Razor shook his head, though he thought he knew what the burglar meant, even though it was impossible.

'You do, but that's beside the point. I have a few problems. Firstly, I haven't found what I'm looking for. Secondly, you have brutally killed my assistant...'

'It was an accident... I think. I don't remember.'

'... and, thirdly, you are a witness.'

'To what? I didn't really see anything. Honest. What are you looking for? Perhaps I can help. There's no money in the house.'

'I don't want your money.'

'There's my wife's jewellery. Let me go, and I'll show you where it is. I have no need for it.'

'You seem very willing to give away your late wife's treasured possessions. But why not? They probably remind you of your guilt.'

'It wasn't my fault... there was this mugger...'

'Really?' said the burglar. 'Then why do you still blame yourself?'

'Who are you?' asked Razor. His head, though still aching, was a little less fuzzy, and he was certain he should know.

'Just a random caller.'

'Who happens to know about Flit's death.'

'She preferred Felicity.'

'How would you know?' Razor, the itch on his nose driving him wild, fought against the ropes, anger taking over from fear.

'I know a great deal. For instance, taking her

to the cinema that night was your pathetic effort to win back her affection after years of neglect.'

'I didn't neglect her.'

'You were never home, except to eat and sleep. Can you deny it?'

'Of course I can. Let me go!' Razor's fury was reaching critical and the only way to release the pressure was to swear, which he did in bucket loads, until his throat dried up, reducing the torrent of cursing to a hoarse trickle.

'When you've quite finished. I didn't come here to upset you.'

'Then why are you here?'

'That would be telling... which may not matter. You have really given me a problem.'

'Good,' said Razor. 'But why?'

'I don't want a witness...'

'But I can't see anything and I don't know anything!'

'... and, finally, I need something to explain Kane's death. I've thought about it and the fact is, and I deeply regret it, that I may not allow you to live. I can see a scenario that should work. It goes something like this. Kane breaks into your house, you confront him and in the ensuing fracas you are both tragically killed. If I set things up in the right way, I'm sure the cops will buy it. Why should they doubt it, Raymondo?'

Slow wheels turned in Razor's brain and something clicked into place. Who knew Flit was Felicity? Who called him Raymondo? Who, according to Kev, had already tried to burgle his house? Who'd been with Kane at the pub? 'Ingenious, Alex,' he said, gratified to hear a sharp intake of breath. 'But, since I'm going to die, can you explain why your voice sounds so funny... I mean the voice you are using now, not your normal one.'

There was a brief pause and Alex spoke, sounding like himself. 'If you must know, I'd stuffed a handkerchief in my mouth. I thought it was working. How did you know it was me?'

'I saw you and Kane at the Watermill... and you just called me Raymondo.'

'That was foolish of me and even more foolish of you to reveal it, since I now have no other option than to kill you.'

'How are you going to do it?' asked Razor, trying to keep his voice calm.

Alex sighed. 'I don't know—I've never done this sort of thing before. Do you have any ideas? Something quick and painless?'

Razor shook his head. He was unsure whether he would still welcome death now there was a faint inkling of hope in his life.

The front doorbell rang.

'Who the hell comes visiting at this time of night?' asked Alex.

Razor shrugged. 'I wasn't expecting anyone.'

Alex swore as the bell rang again. 'Keep quiet and they'll go away.'

'Unless it's the police,' said Razor, hoping for once that it might be.

'Shut up. No, why do you think it might be the police? Have you confessed your despicable behaviour towards Felicity? Or is it about the incident on the bridge? Or something else?'

'What do you mean?' asked Razor. 'I've done nothing… except…'

'Except murder Kane?'

The front door clicked open.

'Hello? I am returned. Is anybody home?' said Kev.

Alex's hand clamped Razor's mouth before he could cry out. 'Keep quiet or die now,' he hissed.

The front door shut and Kev continued his annoying prattle from the hallway. 'If you be not awake, then I'm here to murder sleep. If you are awake, then I bring vittles for the famished… and ale for the parched, for a quart of ale is a dish for a king, wouldn't you say? Though it's not ale, it's lager which was all that was left in the shop… Bloody hell! How did he get here? What's happened?'

Pain exploded into Razor's head. Had he not been bound to the chair, the blow would have floored him. A few moments later, footsteps approached.

'Are you alright, mate?' Kev asked and took off the hood, a cushion cover.

Razor blinked in the light and nodded though blood dripped from his nose down his shirt. He was in his own bedroom. There was no sign of Alex.

'What happened?' asked Kev, looking shocked and worried.

'Alex.'

'The villain… and did he do Kane in as well?'

'That… er… might have been me.'

'T'were well it was done.'

'But I don't know. All I can remember is charging upstairs with the poker… and then this. Can you untie me? My nose is tickling—it's driving me mad.'

'Of course,' said Kev. 'Or rather, no I can't.'

'Why not?'

'He's used cable ties. I'll need a knife.' Kev turned towards the door.

'Don't leave me,' said Razor. 'He's still around.'

'I think not. The window's open, so I reckon he went out that way.' Kev crossed the room and checked. 'Yeah, there are scuff marks on the woodwork... and someone groaning on the lawn.'

'I hope he's broken something,' said Razor with feeling.

'He's broken your trellis and pulled down that nice wisteria.' Kev hurried downstairs and returned with a short, heavy-bladed vegetable knife that sliced through the cable ties with ease.

The circulation returned to Razor's limbs, but he would have struggled to stand without the little guy's help.

'Let's see if Alex is still out there,' said Razor when he'd regained control of his extremities and the pain had diminished. The blood, other than that dripping from his nose, coursed through his body, feeding a growing rage and desire for vengeance. He ran into the spare room and returned, brandishing his cricket bat.

Kev looked at him askance. 'Why, mate?'

Razor laughed. 'I intend to find Alex, and when I do, I'll crack his head like an egg. He deserves it—he wanted to kill me.'

'Then you'll have a genuine reason for running from the police. With his record, they'd believe Kane died accidentally, or because you were defending yourself, but beating a fleeing man to death is murder, even if you were provoked earlier.'

Although he knew Kev was right, Razor struggled to suppress the fury inside.

'Before you do anything else,' said Kev, 'I would recommend contacting the emergency services. If you don't, it will look as if you've got something to hide.'

Razor shouldered his bat, remembering how he'd bought it just after moving to Willoton and thought he might join the village cricket team. It was still unused. He forced the fury back to anger and tried to think. 'Good point, but you'd better call the police while I look for Alex before he gets too far away. I promise not to take a swing, unless he has a go at me first.'

'I can't do that,' said Kev.

'Why not?'

'You haven't paid the bill so your telephone has been cut off, and you smashed your mobile.'

'Good point. Perhaps Kane has one?'

'Perhaps,' said Kev. 'Go and see.'

'Not me.' Razor's squeamishness overwhelmed him.

'Nor me. I will not touch him while he is yet warm.'

An idea popped into Razor's head. 'You could use the one in the village. It's a museum piece with a dial, but it still works.'

'But I have no loose change.'

'You won't need any. Just dial 999.'

Kev looked embarrassed. 'I can't talk to the police.'

'Don't be so damned stupid! It's not difficult.' Angry, Razor swung the bat and knocked a splinter of wood from the door frame. At least he hadn't taken a swipe at Kev. As he forced down the rage, he could almost believe he could hear Flit's voice telling him to adopt a calmer outlook. It gave him a sense of power and decisiveness he'd believed lost. 'Alright, Kev, I don't understand your problem, but I'll accept that you can't, or won't, do it. That being the case, I'll check the bastard isn't lying injured somewhere. If he is, I'll come straight back and call for the emergency services myself. How about that?'

'Okay,' said Kev. 'I'll come too.'

'Don't bother, I can handle this and I don't need a guardian angel. If he's injured, I won't hurt him anymore, but I will defend myself if I must.'

Without waiting to even put on shoes, Razor marched downstairs, intending to be true to his word, even though part of him hoped Alex might provoke him into mindless, vengeful violence.

Kane's crumpled corpse sprawled at the bottom of the stairs like a grotesque rug. Averting his eyes, though his gorge rose, Razor stepped over, made his way into the kitchen, unlocked the back door and strode out into the darkness, swinging the cricket bat like a battle axe. Fearing that only blood would quench the primeval rage burning inside, he hoped Kev's wise counsel might damp the murderous impulse should he come across Alex.

Razor called out for Alex without reply. Other than a distant shriek from Launcelot, the only sounds were his own heavy breathing and the murmur of the wind.

He tried again. 'Alex, mate, are you hurt?'

No answer, but had that faint murmur been the wind, or a muted groan?

'We ought to talk,' said Razor.

The faint noise, now more like a hum, sounded as if it was coming from the shadows of the house to his right. As Razor stepped towards it, his bat raised, his socked foot smacked into the ruined trellis. He yelped, stumbled and fell into Flit's prized wisteria with all the grace of a concrete slab. The hum became an angry buzz. He groaned.

A soft, soothing voice reached his ears. 'If you stay still and take care, I think you'll be alright, my lovely.'

'Miranda, is that you? I stubbed my toes.'

'Serves you right for not looking where you're going and for running around in your socks. Why?'

'Why what?'

'Why were you running around in your socks while wielding an offensive weapon?'

'It's only my cricket bat!'

'I know little of the game, but I know you don't play it on your own in the dark while shouting.'

'Perhaps not, but it's not an offensive weapon—it's defensive.'

Miranda's silence was sceptical.

Razor couldn't see her unless she was the slightly darker shade of night. 'What's that buzzing noise?'

'Wasps.'

'Oh, hell!'

'The poor things' nest appears to have come down with that trellis and you've put your foot in it.'

Razor squirmed. 'They're on my legs—they're crawling up my trousers!'

'Well, don't provoke them,' said Miranda.

Razor's question erupted like a shriek. 'What can I do?'

'Calm down. They'll be lethargic in this cool weather—until your body heat warms them up.'

'Then what?' Razor squirmed.

'Then they might become a little frisky.'

Razor swallowed, and only Miranda's presence stopped him from springing to his feet and running around swatting and screaming.

Her cool, soft hand helped him to stand. 'It'll be easier to deal with them in the light. Come along.'

He adopted a slow, stiff-legged shuffle as she

led him towards the back door. They stepped inside. Miranda removed her black cloak while Razor kept as still as a statue below, while his upper body writhed with terror. He prayed for a quick and painless escape from the crawling, prickling sensation all over his calves.

'Ah mistress, what's here?' asked Kev, looking up from a book.

'Mr Razor's trousers are full of wasps,' said Miranda.

Kev looked him up and down and chuckled. 'Why, what a wasp-stung and impatient fool, art thou.'

'The wasps are relaxed and not inclined to fight,' said Miranda.

'T'were well done,' said Kev with a nod, and glanced at Razor. 'Did you find him?'

'Find who?' asked Miranda.

'Alex,' Razor explained, forcing himself not to scratch. 'He's a friend... or was... sort of. I wanted to ask him something, but he'd gone.'

'And the cricket bat?'

'It really was for protection... he'd tied me to a chair and hit me earlier. That's why I'm so bloody and battered...'

Miranda's look was dubious.

'... but that's not important now,' Razor

continued, 'I've got wasps!'

'His tale is strange but true,' said Kev. 'It appears Alex jumped from the window when I turned up. I didn't know I was so scary.'

'Stop fidgeting and drop your trousers,' said Miranda.

'You impudent hussy!' said Kev, mock shocked.

'This is... er... a little embarrassing,' said Razor, fiddling with the waist button and zip.

'Nonsense, my lovely. I've already bathed you. Anyway, you can trust me—I'm a doctor.'

'No, you're not,' said Kev, shaking his head. 'And you shouldn't pretend... remember Bournemouth?'

Miranda smiled. 'No sudden movements now.'

Razor let his trousers down, hoping he wasn't blushing too much.

'Step out of them carefully.'

Herds of yellow and black stingers rampaged all over his lower limbs, and he could not suppress a childish squeal. He suspected it had not impressed Miranda.

'Come, come, you wasp; i' faith, be not too angry,' said Kev, bending and holding out his hand. Several of the yellow-jacketed villains crawled aboard and he took them to the back door and out into the garden.

'Why didn't you just kill them?' Razor asked when he returned.

'Because there was no need,' said Kev. 'None has stung you, have they?'

'Not yet,' said Razor, unwilling to appear too pathetic in Miranda's eyes, and doing his utmost to keep a brave and calm expression on his face. Kev reached out his hand for more of the insects, who were, much to Razor's astonishment and relief, peaceful.

'There you go, mate,' said Kev after transporting them. 'I have successfully removed all the little blighters and returned them to the nest, though the poor devils won't last much longer at this time of year.'

Miranda, who'd been observing the procedure with amusement, ran her gaze over Razor. 'You're covered in mud and blood. Go upstairs, wash yourself and slip into some clean clothes. And then you can come back down and slip into a dry martini.' She winked.

Razor wasn't so sure about Miranda's suggestion—after a James Bond film fiesta, he'd once ordered a vodka martini, shaken not stirred and had not enjoyed the experience.

Sophistication, despite attempts to impress at Burke and Coe, did not suit him and beer remained his tipple of first choice, though he enjoyed a good malt whisky on occasions.

Amazed and mystified that he'd survived the encounter without a single sting, he trudged upstairs, stripped and washed before putting on some old jeans, a sweatshirt and a battered pair of trainers he'd forgotten he owned. On returning to the kitchen, he found Kev and Miranda chatting at the table. Her grin caused Razor a moment of embarrassment, not to mention a tremor of excitement before habit kicked in and made him berate himself, though he'd started to accept Flit's loss and knew she wouldn't have wanted him to live the rest of his life like a monk. Sucking in his belly and standing tall, he grinned back, thinking how pretty Miranda looked, despite her dark shapeless clothing and pale face. He knew so little about her but with luck, he'd find out more.

'I think I'll pass on the dry martini,' he said, 'but I'd like something.'

Kev opened the fridge. 'Lager?'

'Since there's no bitter. If either of you want anything else, there may be wine in the cabinet in the lounge. There's no whisky.'

'We're fine,' said Kev, handing a can to Razor.

'Who is Alex and why did he tie you up?' Miranda asked as Razor took a seat.

'He was my wife's colleague and...' said Razor. He might have said more, but was struck by a sudden thought. 'What happened to Kane?'

'Would that be Kane Cullum?' asked Miranda, her beautiful eyes fixed on Razor who nodded.

'He looked messy lying there,' said Kev, 'and was also a tripping hazard. He'd cooled a little, and I'd found some rubber gloves, so I tidied him away.'

Razor wondered if he was dreaming—you did not just tidy away bodies.

'There was less blood than you might have imagined,' Kev continued.

Razor's face must have shown his bafflement.

'Which means the poker in his neck didn't kill him, mate.'

'Then what did?' asked Razor, disconcerted by Kev's casual attitude and Miranda's lack of concern.

'A broken neck,' said Kev. 'His head was all floppy.'

'From the fall?' asked Razor, shuddering.

'I'd guess so, mate, but what puzzles me is that

the poker had clearly been driven in post-mortem.'

'Alex must have done it,' said Razor, hoping that was true. 'But why?'

'To make sure he was dead?' Kev suggested.

'Or stayed that way,' said Miranda with a grin.

Although Razor took it as a joke, something about the way she'd said it worried him. To hide it, he took a massive slurp of lager and spent the next minute choking and spluttering, with Kev thumping his back and Miranda watching the theatricals with apparent amusement.

'Enough!' Razor gasped when Kev's pounding seemed likely to drive his lungs through his front.

'Are you better now?' Kev asked.

Afraid of further violence, Razor nodded, though his eyes were dripping, and he was still prone to paroxysms of coughing. He turned to Miranda. 'Did you know Kane?'

'Sadly, I was acquainted with both him and his horrible brother. I do not mourn their passing.'

Razor would have liked to spend the rest of the evening with her but there was business to attend to first. 'I'd better look for Alex—I need to talk to him. Where's my bat?'

'In your belfry?' said Miranda.

Razor got to his feet. 'My cricket bat!'

'It's where you dropped it, I expect.'

He walked to the back door and looked out. 'It's so dark.'

'The sort of black night that's perfect for a ghouls' night out,' said Miranda, straight-faced.

'True enough,' said Kev, as Razor turned to stare at her, 'though I doubt they'd venture this far from town when there are plenty of closer feeding places. They're not great walkers.'

'You two are crazy,' said Razor, trying to laugh it off.

Miranda smiled but Kev stayed serious. Razor sought sanity in practicalities. 'Do either of you have a torch? I've lost mine.'

'I've got a small one,' said Kev.

'So I've heard,' said Miranda, raising her eyebrows.

Kev looked pretend affronted as he drew a torch from his pocket. 'It's bright for its size.'

'Which is more than could be said of you.' Miranda grinned.

Razor took it with thanks and went into the garden. The first thing he noticed, other than the legion of foraging slugs on nocturnal manoeuvres, was that his cricket bat had gone.

The second was a trail of footprints in the sodden grass leading towards the fields at the back.

Razor took up the pursuit, confident he'd catch him, but less certain what would happen afterwards. If Alex was stupid enough to believe he'd got away with burgling Razor's house, tying him to a chair, hitting him and leaving a dead thug at the bottom of the stairs, then he had another think coming, and although the still small voice of reason suggested that a sensible man would call the police, a cold hard lust for vengeance shouted it down. 'Ready or not, here I come!'

Moonlight came and went as clouds scudded past, but Kev's little torch cut through the darkness and drizzle, though its beam was not as wide as he might have wished. Razor picked out Alex's trail up to the garden wall and along the river side. He followed, alert and excited, chuckling when he reached a spot where the bank had crumbled—the marks suggested Alex had got a shoe full of cold water. A muddy patch of flattened grass showed where he'd scrambled out.

Razor followed. He'd supposed Alex would run for home, but his trail turned across a ploughed field, heading upwards towards Willoton Ridge. After a few minutes, he began to suspect Alex was heading for the old pillbox, though why, when his home was nearer?

As he approached the scrubby woodland around the summit of the ridge, Razor stumbled on a tussock. He fell to his hands and knees. A dazzling flash cut through the darkness, accompanied by the retort of a gun.

He pressed his body to the ground and switched off the torch.

19

Razor moulded himself into the mud and lay still, waiting for whatever came next.

Nothing happened.

After a few minutes, he could almost have believed he'd imagined it. Had it been an isolated flash of lightning and the rumble of thunder? Or another careless shot from Farmer McGill out hunting? He rather hoped the latter might be the case—it would mean the old farmer was alive and well, and that Razor's exertions had been successful. But deep down he knew the real truth—Alex had tried to kill him. Somehow he'd known the shotgun was concealed up there; the stinging of the side of Razor's neck and a trickle of blood confirmed he'd come close to succeeding.

Since staying there meant he was still in range, it made sense to get away—though how far away did he have to be for safety? Slithering like a snake, Razor started down the hill.

The treacherous clouds parted and the moon shone through.

'I can see you, Raymondo,' said Alex. 'The game's up. Get to your feet, put your hands on your head and don't try anything silly.'

Hoping he was muddy enough to merge with the field, Razor stayed still, but squelchy footsteps approached. Alex was standing over him, gripping the shotgun, finger on the trigger, McGill's cartridge bag slung over his shoulder.

'Get up. Now!'

Razor stood and placed his hands on his head. Although he trembled, his mind felt clear of fear and he wondered if it had always been braver than his cowardly body.

'That's better,' said Alex. 'I can't bear to see a grown man grovel.'

'I wasn't grovelling. I was trying to remain inconspicuous.'

'To be fair, Raymondo, it wasn't a bad attempt. I almost thought I'd imagined you. Why were you following me?'

'I wanted to talk.'

'A nice little chat between old friends?' Alex laughed.

'I have a few questions.'

'Fair enough. I have one for you too, but, please, ask away.'

'Would you mind pointing that thing elsewhere?'

Alex glanced at the shotgun and shook his head. 'I don't believe I can trust you. You were threatening to smash my head in not so long ago.'

'I wouldn't have,' said Razor. 'The bat was for self-defence.'

'Liar. I could hear you muttering—you're quite inventive.'

'You were still in the garden?'

'Behind the rockery. I've never dropped from an upstairs window before, and my ankles hurt.'

'Are you alright?' Razor asked.

'Pretending concern? She said you did that.'

'Who did?'

'Felicity. She was a good woman and deserved better than you.'

Razor clenched his fists, cold fury reasserting dominance over his emotions. 'Someone like you, you mean?' He took a step forward.

Alex raised the shotgun. 'Don't even think about it.'

Razor forced himself into a superficial calmness. 'I never understood what she saw in you.'

'What do you mean?' asked Alex.

'You and Flit.'

'We were colleagues. That's all.'

'Yeah… right,' Razor growled.

'It's true. We were friendly, but nothing more.'

Razor shook his head. 'Then why did she spend so much time with you after work?'

'If you'd ever paid attention to her, you would have known what a mess the company was in. We were doing our best to stop it going under. It meant we often had to work late.'

'You were having an affair.'

'Don't be ridiculous,' said Alex.

'What do you mean ridiculous? She was an attractive woman.'

'Attractive? Is that all you can say? She was gorgeous.'

'So why ridiculous?'

Alex sighed. 'I can't have… relationships anymore.'

'What the hell do you mean?'

'I had a motorbike smash a few years back. There was nerve damage. The thing is I can't… well, you know?'

Razor almost felt sympathetic, almost believed the preposterous story. 'Flit said you had lots of girlfriends.'

'Yes, but all strictly platonic. Felicity—she

hated you calling her Flit, was good fun. I never understood why you neglected her.'

The wind brought a spattering of rain. Dark tendrils of cloud flickered across the moon and Razor bared his teeth like a dog, anger masking the underlying guilt. 'I never neglected her, and if I wasn't with her as much as I wanted it was only because I was working so hard to make money so we could have good times together.'

Alex shook his head. 'Come off it, Raymondo. Stop trying to pretend you were a good husband. FYI you weren't.'

'I did my best.'

'Once maybe, before you turned into a money-grubbing workaholic.'

'Everything of mine I gave to her.'

'Except the things she wanted. You were hopeless.'

A scudding cloud blacked out the moon. Razor lunged, grabbing the shotgun by both barrels and twisting it from Alex's grip. As it dropped, Alex fought back like a maniac, battering Razor with a deluge of punches. Although Razor's extra weight and strength took Alex to the ground, he would have been in trouble had he not used his head—he rammed it into Alex's face. The moon came back out, shining a spotlight on Alex, who was spreadeagled in the mud, groaning.

Razor had won the battle at the cost of a split lip and a grazed forehead; he was grinning as he got to his feet—he'd come out on top in a real brawl again. He punched the air and whooped before he remembered the shotgun.

Too late.

Fast as a striking snake, Alex rolled over, grabbed it and took aim. Razor backed away, hands up.

Alex got to his feet breathing hard. 'Sorry, Raymondo. I don't want to do this, but I've got to end it now. I'll tell the police you attacked me and threatened me. In the ensuing struggle the gun went off and, regrettably, you were killed. The best part is that it's essentially true—and I have the bruises to prove it. I will, of course, also ensure you're blamed for Kane's sad demise. I never intended to hurt anybody, but you've forced me into an impossible position, and when I've finished with you, I suppose I'll have to work out what to do with your little friend.'

'I suppose so,' said Razor, gulping, breathing hard and failing to find comfort in knowing the end was nigh. 'I can see how murdering me would seem logical from your point of view. Oh, well, you've won and I've lost. Do what you must, but would you mind answering just one question first?'

'Maybe. Unless it's about numbers. I was never much good with them—not a good thing for an accountant to admit.'

'What were you looking for if it wasn't money?' Razor asked.

'Something else.'

'Go on.'

'A memory stick.'

'One of those data things you put in a computer?'

'Well done, Raymondo. Felicity said you were a duffer with technology.'

'I know what I need to know… but why did you want it?'

'Let's just say Felicity had put something on it that I'd rather wasn't left hanging around for any Tom, Dick or Raymondo to find.'

'But if it was in our house, how come I've never seen it?'

Alex scoffed. 'You have to ask? Tidying up was never your strong point, was it?'

'But why didn't you ask me to help find it? I would have done. What's on it? What have you done?'

'I have no intention of telling you,' said Alex, his voice hardening. 'Enough of this banter. I hope you are prepared to meet your maker.'

Razor watched as Alex brought the gun up to his shoulder.

'This thing's got a hell of a kick,' Alex remarked as if enjoying a normal conversation. 'It knocked me flat on my back last time.'

'Good,' said Razor, 'and I hope it gave you a bloody good bruise.'

'Be nice,' said Alex. 'Again, Raymondo, I'm sorry. I wish things hadn't worked out like this though you probably deserve it for what you did to Felicity.'

'What did I do?'

Alex shook his head and took aim. Razor imagined his finger tightening on the trigger and awaited death. Perhaps it was for the best. Perhaps he deserved to die, but even in his final moments, he couldn't stop thinking about what might be so important to Alex that he was prepared to kill for it. Not that it mattered anymore because he'd never know. He wished Alex would get on with it—the waiting was always worst. At least he hoped so.

A shadow, as fast and lithe as a cat, darted

across his line of vision.

He never heard the bang.

Razor could taste blood from a split lip, but there was no pain elsewhere—at least no more than previously. Not having expected to be anywhere, it was confusing to be somewhere smelling musty and damp. The blanket enfolding him was warm as he sat up and stared at the old brick wall in front. 'Where am I?'

'The old pillbox on the ridge. Thou has slept well, my lord.'

'Kev?'

'That's right, mate.' Kev walked round the ricochet wall. 'How are you?'

'Okay in the circumstances. What am I doing here? Alex was going to blow me away. He couldn't have missed.'

'The evidence suggests he could have.' said Kev.

'But he was pointing the gun right at me from two steps away.'

'Perhaps you were snatched from harm's way.'

Razor forced a laugh. 'By what? My guardian angel or something?'

'She's no angel.'

'Miranda?'

'Who else?'

Just to see her and talk to her was everything Razor wanted in that moment. 'Where is she? I'd like to thank her. Is she alright?'

Kev shrugged. 'Not sure.'

'You're not sure where she is or whether she's alright?' asked Razor, experiencing a sudden chill of fear.

'I reckon she's alright, mate, but she comes and goes as she wants. Sometimes I don't see her for months.'

'Months?' said Razor, disappointed. 'Why? What does she do? Where does she go?'

'I've never asked. I doubt she'd tell me.'

'Has she got something to hide?'

Kev shrugged. 'Perhaps everybody has something to hide, but she hides it well. Don't worry—she will turn up sooner or later. Probably.'

Razor had no choice but to accept the situation. He tried to think. 'What are we doing in here?'

'It was the nearest shelter when the rain came back, and it wasn't a gentle rain from heaven— it absolutely pissed down.'

'And Alex?'

'Is at rest,' said Kev.

'She killed him?'

'What kind of woman do you think she is?'

'A dangerous one,' said Razor. He might also have added a powerful one, a pretty one and an exciting one, before listing all the other qualities he hoped he saw in her and found delightful.

'True. I suspect she may have killed Liam in the wharves—she won't say, but she had reasons. Though she looks like an innocent flower, she is deadly as a serpent underneath, if only to those that deserve her wrath.'

'Talk properly. What's she done to Alex?'

'Rendered him immobile. I know not how, but I doubt she sang him sweet lullabies.'

'Where is he?'

'On the far side.'

'Is that some bizarre way of saying he's dead?'

Kev laughed. '... he's on the other side of the wall.'

'Oh, right.' Razor scratched his head, dislodging a small spider. He shuddered. 'Have you any idea what happened?'

'No, mate. I wasn't there.'

Razor nodded, though something made him

suspect Kev of knowing more than he was letting on—not for the first time.

'Do you fancy a coffee?' Kev changed the subject. 'I brought a thermos.'

'Please.'

'It's only instant, and there are also cheese and pickle sandwiches, if you're peckish. I know I am.'

'That would be great.' Razor's stomach rumbled as Kev went behind the wall to fetch them. 'Any idea of the time? My watch has stopped. I hope it's not broken—it was a birthday present from Flit.'

'We heard the chimes of midnight an hour ago or more, and thus from now until the break of day we must abide four or five hours.'

'Where's the light coming from? Candles?'

'Our source of illumination until we say good morrow to the sun is a paraffin lamp,' said Kev returning with a bag.

'If we get to see the sun tomorrow. Listen to that rain!'

'Yeah, it's bad,' said Kev. 'I wouldn't recommend going out and reckon we're stuck here until we see this morning's face.'

'With Alex? He's still dangerous.'

'I know, mate,' said Kev, a worried look

328

crossing his face. 'I wish Miranda was still here.'

'But she's...' Razor paused, pulling the blanket closer. 'So do I.' He accepted a cup of coffee and a sandwich.

Afterwards, feeling more alive, he got to his feet and walked around the pillbox to stretch his tired muscles. It was infuriating to see Alex, tucked in a blanket, sleeping, with only his face poking out. He was smiling like a saint, as if he hadn't just attempted murder.

'Kev, where's the shotgun?' Razor whispered.

'It's hidden along with the cartridge bag,' said Kev.

'Where?'

'I don't know, mate, I didn't hide them. Why do you ask? You don't want it, do you?'

Razor shook his head. 'I'm worried about Alex getting his hands on it again.'

'But you don't want to use it?'

'Why would you even think such a thing?'

'Because you were going to smash his skull in a couple of hours ago.'

'Well, I won't do it now. However, I'd like to have it handy—as insurance in case he tries anything.'

'When he wakes, he may indeed try

something, but there are two of us and you're bigger than him.'

'Still,' said Razor, 'the gun would have been a useful backup.'

'Have you ever fired one?'

'Of course.'

'When?'

'At the Country Fayre, two or three years back.'

'How did you get on?'

'I was shooting at clay pigeons and they moved ever so fast, but the guy in charge said I came really close to hitting one.'

'Well done,' said Kev. 'What about the kick?'

'Yeah, that was unexpected. I only fired ten shots and got an amazing bruise on my shoulder.'

Kev nodded. 'So what you're telling me is that you repeatedly missed your target and hurt yourself. Besides, they use low-recoil cartridges at events like that, not the heavy ones used by hunters. If you fired it, I reckon you'd end up on your back or with a haematoma. I also suspect your chances of hitting a target would be remote, so it's better it's out of harm's way.'

Razor scratched his chin. 'Okay, but when this

is over I'd like to return it to Mr McGill.'

'Farmer McGill died,' said Kev.

'I didn't know,' said Razor, shocked and flooded with guilt—he'd known he should have done so much more.

Kev continued. 'The lady running the shop said the old boy had suffered a massive heart attack. Somehow he found his way home, but when he got there, he ran into a burglar who tied him up. When Mrs McGill returned from her yoga class, it was too late.'

'I hope they catch the bastard,' said Razor.

'I suspect it might be too late for that,' said Kev.

'Why?'

'Well, can you think of a housebreaker around here who met a sticky end tonight?'

'You mean…'

Kev nodded. 'Kane. Burglary with violence was always top of his CV, and he has—had no conscience whatsoever.'

'Why did you move the body, and where is it?'

'After all the time I spent tidying up your house, I couldn't bear the mess. I stuffed him in the broom cupboard.'

'I have a broom cupboard?'

Kev nodded.

Razor, feeling weirdly euphoric, tried to be serious. 'We'll have to do something about it when we get back.'

'The broom cupboard?'

'The body!'

'That's to worry about later, mate. Happy is the man who has broken the chains which hurt the mind, and has given up worrying once and for all.'

Razor didn't know what to say until something scratched at the door. 'What the hell is that?'

'Badgers?' Kev suggested.

It sounded bigger to Razor.

The door juddered open a notch.

20

The ancient hinges creaked and the rusting door slammed shut. Nothing had entered except a blast of night air.

'Wind?' Razor suggested, his heart racing.

'Sorry about that—it's my nerves.' Kev gave an uncertain chuckle.

'It's a heavy door,' said Razor. 'Could the wind really have done that?'

'I know not,' said Kev, biting his lip.

'There's a nasty draught in here,' Alex whined, making them both jump. 'I'm cold.'

When Kev handed him another blanket and a cup of coffee, he took them without a word of thanks.

Razor noticed and his uneasiness edged towards anger. He knew it happened too often, and he could slip into it as easily as he could into a favourite T-shirt. In a moment of insight, he knew he hadn't always been this way—it had only developed after his promotion at Burke and Coe, when work and pressure had piled up. Although in theory his new position had allowed him to delegate, he'd found power addictive and had hated giving any away and losing control. Within weeks, the fuse on his temper had shortened though on the whole he'd retained enough self-control to avoid inappropriate outbursts at work. Too often, he'd vented his frustrations onto Flit. Shame and regret filled him. Alex was right—he really hadn't been as good to her as he'd believed.

As if on cue, Alex moaned about the coffee being too hot.

'Shut up!' Razor roared, his voice reverberating. 'I've had just about enough of you. Give me one reason and I'll...'

Alex stared, open mouthed, a trickle of coffee on his chin.

'Calm down, mate.' Kev placed a hand on Razor's arm. 'The man's had a trying night, and it's no wonder he's upset.'

'Yeah, he tried to shoot me, but okay—as long as he keeps quiet,' said Razor, mastering the rage. 'I've had some trying months, so he'd better not bother me anymore tonight.'

'I'm sure he'll behave,' said Kev, giving Alex a look.

Alex nodded, his eyes wide.

Though having the upper hand made part of him feel superior and strong, the better part of Razor hated how easy it was to fall into bad old ways. He resolved to transform into a better person when this business had run its course. Looking back on recent days, he suspected he might not be made of the right stuff for a hero, but nothing could stop him becoming a good Samaritan—there were always people needing a helping hand. Furthermore, he might impress Miranda.

'I'll take a look outside,' said Kev. 'I don't know why the door opened, but it could have been a homeless person looking for shelter and when they saw it occupied, they left. It's too horrible a night for anyone to be out.'

'Alright, but be careful,' Razor agreed, trying to be charitable though not fancying sharing the confined space with a wet tramp.

Kev pushed the door. Nothing happened. He tried again and grunted.

Razor sighed and nudged the little guy out the way. He shoved, barged and jiggled the door. 'It's stuck,' he concluded.

'We can't get out,' said Kev.

'What's happening?' asked Alex.

Razor glared. 'Didn't I tell you to shut up?'

Alex cringed.

'This might mean real trouble,' said Kev. 'There's no other way out.'

'The windows?'

'They're embrasures for shooting from and they're far too small.'

'Let's see. I'll give you a leg up.' Razor squatted and linked his fingers into a step.

Though Kev looked sceptical, he gave it a try. 'No chance, mate. I can't even get my shoulders through, never mind anything else.'

Razor set him down. 'Oh well. If we must, we can break through the wall—the old bricks are already crumbling.'

'Yeah, but that's just the lining. They built these things with a core of reinforced concrete—we'd need a sledgehammer at least.'

'Or we could use Alex's head,' said Razor with an evil grin.

Alex winced.

Kev slumped into a corner. 'We're stuck here.'

'No, I reckon Miranda will turn up,' said Razor, with a glow, hotter than the heat of anger filling his heart.

Kev brushed a cobweb from his face. 'She might never come this way again. I don't suppose Alex has a mobile?'

'I did, but I must have dropped it when I went out the window,' Alex whispered, keeping a wary eye on Razor.

'So what are we going to do?' asked Kev.

'Sleep on it,' said Razor and yawned. 'We weren't going anywhere tonight, anyway. We'll be fine.'

Kev looked unconvinced, but Razor had confidence they'd find a way out in the morning when they could see what they were doing and, if they couldn't, they could always shout for help. Someone would hear them—there were numerous dog walkers in the vicinity. It was just that he hadn't seen many round here.

Alex groaned. 'We can't stay here all night. It's crawling with spiders.'

'Frightened of a poor little spider? It wouldn't hurt a fly,' said Kev and grinned.

'Idiot.' Razor forced a chuckle, trying to appear nonchalant.

Alex bit his lip and stared at the big black hairy thing dangling over his head. 'I want to get out.'

'You've got far more to worry about than that, and if you don't stop moaning, I'll give you something to really moan about,' Razor threatened, echoing a phrase his grandmother had used. She'd never meant it.

Alex clutched his blankets and rolled against

the wall.

Although Razor's exhausted body craved sleep, he feared Alex and had no wish to wake up with his head smashed in by a brick. 'We'd better keep an eye on him, Kev,' he said in a loud voice. 'We'll take turns.'

'I don't think it's worth it.' Kev reached for a blanket.

'Explain,' said Razor, aware of Alex listening.

'He's no fool and has no wish to be entombed. We'll stand far more chance of getting out if all three of us work together. If anyone is incapacitated, there'll be little chance of the others escaping. Am I right?'

Razor nodded.

Kev glanced at Alex. 'You won't try anything, will you?'

Alex shook his head.

'Good,' said Kev.

A question that had been skulking in the dim recesses of Razor's brain stepped forward. 'How did you know about the shotgun?'

Alex looked up. 'I overheard Kane telling one of the gang about it on his mobile. He'd stumbled across it when he was hiding stolen goods up here. That's all I know because I made sure to distance myself from that sort of thing.'

Razor nodded. 'Okay. We should try to sleep now.'

'I'm... er... sorry, but I need the bathroom,' said Alex miserably. 'I can't hold it much longer—what should I do?'

'Use the corner,' said Razor.

Alex unwrapped himself from the blankets, looking thin and feeble as he unbuttoned his trousers. 'There's no paper.'

'Then you'll just have to improvise.' Kev grimaced at Razor and they left Alex to his side of the partition.

After a noisy, smelly interlude, they settled down. Razor thought of the happy times with Flit before his ambition drove a wedge between them.

The lantern flickered and went out. 'What's it done that for?'

'Ran out of paraffin I expect,' said Kev. 'There wasn't much left when I came out, but it was the only thing I could find at your place, apart from smelly candles.'

'It's mine is it? I didn't know I'd got one. What about the torch you gave me?'

'Not a clue, mate—you had it last. I just wish I'd brought some candles, but I was already overladen.'

'So, we're stuck in the dark. Great.'

'Until the morning steal upon the night, melting the darkness.'

'Better make the most of it then. I'm glad you brought some blankets. Are there any more?'

'Sorry. Miranda suggested I might need some, but I could only carry three,' said Kev. 'Alex has two.'

Razor sighed. 'I have no intention of going round his side in the dark.'

'Nor me, so we'd better make the most of the one we've got.'

They groped around for dry leaves, scooped them into a pile, and lay down side by side, covering themselves as best they could. Despite the cold and the rain drumming outside, Kev was soon dozing. Razor did his best not to disturb him though the leaves flattened into awkward bumps and there'd never been enough for two bodies. He shivered beneath a meagre portion of blanket, his brain wide awake, his body exhausted.

His mind kept looping, bringing up old memories and examples of his own insufferable behaviour. Deep down, he'd always known Flit had little interest in money, and that his attempts to show off by laying the rewards of long hours of labour at her feet had not impressed her. Too often he'd been away on business or had come home late, scarcely giving a thought to her needs and how she occupied her time. There'd been many occasions during the last months of her life when she'd tried to engage him in a proper conversation and tell him something important, but his own cares had consumed almost all of his attention. Even so, he'd known something wasn't right and that Alex was involved, which was why he'd suspected an affair—it was part of the reason he hadn't wanted to listen.

Fearing losing her, he'd devised the brilliant plan of treating her to a night out, just like they used to enjoy. He'd hoped it would draw them back together. In retrospect, it seemed a feeble response though he had only intended it as a first step on the way to improving things between them. He should, however, have let her know. Instead, he'd decided to surprise her, and had come home early, filled with his own virtue. She wasn't in, her mobile wasn't working, and when she got back, it was too late for the theatre and the meal he'd planned. His disappointment had turned to fury, even when she pointed out that the battery on her mobile had died and she'd had no way of knowing he'd return three hours earlier than normal. He'd as good as accused her of having an affair. It was now clear she'd been innocent. Even if she'd wanted one, Alex was incapable of sex.

Or so he said.

Razor's thoughts returned to the past. A week after the failed theatre trip, when his temper had cooled, he'd suggested a visit to the cinema. This time, he told her in advance, made the effort to leave work on time, picked her up at home and drove them to Glevchester. How could it have gone so wrong?

He tried not to toss and turn, hoping the itch on his belly was just that and not a wriggling centipede or worse. Before meeting Flit, he'd been a lonely young man in a strange new town. She'd brought happiness into his life, until he'd started taking her for granted and had allowed ambition to turn him into an angry, workaholic pig. After that, he'd played the role of grieving widower, suicidal hero and had then come perilously close to becoming a thug—even if he could just about convince himself that those who'd experienced the blunt force of his rage had deserved it.

Throughout it all, thoughts of Miranda kept coming back. She was amazing, despite unfashionable clothing, a complete lack of makeup and appearing to have never visited a hairdresser. Still, something about her troubled and intrigued him. First, her apparently frail body held so much strength. Second, she kept turning up when he was in trouble. Third, she, like Kev, seemed so blasé about death. He didn't understand her and, in truth, was a little afraid of her. Nevertheless, he wished she was sharing the blanket with him—he'd put money on her not snoring and twitching as much as Kev.

'Shut up!' Razor muttered, trying to get comfortable without waking him.

More thoughts entered the loop. How had the door opened? Had someone really been out there? Had that person blocked them in? Could they escape, or were they doomed to a horrible lingering end? He didn't fear death, but had always hoped not to be around when it happened.

Had he dozed off? Perhaps. He could no longer hear the rain though Kev was still snoring. The pillbox held such darkness he wondered if he might have gone blind. He shivered and tugged at a corner of the blanket, gaining temporary control of a fragment until Kev rolled over and seized it back.

Somehow sleep found him.

The world was silent when Razor awoke. Grey morning light filtered into the pillbox and his breath steamed. He was under three blankets and though they felt damp, he didn't wish to leave the comparative warmth. Groggy and yawning, he staggered to his feet, calling for Kev without a reply. He was all alone. When he tried the door, it swung open easily. The world outside was swathed in fog and looked as cold and murky as the North Sea in winter. He relieved himself into a bush and shouted, but the fog absorbed his words like a sponge and no friendly voice reassured him. Questions tumbled round his head like balls in a bingo cage. Some bounced within reach. How had the door unstuck itself? Where were Kev and Alex? Why had they abandoned him? Were they now working together?

He found no answers and no sound penetrated the murk, other than occasional drips from the trees. Hungry and chilled, his clothes clammy, he decided to go home. It would be impossible to get lost—all he had to do was keep walking downhill and he'd soon reach the village. Anyway, the fog was sure to clear.

After a dozen or so steps, he looked back, but there was no sign of the pillbox, and it wasn't long before he'd completely lost all sense of direction—he couldn't even tell if he was heading upward or downward. He ploughed on, beads of moisture dripping down his face, and hoped to stumble across somewhere recognisable. It felt like he'd been wandering for hours when a faint glow appeared ahead. It was the sun, but it should have been behind him. Then, for an instant, he was blinking in bright, warming sunshine, with the fog spread below like a cape.

He was still on the ridge, just in front of the pillbox. Dropping to his knees, he howled his despair and frustration, and the fog swirled back, enfolding him like a soggy bath towel.

He smelled flowers.

'Good morning,' said Miranda.

He was back on his feet in an instant, his face red hot. 'Where are you?'

'Here.'

'I can't see you.'

'Walk towards my voice.'

He fancied he could make out a darker shade in the murk.

'You look exhausted,' she said. 'Let's get you home. Follow me.'

'What about Kev and Alex?' he asked.

'They are in your house, drinking your whisky. Kev asked me to look around and I found a bottle of the stuff.'

'I'm amazed there was one. I hit it rather hard after Flit's funeral—she was my wife you know.'

'I know.'

'She died,' said Razor. 'I guess that was obvious. Otherwise she wouldn't have had a funeral.'

'Keep walking, Mr Razor, and maybe you'll be back in time for lunch.'

'Kev's a great cook,' said Razor, much cheered by the idea.

'Sometimes, but whisky is his weakness. His ability to cook varies inversely with how much he's taken. He drinks it as if it were beer.'

'What do you mean?'

'He swigs it by the pint. Especially the good stuff.'

Razor kept walking, comforted by her

nearness, but wishing he could see her. It was strange, now he came to think about it, that he'd never seen her in full daylight. It was also odd that she seemed to know where she was going. 'Where did you find it?' he asked, because he liked hearing her voice.

'The whisky? In a recess between the rafters in the attic.'

'I didn't know there was one,' said Razor, 'so it couldn't have been mine. Nor Flit's—she hated the stuff. What sort was it?'

'The Scottish sort,' said Miranda.

'Did it have a name?'

'Something Scottish. The bottle was in a white cardboard tube with a metal lid. There was a man's sweater in a tartan plastic bag next to it.'

A thought struck, happy and sad at the same time. 'I bet they were my birthday presents. She must have got them for me. I wonder how she found that hidey hole? Come to think of it, how did you find it? What were you doing up there?'

Miranda didn't answer for so long Razor feared he'd lost her.

'I was searching for something,' she said.

Razor turned back towards her voice—he'd been about to start walking in circles again.

'What?'

'Whatever Alex and Kane had been looking for.'

'Right… and how did you know what to look for?'

'I didn't. However, it was clear they had been searching, and since they'd failed to find it, whatever they wanted was well hidden. I'm good at finding things—and hiding them.'

Razor recalled all the times he'd caught Alex in the house and accepted his explanation that he was just tidying up, even though nothing ever appeared any better. 'Alex's attempts to find whatever it was were becoming desperate, so I guess it was important. Did you find it?'

'I believe I did,' said Miranda.

'What is it?'

'I don't know.'

Razor's rising excitement deflated. 'Then how do you know it was what they were looking for?'

'Because it was hidden.'

'So was the whisky, but they wouldn't be searching for that—unless it was a very rare and expensive one. It wasn't was it?'

'I wouldn't know, but even the rarest and

costliest drink becomes worthless once it's inside somebody.'

Razor trudged behind, concentrating on keeping her blurry outline in sight, and worrying about what else she might have discovered while searching through his house. They reached flatter, smoother ground and he heard running water. 'Is that the river?'

'Yes,' she said. 'You're nearly home.'

'Thank god for that. I'm knackered. Thanks for coming for me.'

'You're welcome. Here's the footbridge, Mr Razor.'

Razor followed her voice into the lane to his house.

The fog cleared and Launcelot's eerie cry made him jump.

There was no sign of Miranda.

She did not reply when he called her name and although bright autumn sunshine eased his freezing bones, her absence left a chill in his heart as he trudged the final few steps.

21

Razor entered by the unlocked back door. After removing his mud-encrusted trainers, he washed his hands and slurped down two full mugs of water before looking into the lounge.

Kev, flat out on the sofa, was snoring into the book propped up on his nose. Alex lay asleep on the carpet by the radiator, an almost empty special edition bottle of Laphroaig whisky at his side, a chunky hand-knitted Aran sweater wrapped around him. Razor had coveted such a garment since visiting the bleak but beautiful Aran Islands with Flit soon after their wedding, when money was tight, luxuries beyond their means and just being together was enough. He couldn't decide whether he was angry with Kev and Alex for guzzling his favourite whisky and purloining his sweater or just happy because Flit had still cared enough to buy him thoughtful presents.

After thinking about it for a few moments, he decided against giving Alex a good kicking. Instead, he seized control of his sweater, marvelling at its weight, its softness and the intricate patterns of the knitting. Next, he finished the last drips of whisky, appreciating its smoky, peaty flavours and the glow it gave him before remembrance of everything he'd lost and of the loneliness of life without her made tears well up. Practicalities took over. He returned to the kitchen, made tea and cheese on toast, and by the time he'd satisfied his stomach, he felt warm and as if life might be worth living. Sooner or later, he'd have to contact the police and explain about the body in the broom cupboard, among other things.

He pushed the thought to the back of his mind.

With Kev and Alex still out for the count, he treated himself to a long, soothing bath, luxuriating in the simple pleasures of hot water and soap, and trying to recall the good old days and Flit. Despite this, Miranda's image kept intruding, offering hope that life might provide another taste of the sweet pleasures he'd once so idiotically taken for granted.

Thoroughly cleaned, he stepped from the bath and towelled himself dry as the muddy brown bathwater ran away. Then, for the first time in his life, he wiped round the bath and returned to reality, though with hope that Miranda would turn up again very soon.

After dressing, he headed downstairs. She wasn't there, but Kev, though red-eyed and bleary, was awake. 'You found your way back then?'

'No thanks to you,' said Razor. 'You abandoned me to the fog.'

'Fog? It was a fine, sunny day when we left.'

'Why did you leave?'

'Alex wanted breakfast.'

'You could have woken me.'

'I tried, but you told me to get lost... though not in such polite terms.'

'I don't remember,' said Razor, 'but if I did...'

'You did.'

'... then I'm sorry. How did you open the door?'

'Easily—it wasn't stuck.'

'But it was solid last night,' said Razor.

'I can't explain that. I am in the darkness of ignorance.'

Razor sat down beside him on the sofa. 'While you two were enjoying my best whisky, I was stuck in a fog so thick I could barely see my own feet. I don't know what would have happened if Miranda hadn't turned up.' He shivered.

Kev looked up. 'Miranda?'

'She brought me back.'

'I thought she might have,' said Kev.

'You sent her?'

'She's not one to be sent by any man. Over hill, over dale, through bush, through briar, through flood, through fire, she wanders everywhere. Though she turns up unexpectedly, she does turn up, and in your case she appears when you need her most. You are one of the lucky ones.'

'I'm glad she does. Is she back yet?'

'You mean back here?' said Kev. 'No.'

'When do you expect her?'

'When she turns up and not a moment sooner. She is a free spirit; she has the spirit to do anything.'

Razor rolled his eyes. 'Are you talking Shakespeare again?'

'Partly, mate. The bard has a way with finding the right words.'

'How do you know so many quotes?' Razor demanded.

'I was an actor in a previous life.'

'Why not now?'

'All the world's a stage, mate, and all the men and women merely players. They have their exits and their entrances and one man in his time plays many parts. Time moves on and changes all men. Familiarity lessens what was once important. The thing is I'd played all the theatrical roles I'd ever wanted to, and it was time to move on.'

'So you became a thief.'

Kev shrugged. 'I'm sorry we drank your whisky.'

'It's alright,' Razor admitted. 'I didn't know I'd got any.'

'But if we hadn't already drunk it, we could drink it now.' Kev looked comically distraught.

Razor laughed. 'Good point, but Miranda said she discovered more than whisky.'

'She found a nice sweater.'

'And the other thing,' said Razor. 'She told me she'd found what Alex was looking for.'

Alex twitched at his name, but showed no other sign of consciousness.

'She did find something,' said Kev, 'but I don't know what. It's small.'

'Show me,' said Razor.

'I haven't got it...'

'Then where the hell is it?'

'I was trying to say I haven't got it on me.' He glanced at Alex who was still fast asleep. 'Miranda considered it prudent to conceal it again. It's behind a jar of pickled pigs' feet.'

Kev, swaying a little, crossed to the cupboard under the stairs where Flit used to store tins and bottles of unusual cooking stuff. He pulled out something small and silvery and returned. As Razor stood up, holding out his hand, Alex barged into him, knocking him to the carpet.

'Are you alright?' asked Kev, looking down with concern as the front door opened and slammed.

'Yeah... I think so,' said Razor, checking.

'Then stop groaning.'

Razor sat up. 'Did he take it?'

'He took what was in my hand,' said Kev.

'Then I'd better catch him.' Razor pulled himself upright.

'I wouldn't worry—he'll be back.' Kev smiled.

'What are you grinning at?'

'I guessed he was feigning sleep, so swapped the real thing for a cigarette lighter.' Kev reached into his pocket. 'This is what he wanted.'

'It's a USB flash drive,' said Razor, taking it. He paused. 'Why did you have a lighter? You don't smoke do you?'

Kev shook his head. 'No, I found it in the cupboard, next to the cigarettes.'

Razor frowned. 'That's weird—neither of us smoked. Well, Flit used to, but gave up because I didn't like it.'

Kev said nothing.

Razor bristled at the way he didn't say it. 'You think she started again, don't you?'

'I have no idea, mate.'

'Why would she? And why would she hide them?'

'On such topics I confess ignorance, that curse of god—though they weren't hidden.'

'They might as well have been,' said Razor. 'I'd never look in there. Perhaps they belong to Alex.'

'Perhaps,' said Kev, looking unconvinced.

Razor didn't believe it either—they had to be Flit's. She'd started smoking again, and he'd failed to notice even though he'd hated the taste of stale cigarette smoke on her lips before she quit. When had they last enjoyed a proper kiss? All he could recall in the months before her death were quick pecks on her cheek as he hurried to work. If Kev had not been there, he would have cried again. Instead, he sniffed, pulled himself together and examined the USB stick.

'Why would anyone want to steal that?' asked

Kev. 'Is it valuable?'

'Not as such, but I assume it contains information that's important to him.' Noticing Kev's expression, Razor laughed. 'Good God! You are a genuine ignoramus. This little stick contains electronic data that can be read when plugged into a computer.'

'I see. Do you have a computer?'

'Of course… at least I think so. I let Alex borrow Flit's laptop—he said there was important work stuff on it. Funny, I don't remember him bringing it back. However, I think my old one is still upstairs. I haven't used it since… you know?'

He led Kev to the room they'd kept as an office. Once upon a time, it had been tidy and organised. Now, papers, folders and books lay strewn across the carpet, all the drawers were out and empty and all the shelves were bare. 'They've ransacked it!'

'I believe you,' said Kev, 'even though it looks much like the rest of your house when I first got here. Where's your computer?'

'It was on the desk,' said Razor, paddling through the sea of paper until he stubbed his toe on something hard. When he'd finished swearing, he bent down and retrieved his old laptop from the litter.

'Now what?' asked Kev.

'I'll boot it up, if it's not broken,' said Razor, putting it back in its rightful place and pressing the button. When, somewhat to his surprise, it had started normally, he plugged in the USB stick. 'Let's see what we've got.' He put his leather swivel chair back on its feet and sat down, filled with excitement and trepidation. 'There are some files.'

'What do they say?' asked Kev, leaning over his shoulder.

'Let's see.' Razor clicked. 'Dammit, it's asking for a password.'

'Meaning?'

Razor sighed. 'It means I can't access the data... that is I can't see what's on it, unless she wrote the password down somewhere, or I can guess it. If I can't, the contents might just as well be in Timbuktu.'

Kev's face suggested bafflement. 'Why would they be in Timbuktu?'

'I just mean the data is inaccessible.'

Kev looked glum for a moment and then brightened. 'Perhaps Alex knows it.'

'Unlikely, and even if he does, why would he tell us?'

'We could persuade him.'

'How?' asked Razor, wondering if Kev was hinting at violence.

'By letting him have the stick thing, but only after we've seen what's on it.'

'I doubt that would work and, anyway, he's scarpered.'

'He won't be far away. He put so much effort into trying to find it that he won't give up easily. I had to get him drunk to stop him searching.'

'And, of course, you had to share the bottle,' said Razor with a grin.

'It's rude to let a guest drink alone.'

Razor felt frustration rising. 'There's no use talking about it if he's not here.'

Kev was smiling. 'I have a feeling he'll turn up soon. He's desperate.'

'Miranda thought the same.'

'Yes, he's gone from searching when he could claim a legitimate reason for being here, to ransacking the place and resorting to violence. Now he's apparently prepared to kill, so, yes, I'd say he's desperate.'

'I wonder why?'

'So do I,' said Kev, 'and also why now? He's had months. What's changed?'

Razor shrugged. 'I've no idea. He's strange. Why did he stay here and get drunk when he could have got away?'

'I may have hinted that I'd found it and that someone was taking it to the police.'

'Nice work,' said Razor. 'Let me try something.' He tapped at the keyboard. 'Bloody hell, I'm in!'

'How?'

'She'd used my first name... not the most secure password.'

Kev leaned over Razor's shoulder and peered. 'What's all that about?'

'It's a directory—a list of files with dates.'

'Is that all?' asked Kev. 'I was hoping for something interesting.'

Razor clicked on the first file. 'Let's see what we've got.'

Some hours later, he got up to switch on the lights, surprised to be alone apart from a mug of tea on the desk. He took a slurp—it was cold. Reflected in the window, his image looked keen and alert, much like his old self, apart from the bristly head and bruises.

Kev sauntered in. 'Are you alright, mate?'

'Yeah. Thanks for the tea.'

'You're welcome. I didn't think you'd noticed. Have you found anything?'

'I have. I've looked through several files and they are very interesting indeed.'

Kev glanced at the screen. 'It's just rows of numbers.'

'Numbers that tell a story.'

'What story?'

Razor, excited and back doing something he understood, paid no heed to the creak on the landing. 'This is evidence that Alex was up to no good.'

'In what way?' asked Kev.

'He's guilty of...'

'Embezzlement on a massive scale,' said Alex, strolling in.

'Told you he'd be back,' said Kev unnecessarily.

'Flit found out didn't she?' said Razor turning to face Alex. 'That's why she was spending so much time with you.'

'Her name was Felicity and, yes, Raymondo, she found out. She led me to believe she was interested both in me and in a share of the money. I admit to being flattered by her attention, but it turned out she was honest and loyal to the company as well as to you. She took

361

me in completely, and it turned out that she was brilliant at hiding stuff.'

'My name is Raymond and your game is up,' said Razor. 'Why are you here?'

'I want the memory stick.'

'No chance.'

'I thought you'd say that, but let's not be hasty. Perhaps you'll be interested in hearing my proposition?'

'Why should we?' asked Kev.

'Yes, why should we?' asked Razor. 'I have the information and from what I've seen, and I've only had a cursory look at about a tenth of it, you're screwed.'

'What do you intend doing?' asked Alex.

'I'll hand it to the police. You'll be looking at a long stretch in prison.'

'You're probably right, but there may be a better option—you could not tell the cops and I could split the proceeds with you both.'

'How?' asked Kev, looking interested.

'Half to me. After all, I did the work and took the risks, and the rest split how you like. It'll be safe money.'

'Not a bad offer. From what I've seen, we'd all be millionaires, or thereabouts,' said Razor.

'Thereabouts,' said Alex. 'I could manage on

half of the profits, though obviously I had wanted more. Of course, if they'd promoted me like they should have, I wouldn't have had to do it.'

Razor laughed. 'Of course you wouldn't.'

'I deserved that promotion for all the work I'd put in for the company. Since they were too stupid to see it, I struck out on my own. When you come to it, it's every man for himself and loyalty is for idiots. Now, what do you say to the deal?'

Razor shook his head. 'Not a chance.'

'Let's not be hasty,' said Kev.

'Your little buddy has way more sense than you. Give me the stick, I'll take it, get away and wire you your share. How about that?'

'Bloody hell, Alex. How stupid do you think I am?' said Razor. 'Do you honestly think I'd fall for such crap?'

'Not really, but I hoped you would. I wouldn't cheat you.'

An incredulous noise, half snort, half laugh burst out of Razor. 'Sure you wouldn't and even if I believed you, the data is still going to the police. I'm honest, like Flit was.'

It was Alex's turn to snort. 'Now, you're having a laugh! After all this time I can't believe you're still denying what you did to her.'

'I did nothing,' said Razor, getting to his feet, his fingers bunched into steel fists.

'You could have been brave, but you chose to let her die under a lorry.'

Razor slumped back into his chair, a piercing chill stabbing through his guts. 'Shut up!'

'What does he mean?' asked Kev.

'Nothing. He's lying.'

Alex sneered. 'Does the truth hurt, Raymondo?'

Razor, close to tears, trying to block his ears and fearing he might whimper, wanted to hurt Alex, to shut him up forever, but his strength had drained away and the half-healed wound in his soul was bleeding again.

'I'll tell you what he did,' said Alex glancing at Kev. 'When the mugger accosted them in the alley, that cowardly piece of shit cowering in his chair ran away, leaving his wife behind.'

'She ran with me,' Razor murmured.

'You never even looked back. Even when she fell, you could have pulled her to safety, but...'

'I tried,' Razor's voice cracked. Tears trickled down his face.

'Liar!' Alex screamed. 'She reached out, but you let her die.'

'No!' Razor's legs buckled. He fell to the floor and curled up amid the papers. He'd heard it all before and the screaming face of his nightmares came into focus—it had been Alex all the time. Distorted memories of the night after the funeral returned, of getting drunk into a stupor and Alex, his face distorted by rage and contempt, bellowing accusations at him until he passed out. It was unbearable. What a snivelling, useless coward he'd been.

'Hold on a minute,' said Kev. 'How do you know all this? Unless you were there?'

Razor couldn't breathe as he awaited Alex's reply.

It took a moment as long as time. 'Yes, I saw it happen.'

'You were there? But you didn't help,' said Razor, sitting up. 'You didn't even come forward as a witness. Why not?'

'I had no wish to implicate myself.' Alex sighed. 'The truth is I guessed Felicity was onto me and set up a tracker in my office. I caught her copying the files. She said she was going to show them to the boss. Obviously, I didn't want that. I argued with her, but she wouldn't listen to reason and I thought I'd had it. Fortunately, the boss was at a conference, so she couldn't do it straight away. Even so, I thought I'd had it until I overheard her telling one of the secretaries she was going to the cinema with you. I came up with a plan and it might have worked if she'd gone straight to meet you, but she didn't—she came back here first and hid the USB stick.'

'She wanted to change,' said Razor, remembering how lovely she'd looked that night in her new dress.

'Were you the mugger?' asked Kev before Razor could think straight.

'Of course not—she'd have recognised me. I gave the job to our late lamented friend, Kane.'

'I doubt anyone's lamenting him,' said Kev.

'No, probably not. I went to school with him and his brother, you know? I kept in contact because their skills occasionally came in handy. Kane should have been the right man for the job, but he goofed. No one was meant to get hurt.' Alex laughed. 'Well, that's not quite true. I'd asked him to hurt you, Raymondo, a bit—quite a bit in fact, but not her. Despite everything, I still liked and admired her. But enough. Give me the stick and I'll say no more about your pathetic cowardice.'

Razor roused himself and got to his feet.

'Come and take it, if you dare.'

'I feared you'd be unreasonable,' said Alex and shrugged. 'I can't beat you in a fight and you know it, so I must take other actions.'

'What actions?' asked Kev, his face radiating suspicion.

'Destroy all the remaining evidence.' Alex pulled a plastic bottle from under his jacket. 'I've already dealt with Heartfields.'

'No!' said Kev, catching on before Razor's brain could register fear.

Alex, grim and determined, unscrewed the bottle and squirted the contents around the room.

'It's petrol,' Kev yelled. 'Get out of here!'

But Alex already had the lighter in his hand.

'Don't be a fool,' said Razor, his eyes widening and his mouth drying as he saw the danger. 'I'll give you the stick.'

'Too late. Sorry,' said Alex, clicking the lighter.

A flash. Fire was everywhere. Time went into slow-mo as Alex lit up like a bonfire and staggered around, shrieking and smashing into things. Kev backed into a corner, the papers around his feet igniting. Razor's shirt front smouldered and his skin hurt. Death would take him now he'd stopped looking for it, and in a most horrible way. He fell out the doorway onto the burning landing.

There was no hope.

A small dark figure darted towards him.

22

Acrid smoke caught the back of his throat and Razor gave in to an uncontrollable bout of coughing. Pain gripped him in a tight embrace. A weird, flickering orange light was all around and he opened his eyes to see flames erupting through the roof of Riverside Cottage, his home for four years. He was lying on the lawn and made an attempt to get to his feet.

'Stay where you are, my lovely.' Miranda pressed him back down.

'But... Kev... and Alex,' he said, squeezing out words between coughs. His lungs felt as if they, too, were on fire.

'I know,' said Miranda and ran towards the house.

'No,' he croaked, but she reached the back door and plunged into the inferno. Strong hands grabbed his sore shoulders as he attempted to follow her.

'Don't be a fool, Ray—it's about to go,' said Tom Talbot.

Seconds later, the roof caved in, a fireball burst through the doorway. Razor howled.

Something covered his face. He couldn't move his hands to get rid of it. His eyes opened and focused on a white ceiling and walls and the medical equipment all around him.

'It's alright, sir,' a woman in a green tunic reassured him.

'Where am I?' Razor croaked, his voice muffled by the thing on his face. His face, hands and chest hurt like the devil and he felt wet. He could not sit up.

'You're in an ambulance, on your way to hospital. There was a fire, but you were lucky, though you do have some burns that we treated at the scene. I imagine they are rather sore. You've also breathed in smoke which is why you're on humidified oxygen. I'm Alice. Can you tell me your name?'

'It's... er... Razor... Raymond Holmes... er... call me Ray.'

'Well, Ray, I'll take care of you until we reach the hospital. How is the pain?'

'Bad.'

'Okay, Ray, I'll add a little something to make you feel better.'

'But Miranda and Kev... and Alex? They were still inside.'

'The fire brigade are dealing with it. I'm sure

they'll let you know how your friends are later. Now, take deep breaths. It'll help with the pain, though it might make you woozy.'

Razor inhaled. 'You're right, I am a little wooz...'

Razor awoke with screens all around. A nurse smiled down at him. A doctor studied a tablet computer.

'Good morning, Mr Holmes,' said the nurse.

'Morning?' asked Razor. Where had the night gone?

'Morning!' said the doctor. 'And how are we feeling today?'

'We?'

'How are you feeling today, Mr Holmes? Any pain?'

'Some... not too much... my chest hurts.' He tried to touch it but found his hands were swathed in dressings. They felt stiff.

'Best not to prod anything for the moment,' said the doctor. 'You have several mostly superficial burn injuries and they will feel sore for a few days, though I doubt there'll be any long-term effects. A deeper burn on your chest may take a little longer to heal, but the prognosis is excellent and I doubt there'll be much scarring, if any. Questions?'

'Yes,' said Razor, comforted that medical people were caring for him, though he felt distant and confused. 'Can I get something to eat and drink?'

'I expect so, but it must be soft on account of your throat. You'll be moving to a ward soon, but I'm sure something can be arranged, can't it nurse?'

'Yes, doctor.'

'Excellent. Well, I'd best be on my way. Goodbye for now, Mr Holmes.'

Razor fidgeted in his bed, waiting and listening to the hubbub of the busy hospital ward on the other side of his cubicle's curtains. Drugs subdued his pain. Just before he thought he might expire of hunger, a nice middle-aged lady called Angela came in with a trolley and offered him water and chicken soup. Grateful, he accepted though he needed Angela to hold the glass to his lips and to spoon soup into his mouth.

Later, a smiling grey-haired lady called Doreen helped him up and guided him to the bathroom. Later still, memories of the previous evening returned, at first as vague as a snatch of a night's dream. Tears started—there was no way Miranda and Kev could have survived the roof collapse, but none of the staff admitted to knowing anything about them.

As he settled into the boredom of hospital routine, drugs kept pain at a distance, doctors came and went, asking questions, nodding heads and occasionally prodding, nurses talked to him and Angela fed him more soup and water. Sometimes he slept. Sometimes he listened to the radio. Miranda was on his mind whenever he woke and in his dreams.

He marked the passage of time by the arrival of meals and sleeps. Slowly, his brain cleared as his medications were reduced. A grizzled police officer turned up at his bedside. 'I'm DS Prince,' he said showing an ID card. 'I'm part of the investigation team looking into the fire at Riverside Cottage in Willoton. You are Mr Raymond Holmes, are you not?'

Razor nodded.

'Excellent. Do you mind if I sit?' Without waiting for a reply, DS Prince pulled up a chair, sat down and took a notebook from his pocket. 'Do you feel up to answering a few questions?'

'Yes,' said Razor, 'but, please, can you tell me how Miranda is?'

'I'm sorry, sir, but I don't believe I know the lady.'

'And what about Kev? Kevin Crumb, that is. They were in the house.'

DS Prince shook his head. 'Mr Holmes, I'm afraid I have bad news—the fire brigade recovered two bodies from the house.'

Razor wept.

'Can you confirm who was inside at the time of the fire?' asked DS Prince when Razor was back in control.

'Me, Miranda and Kev.'

'So, there were three of you?'

'Four. Alex was there as well. He started it— the fool used petrol and set himself alight.'

'Was that Mr Alexander Bond of the Manor, Willoton?'

'Yes. How did you know?'

'We have reason to believe he was one of the bodies.'

Razor gulped, grasping at a new hope. 'And the other?'

'A large male who appeared to have suffered a broken neck and another significant injury before the fire. Would you know anything about that and why he was in a cupboard?'

Razor had forgotten until then. 'Oh... that was

Kane.'

'Kane?'

Razor nodded. 'Kane Cullum.'

The detective started. 'Kane Cullum? We know him very well. Who'd have thought it? Can you explain why you didn't mention him earlier, and can you account for how his neck got broken?'

'I can... and I will, but weren't there any other bodies? Miranda and Kev were quite small.'

'I'm assured there were only two.'

'Thank God for that... but I don't understand. She pulled me from the fire, but when she went back for Kev, the roof came down. There's no way she—they could have got out.' Tears started again.

'Yet,' said the detective, 'only two bodies were found. You'd better tell me what happened.'

Razor forced his emotions back under control and took a deep breath. 'Alright, detective—I hope you've got plenty of time.'

He recounted the whole story and over the next two days had to retell it to several other police officers—he wondered if they just wanted to hear his bizarre tale for themselves. All insisted that only two bodies, now confirmed as Alexander Cedric Bond and Kane Frederick Cullum, had been discovered, though, as they all pointed out, the fire had been intense.

The only good news for Razor was learning that the police had never suspected him of attacking the barmaid—the picture in the paper had merely been of someone she'd identified as a possible witness.

Razor lost all hope and retreated to his private hell of grief and loss, almost oblivious to the surrounding hospital, except when they forced him from moping in bed to get up and walk. Losing Kev hurt, for the little guy had proved himself a real friend, but losing Miranda was devastating. Everything he valued was gone.

Despite his misery, DS Prince piqued Razor's interest by mentioning an arson attack on Heartfields Ltd, Flit and Alex's workplace. 'It happened three days before the fire at your cottage. The video was taken by a security camera at an adjoining business.' The detective touched the screen on a tablet and started the clip. A slim man, face hidden between a cap and a scarf, appeared at a window, pouring liquid from a jerrycan.

Moments later the first flames kissed the night sky.

'That was Alex,' said Razor.

'Mr Alexander Bond? Are you positive?'

Razor nodded. 'It's the way he moved. Besides, he said he'd done something to Heartfields.'

'We suspected so. There was no sign of a break in, so we considered it likely that it was an inside job. Thank you for your help.'

'But why did he do it then?' asked Razor.

'We are working on the theory that it was to destroy traces of his embezzlement. Heartfields' directors had become aware of a problem and were planning a major audit in the next two weeks. We will require a further statement from you.

'However, before that, you ought to see this. It might help—though you may find it distressing. It was taken from a traffic camera at the Severn Wharves in Glevchester. I'm sorry it's grainy, but the techies had to magnify it.'

'Go on then,' said Razor, resigned.

The clip showed a main road lined with old buildings with a handful of people in summer clothes walking by. Razor's stomach lurched.

He knew what would happen, but how could a ten-inch screen hold so much hurt and guilt? Yet the different perspective on events ingrained deep in his memory bewitched him and he couldn't look away.

Raymond, wearing the expensive lightweight Italian suit he'd once been so proud of, hurtled from a passage. An instant later, Flit followed, wearing the new blue dress he'd so admired. On screen, Raymond stopped and turned, reaching for her hand, but before they could touch, the heel of her shoe stuck between slabs and she stumbled. The lorry entered the picture, and although the video was silent, the shriek of brakes and her cry as she fell into the road rang loud in his memory.

'Stop!' Razor said, guilt unbearable.

The detective shook his head. The video continued.

Razor knew he'd failed to get to her, believed he'd hesitated because he'd been such a bad husband and suspected her of infidelity. It was terrible to see again, but the screen showed Raymond lunging for her—it looked as if he'd reach her in time, until the huge figure of the masked mugger burst from the passage and crashed into him, leaving him dazed and helpless in the gutter.

DS Prince mercifully stopped the video, but Razor's memory of the events returned as the missing details dropped back into place. It was all there—getting to his feet, dazed and horrified, seeing Flit lying in the road, motionless and bloodied, the ashen-faced lorry driver scrambling from his cab.

DS Prince allowed him a few minutes to recover. 'Do you recognise the man who attacked you?'

'I do now—it was Kane Cullum.'

'Sure?'

'Yes.' Tears drenched Razor's face, yet, despite the grief and the horror, there was a sense of release, of redemption. Maybe he shouldn't have run, but after that first second of instinctive cowardice he'd done his best. Despite everything, his guilt had kept telling him, he would have saved her had it not been for Kane Cullum. Grief for Flit and hatred for Kane overwhelmed him.

DS Prince allowed him a few moments. 'There is one more thing, Mr Holmes—it's taken from a security camera across the road. Do you feel up to it?'

Razor nodded—nothing could be worse than

what he'd already seen.

The clip started with a row of shops shut up for the night.

'Look at the doorway on the far right,' said DS Prince.

A slim figure, both hands to his head, lunged from the shadows and dropped to his knees.

'The time signature of this,' said Prince, 'matches that of the incident involving your wife. Do you recognise the man?'

'It's Alex,' said Razor.

'That is what we thought. It confirms that Mr Alexander Bond arranged for you and your wife to be mugged in order to retrieve the memory stick.'

'You doubted me?' asked Razor. It was no surprise.

'We had to check.'

'How come you've only just found the clip?'

'My colleagues had, of course, collected all relevant video records from the time of the incident, but were unable to recognise Kane Cullum, and there was no reason to suspect the onlooker across the road had anything to do with it. We tried to locate him as a witness, but not too hard as the evidence appeared clear and the inquest would be a formality.'

'Did you find the memory stick?' asked Razor as a random thought popped into his head.

'No, but considering the extent and heat of the fire, we wouldn't have expected to.'

'So, Alex got away with it.'

'Other than burning to death, he did. Still, the Fraud Squad would have liked to have discovered quite how much he took and how he did it.'

Razor nodded, feeling better, though the guilt hadn't quite left him—a horrible suspicion remained that had he paid more attention to Flit, she would have told him about Alex and he could have protected her. Worse, what if she had told him and he hadn't been listening?

During the six days he spent in hospital, he became so used to being addressed as Raymond or Ray or Mr Holmes, he could have forgotten that for a short while he'd been Razor. When well enough to leave, he rented a small but comfortable flat above a hairdresser in the middle of Sorenchester—his insurance company had shown itself efficient if not generous.

Living with regret and loss was hard. He wished he could have apologised to Flit, though knowing he had tried to save her was comforting. The worst part was a yearning ache for Miranda and, despite all the annoying prattle, he missed Kev—and not just for his cooking.

The inquest into Flit's death, a day he'd have once done anything to avoid, came and went. As DS Prince had suggested, it was a formality. He gave an honest account of the incident and the jury returned a verdict of Accidental Death, though acknowledged the criminal activities leading up to it. No one blamed Ray.

It was a relief, though it did not entirely eradicate his guilt—he should never have taken her for granted. Still, he could now accept that she was gone, and resolved never to make such a foolish mistake again.

All alone, life held no meaning and Ray feared he might end up suicidal like before. Instead, he took to walking again, using the short hours of winter daylight to search for Kev's house and the secret garden or taking the bus into Glevchester to search for Miranda's mansion. He could find no signs—almost as if he'd imagined them.

Google searches failed to uncover any records of any Kevin or Miranda Crumbs that fitted what he knew. It took a few days before it occurred to him that cousins could come from the aunt's side as well as the uncle's and might not share the same surname. In desperation, he searched for Uncle Bob, hoping he might have been Dr Robert Crumb. Again, he found no likely candidate. All he could discover about the Sorenside Brewery fire was that it had occurred on 1st April 1999 and that the fire brigade had been slow to attend because they'd thought it a hoax.

One day in late November, he thought about Rocky. Might he be able to help? After all, he'd mentioned knowing Uncle Bob.

Wrapped up against a cold northerly wind, Ray walked to The Olde Toll House, enjoying the fresh air and his aching muscles. No one was home, but Rocky had pinned a note to the repaired and repainted front door.

In Norway, out standing in my fjord—back in the spring.

Disappointed, he turned for home, taking an indirect route along lanes, byways and footpaths to give himself more thinking time. In summer, it would have been a scenic walk, but snow flurries grew more persistent, blowing into his face. With the afternoon darkening, he realised he'd taken a wrong turning. It wasn't much to worry about—he could hear the main road not far away and from there it wouldn't take too long to get back to his flat. A tall dry stone wall blocked his way.

He scrambled over and dropped into what he soon recognised was Fenderton churchyard. He and Flit had once attended a carol service there. It had been a happy evening, shortly before his promotion. He recalled the pleasure of belting out the old favourites by candlelight, sipping mulled wine and kissing her beneath the mistletoe in the porch.

Something was nagging at his brain as he headed towards the lychgate. He stopped, turned back and examined a small, plain gravestone.

In memory of Kevan Crum

who shuffled off this mortal coil

1st of April 1999 aged forty-two

The similarity of the name, the date and the weird quote—one of Shakespeare's he suspected, gave him a momentary frisson. But it was clearly just a coincidence. With a sigh, he started homeward.

As the nights lengthened and darkened, December blew in. The shops displayed their version of Christmas cheer, the streets filled with lights and the children grew excited. One chill evening, with snow threatening, Ray returned to his joyless flat from another fruitless day trudging the streets, looking for a friendly face. As he opened the door, he almost trod on a small brown envelope on the doormat. He picked it up and read the attached note.

The handwriting was Miranda's.

Dear Mr Razor,

Kev thought you might want this.

See you soon,

M.

The memory stick dropped into his hand.

Hope returned, bringing a smile to lips long out of practice.

It was time to start living again.

Acknowledgements

Once again, I would like to thank the members of Catchword for their support, guidance and encouragement: Liz Carew, Meg Davis-Berry, Gill Garret, Derek Healey, Richard Hensley, Pam Keevil, Dr Rona Laycock, Pam Orr, and Jan Petrie.

I would like to thank Ultimate Proof for proofreading and Books Covered for the covers.

Writers at the Goods Shed and the members of Gloucestershire Writers' Network have also provided much appreciated support.

Finally, a huge thank you to my family, to Julia, and to The Witcherley Book Company.

Wilkie Martin

Wilkie Martin's novel, *Inspector Hobbes and the Blood*, was shortlisted for the Impress Prize for New Writers in 2012 under its original title: *Inspector Hobbes*. As well as novels, Wilkie writes short stories and silly poems, some on YouTube. Like his characters, he relishes a good curry, which he enjoys cooking. In his spare time, he is a qualified scuba-diving instructor and a guitar twanger who should be stopped.

Born in Nottingham, he went to school in Sutton Coldfield, studied at the University of Leeds, worked in Cheltenham and now lives in the Cotswolds.

https://wilkiemartin.com

Get Wilkie's Newsletter and Join His Unhuman Readers

Sign up for Wilkie's Readers' List and get a free download copy of *Sorenchester Book Maps* and see where everything in his *unhuman* series takes place. You can also download a free copy of *Relative Disasters* – his little book of silly verse, and *Hobbes's Choice Recipes* by Wilkie, as his character A.C. Caplet.

Be among the first to hear about Wilkie's new books, publications and products, and for exclusive giveaways.

Join here:

http://go.wilkiemartin.com/join-readers-list

(Note: Note: The sign-up downloads may vary – follow the link for the latest offer.)